MISS DARCY'S PASSION

When Dominic Sanford's parents die in a carriage accident, he is packed off to Scotland to be brought up in his uncle's household. Years later, he returns to his dilapidated estate that borders Pemberley. His father's journals have recently come into his possession, raising questions about his parents' deaths . . . Upon seeing Dominic for the first time at Colonel Fitzwilliam's wedding, Georgiana Darcy feels an immediate attraction. As she assists him in delving deeper into his family's history, they uncover a fiendish web of organised criminality. But Georgiana unwittingly plays a major role in the miscreants' plans — by involving her, Dominic has placed her directly in danger's path . . .

Books by Wendy Soliman
Published by Ulverscroft:

LADY HARTLEY'S INHERITANCE
DUTY'S DESTINY
THE SOCIAL OUTCAST
THE CARSTAIRS CONSPIRACY
A BITTERSWEET PROPOSAL
TO DEFY A DUKE

THE MRS. DARCY ENTERTAINS SERIES:
MISS BINGLEY'S REVENGE
COLONEL FITZWILLIAM'S DILEMMA

WENDY SOLIMAN

---◆---

MISS DARCY'S PASSION

Complete and Unabridged

ULVERSCROFT
Leicester

First published in Great Britain in 2014

First Large Print Edition
published 2015

A catalogue record for this book is available
from the British Library.

ISBN 978–1–4448–2438–4

Published by
F. A. Thorpe (Publishing)
Anstey, Leicestershire

Set by Words & Graphics Ltd.
Anstey, Leicestershire
Printed and bound in Great Britain by
T. J. International Ltd., Padstow, Cornwall

This book is printed on acid-free paper

1

The plethora of red coats crammed into Lambton parish church brought warmth and colour to a chill November morning. A buzz of expectancy rippled through the congregation as Lord Briar walked the bride down the aisle. Several smothered exclamations of admiration were heard above the organ music; a reaction to the bride's beautiful and highly unusual gown of figured cream silk, trimmed with swansdown, tiny seed pearls, and a scarlet velvet sash. The full length over-dress was also trimmed with scarlet velvet and exquisite lace. She wore a matching bonnet with a tiny veil that shaded her eyes. Scarlet slippers peeped from beneath her hem. Colonel Fitzwilliam watched her approach with a smile of absolute captivation gracing his features.

'Breathtaking,' Lizzy Darcy said *sotto voce*.

'You were a more radiant bride,' her husband replied.

'Thank you, but you are biased. Celia Sheffield is remarkably beautiful, and looks very happy. Colonel Fitzwilliam is a fortunate man.'

The bride reached the altar, the service began. Bride and groom exchanged their vows in firm voices and were declared man and wife. As they left the church to return to Briar Hall for the wedding breakfast, the newlyweds were required to negotiate a red-coated honour guard, sabres crossed to form an archway. The Darcys made their way to their carriages in their wake, moving slowly in deference to Jane Bingley's first appearance in public since her confinement.

'How long ago our wedding day now seems, Lizzy,' Jane remarked as their party sheltered in the porch until the carriage pulled up at the door.

'You were equally as radiant as Mrs. Fitzwilliam, whereas I . . . '

'Oh, Lizzy, what nonsense you speak sometimes.' Jane touched her sister's arm. 'All brides have a duty to shine. You and I had more occasion than most to do so, given the obstacles we had to overcome to achieve our hearts' desire.'

'That is undeniable.' Lizzy flapped a hand. 'Take no notice of me. Having the appearance of a bloated mackerel does not make one feel attractive.'

Jane smiled. 'How do you feel?'

'I was about to ask the same question of you,' Mr. Bingley said, joining them and subjecting his wife's face to an exacting examination.

'Do stop fussing so, Charles,' Jane replied affectionately. 'I feel perfectly well, and would not have missed today for any consideration.'

'I envy you,' Lizzy said, patting her rapidly expanding waistline. 'You got it all over with *and* somehow managed to prevent our mama from descending upon you.'

'That was only because Mary was taken unwell. In all honesty, I should not have minded if she had come north to welcome the birth of her first grandchild.'

Lizzy quirked a brow. 'Really?'

Jane offered a serene smile. 'My temperament makes it easier for me to withstand Mama's fussing than yours ever will.'

Lizzy shrugged. 'I can hardly disagree.'

'I would not wish illness upon Mary as a reason to prevent Mama from coming,' Jane said, frowning. 'However, Mama writes that our sister is getting better.'

Lizzy would mind if their mother interfered in her confinement — that was the difference between her and her kind-hearted sister. It didn't show Lizzy in an especially flattering light, but she knew how much of a strain it would be for Will — for them both — to have her mother at Pemberley for a prolonged period. Fortunately, Mama was not fond of travelling in winter, so perhaps she would be persuaded not to make the journey.

'And how is my niece?' Lizzy asked.

'Emma is absolutely perfect,' Jane replied, beaming.

'And definitely has nothing wrong with her lungs,' Mr. Bingley added with an equally proud smile.

'No difficulties then?'

'Just one.' Mr. Bingley's smile gave way to a confused frown. 'I cannot fathom why my sisters have not hastened north to welcome the new addition to the family. It is most peculiar.'

Will joined Lizzy at that point and overheard their conversation. 'We shall have to tell them,' he said in an undertone as he conducted Lizzy to their carriage.

'Yes, they will hear something sooner or later. It would be better if it came from us.' Lizzy sighed, not looking forward to causing her sister pain, or giving her reason to think badly of anyone — a situation which Jane would find troubling. 'When shall we do it?'

'They are coming back to Pemberley after the wedding breakfast. I shall speak with Bingley alone. You tackle your sister.'

Lizzy grimaced. 'Yes, very well.'

Kitty and Georgiana joined them just as Will helped Lizzy into the carriage.

'Sorry,' Georgiana said. 'We were delayed by some of our neighbours who are not invited to the wedding breakfast.'

'The couple wished to keep the affair private, but it seems half the colonel's regiment is here.' Lizzy settled into the corner of the seat, making room for her sisters and Georgiana. With Will and Mr. Bingley also in the carriage, it was a tight squeeze.

'Fitzwilliam is still a serving solider,' Will reminded them.

'I thought he had resigned his commission,' Kitty remarked.

'He is no longer on active duty but still holds his rank and is entitled to wear his regimentals. His officers would expect to be invited to his nuptials,' Will explained.

'Lydia would be in seventh heaven if she could have seen all those red coats,' Jane said, as the carriage moved away from the church porch.

Lizzy rolled her eyes.

'Who was the gentleman I saw you speaking with a moment ago, Fitzwilliam?' Georgiana asked her brother. Lizzy wished Georgiana would follow her own example and address Darcy by an abbreviation of his name. Fitzwilliam was so long-winded, and caused confusion between Darcy and today's bridegroom, Colonel Fitzwilliam. Besides,

Will suited Lizzy's husband so much better. 'I do not recall seeing him before.'

'That is Mr. Dominic Sanford.'

'A member of the Sanford family who own the manor house that adjoins Pemberley?' Georgiana smiled. 'I can't recall a time when the house was occupied. It is terribly neglected. There is some sort of mystery about the family, I believe.'

'A mysterious family?' Lizzy asked, her curiosity piqued.

Will laughed. 'Sorry to disappoint you, but there is no mystery. Fitzwilliam and I knew Sanford when we were boys. His parents were killed in an accident, so the house was closed up and Sanford was sent away to Scotland to live with relatives.'

'He looks younger than you are,' Georgiana said in a considering tone.

'He is, by several years. Fitzwilliam happened to see him in the village a week or so ago and felt obliged to invite him to the wedding.'

'Does he plan to stay for long?' Georgiana asked.

'I have absolutely no idea,' Will replied. 'It is the first time I have seen or spoken to Sanford for fifteen years.'

'If he means to open up the house,' Lizzy said, 'he must be in a position to pay for the repairs and for its upkeep. He certainly appears gentlemanly. I look forward to knowing him better. I shall invite him to dinner.'

'You should not be considering entertaining when you are so close to your confinement,' Will admonished.

'Nonsense, I have several weeks to go yet.'

'Lord have mercy.' Will shook his head. 'Was Jane this stubborn, Bingley?'

Mr. Bingley flashed a rueful grin. 'It's a family trait, I'm afraid, Darcy.'

'We don't like to make invalids of ourselves,' Jane replied with a sweet smile.

'I believe Mr. Sanford has attracted Georgie's interest and she would enjoy seeing him at Pemberley,' Lizzy remarked playfully.

Georgiana coloured. 'Lizzy, what a thing to say! I merely wondered who he was.'

And couldn't stop looking at him in the church. 'Naturally, my dear.' Lizzy offered up a knowing smile. 'And here we are at Briar Hall already.'

The Darcy carriage joined a procession of others and its occupants waited patiently until they reached the front steps, being in no great hurry to expose themselves to the biting wind. They alighted when the time came and joined the reception line.

'My dear, that gown is a sensation,' Lizzy

said, clasping Mrs. Fitzwilliam's hand in her own and smiling at the bride. 'I wish you all the happiness in the world.'

'Thank you so very much. This time, I feel persuaded I have married the right gentleman for the right reasons.'

'Because you love him?'

'Precisely.'

'There can be no better reason than that.'

Lizzy moved on to Colonel Fitzwilliam and offered him her hand, together with a warm smile. 'Congratulations, Colonel. I am sure you will be very happy.'

'It's really Mr. Fitzwilliam now,' he replied, shaking his head. 'That will take some adjusting, but I cannot regret leaving the army.' He glanced at his new wife with such adoration that Lizzy felt almost like an intruder. 'It's time to move on with my life.'

'Exactly so. I am sorry Lady Catherine didn't feel equal to making the journey.'

'Just because she didn't feel inclined to leave Kent, don't imagine she is lonely.' The colonel smiled. 'I understand she and Sir Marius spend a lot of time together.'

'Anne and I are regular correspondents now, and she told me the same thing. She and Mr. Asquith are also constantly in one another's company.'

Lizzy smiled and moved along the line.

Lady Catherine and her daughter Anne had spent some time at Pemberley at the beginning of the autumn with the intention, on Lady Catherine's part, of securing an engagement between Colonel Fitzwilliam and her daughter, Anne. The moment Colonel Fitzwilliam met their new neighbour, the widowed Celia Sheffield, Lizzy knew Lady Catherine would not get her way. Mrs. Sheffield had inherited her husband's estate in Buckinghamshire but her brother-in-law claimed it belonged to him by right. Colonel Fitzwilliam ensured he did not steal the property from its rightful owner, resulting in today's wedding. The colonel and his bride would be heading to Buckinghamshire within the next few hours to commence their married life together.

The episode had a potentially happy ending for all of Will's relations. Anne and her male tutor, Mr. Asquith, were now unofficially engaged and Lady Catherine was reunited with Sir Marius Glover, a gentleman she had known, but would not admit to having loved, in her youth.

'Now then,' Will said, placing a protective hand on Lizzy's waist and steering her towards an arrangement of chairs close to the fire. 'A seat for you, my dear, and no argument.'

Lizzy affected surprise. 'When do I ever disagree with anything you say, Mr. Darcy?' Will sent her a concerned look, causing Lizzy to capitulate. 'Very well. Jane and I will sit here like two old matrons and allow the young things to dominate proceedings.'

Will barked out a laugh. 'That,' he said, 'I must definitely witness for myself.'

* * *

The doors between the drawing room and dining room at Briar Hall had been thrown open to accommodate the wedding party. Even so, the space quickly became packed with bodies, many of them clad in colourful regimentals. A table groaning beneath the weight of the wedding feast stood at one end of the room and footmen circulated with glasses brimming with champagne. Georgiana and Kitty both accepted a glass as they stood beside Lizzy and Jane, watching the changing sea of faces.

'Mr. Sanford is remarkably handsome,' Georgiana said quietly, so only Kitty could hear her. 'He has an elegant way of moving, and seems comfortable in these surroundings.'

'Why should he not be? I imagine he must be a gentleman, used to good society.'

'Yes, most likely.' Georgiana continued to watch him. 'I wonder what made him decide to return to the district.'

'I expect your brother will find out soon enough.'

'Yes, I expect he will.' Georgiana fanned her face. 'Gosh, what a squash this is.'

'We won't need to stay for long.' Kitty gave Georgiana an appraising look, which is when Georgiana realised she was still craning her neck to follow Mr. Sanford's progress through the throng. 'Should you not be hankering for Major Halstead's company?'

'Not in the least. Major Halstead is merely an acquaintance.'

'Georgie!'

'I know you are enamoured of his friend, Captain Turner, but my feelings towards the major do not go beyond friendship. I have told you before, I want what my brother and your sister have.' Georgiana paused to observe the bride and groom, who were totally absorbed with one another, almost to the point of rudeness. 'And the colonel and his bride, by the looks of things.'

'You couldn't feel such felicity with the major?'

'I like him very much, but that is not enough to satisfy me. Besides, I'm not persuaded his feelings are genuinely engaged.'

'Poor you.' Kitty sighed. 'You are unsure if he really likes you, or if it's your dowry that attracts him.'

'Precisely.'

'Listen to your heart, Georgie. The major hasn't offered for you, and might never do so. Besides, having independent means gives you freedom of choice. You need not marry at all, unless you find the love you crave. I am sure you will know it if you do.'

'That's what Lizzy tells me. But I should hate for people to view me with pity because I cannot attract a husband.'

'Oh, Georgie, what nonsense you do speak! You could take your pick from half the single gentlemen in this room, if you wished to, but — '

'For all the wrong reasons,' they said together, laughing.

'My feelings for Captain Turner are *more* than enough, but he hasn't said a word.' Kitty pouted. 'Infuriating man! Today is the first time I have clapped eyes on him for weeks. He made some feeble excuse about visiting his family, but seeing his ogre of a father always puts him in a bad mood. Even so, since his regiment is now quartered in the Newcastle garrison, it is very bad-mannered of him not to call at Pemberley. Should I drop hints to remind him where we live, do you think?'

'Probably not. He *will* declare himself, Kitty, never doubt it. You just need to exercise some patience. The two of you are made for one another.'

'That is easy for you to say, but — '

Georgiana grasped Kitty's wrist and turned her so they joined in the conversation between her brother and the Bingleys. 'Mr. Sanford is coming this way,' she hissed. 'He must not catch us looking at him.'

'*I* was not looking at him,' Kitty remarked, sounding amused.

'Ah, Sanford,' Fitzwilliam said. 'Allow me to introduce my family and friends.'

Mr. Sanford said all that was right and proper to Lizzy and the Bingleys. At close quarters, he was even more enticing, and Georgiana had never felt such an instant attraction towards any gentleman before. Hair of a deep, rich brown fell across his brow, almost touching equally brown eyes that glowed with unsettling intelligence and great good humour. His beautifully dis-placed features were all planes and angles, as strikingly attractive as his elegant manners and social poise. Georgiana took a moment to admire his straight, aristocratic nose, his strong jaw and full, sculpted mouth. She felt her body hum, as though it had woken from a long slumber that heralded her transgression from annoying little sister to a woman in her own right. The small corner of Derbyshire that represented her world suddenly seemed a very great deal more interesting with Mr. Sanford occupying it.

'I don't suppose you recall my sister, Georgiana,' Fitzwilliam said. 'She was still a toddler when you left Derbyshire.'

'Miss Darcy.' Georgiana bobbed a curtsy. She felt a sizzle of awareness streak through her when Mr. Sanford bowed over her hand, and took it in his. 'I remember a dark-haired infant running amok at Pemberley, plaguing the life out of us boys, but cannot equate that creature to this sophisticated young lady.'

His eyes sparkled with wicked enjoyment as he canted his head and pretended to consider the matter. Not that Georgiana had much experience in recognising wickedness, but she suddenly felt a whimsical desire to behave recklessly. She coloured as she recalled the damage she had caused on the only previous occasion when she had done so. She was older now, wiser, and would not make that mistake again. Even so, there was just something about Mr. Sanford — a combination of worldliness, mystery and danger that made her want to throw caution to the wind.

'Are you sure there hasn't been some sort of mix-up, Darcy?'

Georgiana smiled. 'I am the only sister he has, Mr. Sanford, much as he might wish otherwise. I fear I am a dreadful trial to my poor brother.'

This time his eyes definitely gleamed with interest. 'I hardly dare to ask.'

'That would probably be best,' Fitzwilliam decreed, bringing Kitty to Mr. Sanford's notice. 'This is my wife's sister, Miss Catherine Bennet.'

Kitty bobbed a curtsey and Mr. Sanford greeted her with charm and poise.

'I am glad I returned in time to see Fitzwilliam become leg-shackled,' Mr. Sanford said, nodding towards the bride and groom. 'He seems to have made a happy choice.'

'Leg-shackled, Mr. Sanford?' Georgiana arched a brow. 'You make matrimony sound like a prison sentence, but I know from my brother's example that is not always the case.'

'All single young men are averse to the institution,' Mr. Bingley said, laughing. 'But when they meet the right lady, they soon have a change of heart.'

'Do you plan to stay in Derbyshire for

long, Mr. Sanford?' Lizzy asked.

Georgiana awaited his reply with keen anticipation.

'I plan to settle here permanently, ma'am. I have been travelling extensively these past few years, and am ready to put down roots. On that note, Darcy, I would like to call and see you, if that would be convenient. There are things we need to discuss.'

'By all means.'

What things, Georgiana wondered. She wanted to know a lot about Mr. Sanford: where he had been living all these years, what he had been doing, and what his interests were.

Absolutely everything.

'This is quite like old times, Darcy,' Mr. Sanford said. 'You, Fitzwilliam, and I all in the same room. The only one missing is Wickham. Where is he, by the way? I thought he would be in the thick of things.'

An awkward silence greeted Mr. Sanford's remark. Georgiana was convinced everyone turned to look accusingly at her. That was not possible, of course, since only Lizzy and her brother knew of her indiscretion with Wickham. The guilt that always ate away at her surfaced, and she fastened her gaze on her feet, finding something fascinating about them to hold her attention.

'Did I say something wrong?' Mr. Sanford asked.

'Wickham is no longer welcome at Pemberley,' Fitzwilliam said shortly.

'Ah, I see. Apologies, I did not know.'

'There was no reason why you should, Mr. Sanford,' Lizzy said calmly. 'Tell me, what are your plans for your house?'

The conversation moved on and Georgiana gradually recovered from her embarrassment. She listened to Lizzy and Mr. Sanford conversing, thinking how much she liked the timbre of his rich, earthy voice. She could happily have listened to it for hours on end. Unfortunately, new people joining their circle and good manners dictated that she move to her left to make room for them. That meant moving away from Mr. Sanford. She managed to suppress a sigh when she saw who the new arrivals were, trying to be pleased for Kitty's sake.

'Good morning, Major Halstead, Captain Turner,' Lizzy said.

'Good morning, Mrs. Darcy.'

Major Halstead greeted everyone by name, demonstrating the good manners and easy charm that had first attracted Georgiana to him. He was as good-looking as Mr. Sanford, she conceded, wondering why she suddenly felt as though she couldn't trust him. He lingered over her hand, raised it to his lips and kissed the back of it. She noticed him shoot Mr. Sanford a sideways glance as he did so, as though staking some sort of prior claim.

'Miss Darcy,' he said. 'It seems an age since we last met. Now that the regiment is quartered so close by, I do hope you will permit the captain and me to call upon you at Pemberley.'

'You are both always welcome, sir.' What else could she have said? 'But the weather doesn't always make the roads easy to negotiate.'

Major Halstead flapped aside her concern. 'We are soldiers. A little discomfort does not signify.'

'We will have snow within the next few weeks,' Fitzwilliam said. 'I smell it in the air.'

'Allow me to offer you my congratulations upon the birth of your daughter,' Major Halstead said to Mr. and Mrs. Bingley.

'Thank you, Major,' Mrs. Bingley replied. 'That is most kind of you.'

'What brings you to the district, Sanford?' Halstead asked, standing as close to Georgiana as the proprieties allowed.

Upon learning that Mr. Sanford was a close neighbour of theirs, Georgiana noticed a dark frown invade the major's face.

'Sanford House, you say? The dilapidated property on the western edge of the Pemberley estate.' The major's voice stopped just short of sounding scathing. 'You'll have your work cut out for you there.'

Mr. Sanford raised one shoulder in an elegant shrug. 'Very likely.'

He sounded remarkably unconcerned about the challenge of restoring his family home. Georgiana wondered why it had been permitted to fall into such a state of neglect, but it was hardly a question she could ask without appearing as rude as Major Halstead.

'How long do you plan to stay in the district, Sanford?' the major asked.

'My plans are fluid,' he replied.

Strange, Georgiana thought. When asked the same question by Lizzy, Mr. Sanford gave the impression that he intended to stay indefinitely. Presumably Mr. Sanford had taken exception to the major's bad manners and decided his plans were no concern of his.

'Won't be too comfortable in that house at this time of year,' the major persisted.

'Then it is fortunate it is me who must live there and not you.'

Georgiana wanted to applaud. Mr. Sanford had worded his well-deserved setdown so charmingly that the major couldn't possibly take offence.

After an awkward pause, the conversation became more general. Mr. Sanford's attention was claimed by others who remembered him, including a prominent local family with two daughters to marry off. Georgiana, who had never disliked anyone in her life, suddenly took aversion to that family as she watched the daughters preening beneath the full force of Mr. Sanford's charm.

2

Shortly after the happy couple were waved away from Briar Hall, the Darcy party returned to Pemberley. Jane and Mr. Bingley were planning to stay for an early supper and then make the ten-mile journey back to their new estate before darkness fell. Lizzy could tell Jane was already anxious to return to her daughter.

Georgiana and Kitty took themselves off somewhere as soon as they got home. At Will's suggestion, he and Mr. Bingley headed straight for his study.

'What is it, Lizzy?' Jane asked as soon as they were alone. 'You have not been yourself all day. Are you worried about the baby? About the possibility of it not being a boy, I mean. Charles does not mind having a daughter, in fact he already dotes on Emma, but I am concerned I might have inherited Mama's inability to bear sons.'

'Will assures me it is impossible to inherit such a trait. He also assures me that he has nothing against daughters either, but I can't persuade myself that he speaks truthfully.'

'Charles says exactly the same thing, but all

men secretly desire a son.' Jane looked fiercely resolved. 'And I am quite determined to give him one.'

'It isn't the baby that concerns me,' Lizzy admitted, knowing she couldn't put off what she had to say. 'Although I will admit to feeling a certain amount of discomfort.'

'That I can understand, but it is worth it. There is nothing more satisfying than presenting one's husband with a healthy child.'

'Or more painful.'

Jane grimaced. 'One soon forgets the pain.'

Lizzy waited for the footman who had delivered their tea to withdraw and then poured for them both.

'I have something to tell you, Jane, that you will find deeply upsetting,' she said, having taken a sip of tea and a deep, fortifying breath. 'I wish you didn't need to know, but unfortunately it is necessary.'

'Someone is unwell?' Jane clutched Lizzy's hand. 'Has Mary taken a turn for the worse and no one thought to tell me?'

'No, everyone is well, to the best of my knowledge.' Again Lizzy paused. 'This is to do with Mr. Bingley's sisters.'

'You have heard from them?' Jane's worried expression cleared. 'Charles is very concerned about their unwillingness to come to us here in Derbyshire, especially now they are aunts. He is rather hurt by their neglect, although will not admit it. We wondered if Mr. Hurst had forbidden his wife to spend so much time with us, although he has always been more than willing to accept Charles's hospitality.'

Under different circumstances, Lizzy would have teased Jane for saying something that sounded almost like a criticism. 'No, their absence has nothing to do with Mr. Hurst.' Lizzy took another sip of tea and cleared her throat. 'Something unpleasant happened during the house party we held here at Pemberley in the summer. The one that you all attended at our invitation, and which Lydia forced herself upon.'

Jane looked rather cross. 'This unpleasantness you refer to presumably concerns Caroline and Louisa and yet you did not tell me before now?'

'We could not, at the time. You were in a delicate condition, and we decided it would have been too upsetting for you.'

'You ought to have allowed me to decide for myself,' Jane said stiffly.

'I'm sorry, my dear.' Lizzy touched her sister's arm. 'We did what we thought was right at the time. Do not condemn us until you know the particulars.'

'Then enlighten me.' Jane tilted her head,

her expression now thoughtful rather than offended. 'Is that why Mr. Darcy took Charles out of the way?'

'Yes, he is telling him now.' Lizzy drew another deep breath before starting to speak. This was so very hard. Jane was so sweet, so trusting, and would be very upset by what Lizzy had to tell her. 'Caroline Bingley always felt favourably disposed towards my husband,' she said, deciding upon the direct approach.

'Yes, I think we all knew Caroline hoped to secure Mr. Darcy for herself,' Jane replied. 'I was very sorry for her, but happy for you, of course.'

'Caroline convinced herself that Mr. Darcy had made an error of judgement — '

'No, Lizzy! Even if she thought it, which I am sure she did not, she would never say so.'

'I'm afraid she did worse than that.' Lizzy put aside her tea and clasped Jane's hand tightly. 'She came to the party with the specific intention of making trouble between Will and me. In short, she befriended Lydia when she heard Mr. Wickham was in Lambton.'

Jane's face drained of all colour. 'I do recall us thinking it was an oddity that she and Lydia became friends. Caroline never had a high opinion of our youngest sister, and given

Lydia's wild behaviour in Hertfordshire, I can't altogether blame her for that.'

'Caroline cultivated Lydia's friendship in order to get to Wickham. She was aware of the animosity between him and my husband, but not the reason for it.' Lizzy shook her head. 'Oh my, this is so very difficult. I hate to cause you pain, my dear.'

'I am sure you did nothing to create this situation, but I can't imagine Caroline willfully doing so either. There must be some mistake.'

'Unfortunately not.' Lizzy sighed. 'I will spare you the unpleasant details. Suffice it to say that Caroline bribed Wickham to sneak onto Pemberley land and engineered it so that he and I would be caught in a compromising position by my husband.'

'Dear God, no!' Jane clasped a hand over her mouth. 'She would not go so far.'

'I wouldn't make it up.'

'No, forgive me. That is not what I meant at all, but I am in shock and spoke without thinking.' Jane paused. 'But how? When?'

'Do you remember she suggested we take a turn around the lake together?'

'Yes, actually I do.' Jane nodded. 'I thought it odd at the time, but was glad she seemed to be warming to you.'

'Hardly that,' Lizzy said.

'You invited me to join you and I wish now that I had. I recall there was some difficulty. Mr. Darcy carried you back to the house. You had swooned, and I was so very worried about you, especially when Mr. Darcy wouldn't let me see you.'

'Fortunately, Will recognised the situation for the despicable ruse that it was. Even more fortunately, our uncle Gardiner offered a solution by suggesting Wickham take over the management of one of his warehouses.'

'Lydia knows what he tried to do?'

'Yes, and she surprised me with her mature response. She will keep Wickham honest from now on, if that's humanly possible. She knows this is his last chance.'

'I hope Wickham doesn't give our uncle cause to regret that generosity.'

'As do I.' But deep down, Lizzy couldn't rid herself of the disquieting feelings that she had not heard or seen the last of George Wickham.

Jane shook her head. 'What of Charles's sisters?'

'That was our main difficulty. When confronted, Caroline denied all involvement, but she had written down her financial offer to Wickham. In the event of his not being able to extract money from Will in return for his silence, you see, Caroline had promised to pay him from her own funds. Wickham didn't trust her to keep her word unless she put pen to paper. Fortunately, that written commitment fell into our hands, and so in the end she had to admit it.'

'Such infamy!' Jane looked genuinely distressed. 'Poor Charles. He will be devastated.'

'That is why we avoided telling you before now. We needed time for tempers to cool, and for us to see how Caroline responded to treatment. Mrs. Hurst offered to take her to Brighton for that purpose.' Lizzy sent Jane a reassuring smile, seriously concerned about her sister's pallor. 'She is unwell, Jane. Delusional. So she is not entirely to blame for what she did. She was convinced she was acting nobly by giving Will a way to extract himself from a bad marriage. Mrs. Hurst keeps Will informed of her progress, and it seems she is much better. She has even acknowledged what she tried to do and admitted she was wrong. That is encouraging.'

'Yes, I suppose so.' Jane plucked absently at the fabric of her skirt, her expression dazed. 'I am so shocked I barely know what to say.'

'If we had told you before we knew Caroline was likely to recover, it would have forced you to choose between us and your husband's sisters.'

It was Jane's turn to grasp Lizzy's hand. 'How can you think I would ever turn my back on you?'

'I hope you never would, but I didn't want to put you in the position of having to decide. We also couldn't allow Caroline's actions to go unpunished. If we had, she would have remained with you and Bingley, and would have expected admittance to Pemberley once you moved to Derbyshire.'

'What do we do now?' Jane asked, spreading her hands in a helpless gesture.

Before Lizzy could reply, the gentlemen entered the room, looking grim. Will nodded to Lizzy and managed a brief smile.

'My dear!' Charles Bingley crouched at Jane's side and took her hand. 'Has Lizzy told you?'

'Yes, I can't believe it, but at least it explains why they haven't been to see us.'

'I don't know how to express my apologies,' Mr. Bingley said to Lizzy.

'It is not your fault.'

'I disagree. Caroline was our father's favourite. As the youngest, she was indulged — '

'We understand better than you might imagine,' Lizzy replied, thinking of how Lydia had been pampered by their mother, and the damage caused because her wild behaviour had not been checked.

'I ought to have taken firmer control when I became head of the family, but Caroline has a strong personality, and I am afraid I never really did take her to task when she decided upon some unrealistic course of action.'

'Calm yourself, Bingley.' Will moved to the sideboard and poured his friend a substantial measure of brandy. 'You were not to know what she planned.'

Mr. Bingley shook his head. 'Caroline has a high opinion of herself. She seems to forget our own father made his fortune through trade.'

'Mr. Bingley, please, there's no need for this.' Lizzy smiled her reassurance. 'Will and I have had time to reflect. You cannot reasonably be expected to remain estranged from your own sisters. And, of course, they will wish to visit their baby niece.'

'If you consider Caroline is sufficiently recovered,' Will added. 'She will always be welcome at Pemberley.'

'Thank you, but I am not prepared to have Caroline at Campton Park, much less here, until I have seen her for myself and am satisfied she understands and regrets what she tried to do.'

'You intend for us to go to Brighton?' Jane asked.

'Not us, my dear, only me. You ought to

remain with Emma. It is a long way to travel so soon after your confinement.'

'Very well. If that's what you think best.'

'I have a few matters of business to put in hand and then I shall go. Next week.'

'Your sisters are at Mr. Hurst's residence in London, I believe,' Will said. 'So you will not need to go as far as Brighton, Bingley.'

'Jane, you must come to Pemberley with Emma while Mr. Bingley is gone. I shall be glad of your company. You, Kitty and I can spoil your daughter without Mr. Bingley here to scold us.'

Jane smiled. 'He spoils her more than I do, but thank you, Lizzy. I should like that.'

'And it would put my mind at rest to know you are with your sisters,' Mr. Bingley added, smiling his thanks. 'You are such a good friend, Darcy, to take this so calmly.'

'We cannot choose our families, Bingley.'

'Come,' Lizzy said when Simpson appeared to announce supper. She accepted her husband's assistance to haul herself rather inelegantly to her feet, wondering how she would endure another six weeks or more before her time came.

An hour later, Will and Lizzy waved the Bingleys off.

'I am glad they know,' Lizzy said as they turned back into the house, Will's arm draped protectively around her shoulders.

'I thought Bingley was going to hit me when I first told him.'

'Jane seemed rather offended, too.' Lizzy managed a small laugh. 'I didn't think it was possible to undermine their respective good natures. That they have reason to think less than well of anyone, especially a relation, will be very difficult for them.'

'Enough. Caroline Bingley is now her brother's concern, just as she should be. You, on the other hand, are mine, and you look worn out. Bed for you, Mrs. Darcy, and if I hear you have lifted so much as a finger to do anything for yourself for the rest of the day then you will have me to answer to.'

Lizzy stifled a yawn. She knew better than to argue with her husband when he was in such an intransigent mood and leaned on his supportive arm as she slowly climbed the stairs to her chamber.

3

James Halstead left the wedding breakfast and strode towards the stables at the back of Briar Hall, anger lancing through his veins. For Sanford to return to Derbyshire now, of all times, was beyond infuriating and seriously impeded his personal plans. He was almost in a position to offer for Miss Darcy. He had no doubt she was anticipating his declaration and that she would accept him.

Georgiana Darcy's attitude towards him had cooled a little over recent weeks, it was true, but that was only because his duties had kept him from Pemberley and she was feeling neglected. For all her wealth and privilege, Miss Darcy was shy and insecure, in need of constant reassurance. James understood her well, but also knew his suit would not be successful unless he won over Darcy first, which is why he had not yet declared himself. Georgiana would not go against her brother's wishes and Darcy was a hard man to impress. Such was the way with the landed gentry, James thought sourly. He was frustrated with the amount of time and effort it was taking him to make progress with Darcy. And now, with his wife close to her time, it was even harder to secure his attention. James couldn't afford to wait, so decided to take advantage of Darcy's distraction and approach Miss Darcy direct; to hell with the proprieties. He would play upon her romantic nature, use pretty words, arouse her passions, and leave her to talk her brother round.

Now Sanford had come home and ruined everything. Miss Darcy had barely spared James a second glance today, saving all her smiles for Sanford. Worse yet, Sanford was right next door to Pemberley — within walking distance. James, on the other hand, had his soldiering duties to perform, to say nothing of his other commitments. He needed to act fast, before everything he had worked to achieve slipped through his fingers.

'What's w-wrong, Halstead?' Turner asked, striding towards the stables with him. 'You l-look ready to commit murder.'

'I don't like that way Sanford was looking at Miss Darcy, if you must know.'

'Then do s-something about it. M-miss Darcy l-likes you. Propose to h-her.'

'If only it was that easy.' Halstead grabbed his horse's reins from the groom leading him out and swung into the saddle. 'You get on back. I have to be somewhere.'

'Oh, r-right you a-are.'

Halstead turned his horse in the direction of Kympton village. His destination was a modest cottage on its outskirts which he reached quickly by pushing his horse hard for the entire distance. His knock was answered by the most beautiful woman he had ever seen — and the most conniving. No matter how often he saw her, the sight of her always stole his breath away, and usually took his anger with it. She had a baby balanced on her hip.

His baby.

'What are you doing here in broad daylight, in your regimentals?' She grabbed his arm and pulled him inside. 'Quick, before you are seen.'

'Sanford has returned,' he told her urgently. 'Had you not heard?'

'Damnation, no I had not. How long does he intend to stay?'

Halstead drank in her beauty and allowed it to calm him. Her fiery eyes, her voluptuous body — everything about her fuelled his addiction. He loved her with single-minded passion, but didn't always like her very much.

'He didn't say, but he's probably home to stay. You will have to move the merchandise.'

'Not me, but you.'

'Oh no. I am on the point of proposing to Miss Darcy. I can't take the risk.'

She placed the baby in a bassinet and then faced him, arms akimbo. 'You knew the risks and are in this just as much as I am.'

He stepped towards her, grabbed her upper arms and pulled her against him. Her full breasts half-tumbled from her bodice and James was lost to all reason. He pushed her into the bedroom that adjoined the small parlour and didn't stop pushing until she fell onto the bed.

'Damnation, Rose, why do you do this to me?'

'You do it to yourself,' she replied, moistening her plump lower lip with the tip of her tongue, deliberately taunting him.

'What is it with you and Sanford?' he asked, stripping the remains of her bodice away.

'You know the answer to that.'

James knew better than to tell her that her obsession was dangerous. Instead he pulled off his uniform and they fell on one another, rough, urgent, completely in tune with each other's needs.

'You plan to give all this up when you marry your precious Miss Darcy?' she asked as he buried himself deep inside of her.

'Not this, but the rest.'

'You can't have one without the other.'

James plunged deeper. 'You use me, you

witch, but can't live without what I give you, either.'

'There are other men.'

He scowled at her. 'There had damned well better not be.'

'Can you see your Miss Darcy catering to your baser needs? I saw her in the village the other day. She will not keep you satisfied for more than five minutes, and yet I can make you throb with need, just by looking at you in a certain way. Why pretend? We both know it.'

'I cannot marry you, Rose,' he said, panting as desire overwhelmed all other considerations.

'I don't want marriage. No man will ever control me.'

James believed her. Further conversation became impossible as their passions exploded in a starburst of pleasure. As James dressed he agreed to check on the merchandise, ensure it hadn't been discovered, and make arrangements for its removal; just as they had both known he would.

★   ★   ★

Dominic Sanford rode home to Sanford House and saw to his horse's needs himself. He had yet to employ a groom, or any permanent staff, for that matter. He stabled

Midnight in the ramshackle outbuilding he had appropriated for that purpose. The stable block itself was in need of a new roof, as was the house. But at least the downstairs rooms were habitable, which were more than enough for his simple needs.

'There you are, Midnight,' he said, patting his stallion's neck and filling his manger with fresh hay. 'Don't look so indignant about your accommodation. You will be quite cosy in here, which is more than can be said for me in that freezing cold barn of a house. Whatever made me decide to come back at the start of winter is beyond me. I had forgotten how cold it gets here in Derbyshire when the north wind blows off the sea.'

His horse snorted, attacked the hay, and had no other response to give.

Dominic strode towards the kitchen door and let himself into the house which was now his home. His young, gangly-limbed cross-bred dog hurled himself at Dominic, placed huge paws on his shoulders, and licked his face.

'Hamish,' he said, laughing and removing the dog's paws. 'I'm glad someone's pleased to see me.'

The woman from the village who had been paid by his uncle, from Dominic's inherited funds, to come in once a week to dust and keep an eye on the place, now came in daily. She had already been and gone, leaving a pot of something with an appetising smell simmering on the range. He grabbed a cloth, removed the pot, and placed it on the table. He ate directly from it with a spoon, chuckling as he imagined the reaction of the fine people at the wedding breakfast if they could see his lack of manners.

But they could not see him. Nor did he have any desire for company. What he required were answers to the conundrum that had brought about his return to his childhood home. Not that he would be able to avoid people now that he had shown himself in society and the rumours about his return had been substantiated. Only gentlemen would call, of course, and they would just have to overlook the state of his house. He glanced out of the window and could see Pemberley, huge and magnificently maintained, in the far distance. So close and yet worlds apart. At least the state of the house and his lack of a hostess would give him a legitimate excuse not to return invitations.

Having met Darcy again, Dominic was satisfied he was the right person to confide in and pump for information. Darcy had always been serious and fair-minded, even as a boy. There were changes in him now that he was married. He seemed a little less rigid in his manner, but he was still the same conscientious Darcy. He was also Dominic's closest neighbour, and if anyone could help him, it would be Darcy.

Dominic finished his makeshift meal, scraped the remains into a bowl for the salivating Hamish, and placed it on the floor. The bowl was empty and being pushed around the floor by Hamish's snout before Dominic could straighten up again.

'I shall send your compliments to Mrs. Gibson,' Dominic said, laughing as he moved to the ground floor room he used as a bedchamber and changed into old clothing. He ought to carry on his methodical search of the house for clues. Instead, he felt an urgent desire to be outdoors, despite the cold. He pulled on his old greatcoat, his warmest hat and gloves, and set forth for an exploratory ramble through his woodland.

'Come along, Hamish,' he said.

The dog exploded through the door ahead of him and disappeared into the nearest clump of bushes. Dominic actually had a destination in mind. In the woods, there was a cottage built by his grandfather to house an unwelcome relative. The old gentleman who had lived in it was a curmudgeonly fellow who had frightened the young Dominic. But that hadn't prevented him, Darcy, Fitzwilliam, and Wickham from playing tricks on the poor chap. Wickham. He wondered what he had done to find disfavour with Darcy. The mention of his name had clearly been a *faux pas*, and Miss Darcy in particular appeared embarrassed by it.

He also wondered who was responsible for keeping his woodland in order. To the best of Dominic's knowledge, his uncle had not specifically employed anyone to take care of it. The gardens, his mother's pride and joy, had certainly gone to seed. But the track through the woods was clear of brambles and easily passable. The ground was soft, following heavy rain, and he could see indentations made by several pairs of boots. People had passed this way, and recently, too.

'What the devil?' he said aloud.

Darcy, if Dominic had to guess. No one else had direct access to his grounds. Perhaps Darcy used it as a shortcut when returning home on horseback. It would save him considerable time, and so it would be within his best interests to keep the tracks clear. Dominic would ask him about it when he called upon him, and offer to pay for his woodman's services.

Dominic shivered and increased his pace, whistling to the dog to keep up with him. He threw back his head and smelt the air. Darcy was right. Snow was definitely in the offing, and the wind had picked up since the morning, biting at the few parts of his flesh left exposed. He hoped to find the cottage, which was smaller and considerably newer than the main house, in a relatively good state of repair. He and Hamish could move into it, at least until he got Sanford House's roof patched and the smell of damp and decay out of the house.

His account had been debited for regular maintenance of his family's property, and yet it was obvious that no one except Mrs. Gibson had set foot in Sanford House. Well, it was too late to ask his uncle why not since he was dead. Not that Dominic could imagine him having any need to behave deceitfully. As an eminent surgeon, whose services were in great demand, Uncle Tobias made a very good living and did not need to add to his income through fraudulent means.

Dominic thought of the acquaintances he had made, old and new, at the wedding today. His return to the area appeared to have created quite a stir. No stranger to wistful glances from young ladies, Dominic had received more than his fair share of them today, but he had no particular interest in any he had met. Darcy's sister was a lively little

41

thing, and highly accomplished, apparently. Dominic idly wondered about the major who had overplayed his hand, making his desire to be more than an acquaintance of Miss Darcy's plainly apparent. That didn't come as any great surprise, since Georgiana Darcy was reputed to have a dowry of twenty thousand pounds and must be used to fending off fortune hunters.

The girl had engaged Dominic's mild interest. A combination of vulnerability, lively wit, and luminous eyes saved her from being plain. He had heard it said Miss Darcy was shy and a little aloof, but Dominic hadn't seen it. Significantly she hadn't tried to flirt with him, whereas the two he had been introduced to next, did nothing but flutter their lashes, simper, and giggle. Miss Darcy, on the other hand, spoke intelligently and didn't appear to take herself too seriously.

A very refreshing change.

Ye gods, but it was cold enough to freeze a snowball! Hailstones rained down, bouncing off the brim of his hat. He could see the cottage in the distance, and was encouraged to notice the roof appeared intact. Exploring it could wait until the weather improved. Thoughts of the warm range in the kitchen were far more appealing.

'Come on, Hamish,' he said, turning to retrace his steps.

As he did so he saw a movement on the path up ahead. Whether it was a person, an animal, or the wind bending the branches, he could not have said. It was gone almost immediately, and Dominic wondered if he had imagined it. But Hamish was in no doubt. He growled and streaked off in hot pursuit. Dominic was too cold to stand about and started to walk back. Even if there was something there, Hamish was too young, clumsy, and uncoordinated to catch it.

★ ★ ★

Following his call upon Rose, James Halstead had just left Sanford's cottage when something whirled through the trees, snarling and growling. At first glance, he thought it must be a wolf. Then he realised it was a domestic dog. A very large, nondescript, angry domestic dog, with vicious fangs he appeared intent on sinking into James's backside.

Perdition, would nothing go right for him this day? If he was caught here, he would have a hell of a time explaining himself. Why the devil had he allowed Rose to talk him into coming? Because Rose could make him do anything she wanted, and they both knew it.

James hurled himself against the lower branches of the nearest tree and pulled himself into it just as the dog reached him. The beast took a chunk out of his regimental trousers and broke the skin on his thigh.

That was a close shave! James climbed higher into the tree, its bare branches and his red coat providing little cover if the dog's master — Sanford, presumably — was close on its heels. The dog stationed itself beneath the tree, snarling and growling. James stayed perfectly still and wished himself a thousand miles away. His heartbeat was loud and erratic, and he was already half frozen to death. Damnation, he had removed his greatcoat and stupidly left it in the cottage. If Sanford actually went in there, all would be lost.

James tried to distract himself by considering his discoveries inside the cottage. There was more merchandise concealed in that hovel than was either wise or safe. What could Rose have been thinking? The answer was that she most likely had not been. Her intelligence appeared to fail her wherever Sanford was concerned.

He concentrated his thoughts on his more immediate problems. He couldn't remove the haul until Rose found somewhere else to keep it, and was damned if he would risk being caught with it in his saddlebags. He was expected back at the garrison. His dalliance with Rose, and then making a detour here, had made him late. All he had been able to achieve in his limited time inside the cottage was ensure the merchandise stayed hidden. He had moved a heavy piece of shrouded furniture over the floorboard protecting the entrance to their treasure trove, and must trust to luck that it remained undisturbed.

Still clinging to the tree trunk, the dog all but climbing up it to get to him, James decided he couldn't permit Rose's history with Sanford to cloud her usually sound judgement, or spoil his own reputation. He was a soldier. He knew how to kill quickly and quietly, and he had his dagger with him. If necessary, he would use it on that blasted dog, then on its master. He managed a rueful smile. That would certainly eliminate the competition for Miss Darcy's favours.

In the event, Sanford didn't appear. James heard him whistle to the dog, and to his great relief, the hound eventually gave one final growl before loping off in pursuit of his master.

4

The morning after the wedding, Will and Lizzy sat together in the small sitting room Lizzy favoured.

'I wonder how soon Jane will join us,' Lizzy remarked.

'Sooner than a week, I would imagine. You know Bingley when he makes up his mind to do something. He will find no peace until he has seen his sisters for himself.'

'Poor Mr. Bingley.' Lizzy smiled. 'Still, it will be lovely to have Jane and little Emma here. I can practise being a mama.'

'I am told these things come naturally to a woman, and I am perfectly sure you will prove to be an exemplary mother.'

Lizzy rested her head on Will's shoulder, glad the girls were out for an hour and they had the house to themselves. 'Ah, but shall you be a strict papa?'

'I shall beat our children black and blue, obviously.'

'Because you were treated that way and know no better?'

'Actually, my father seldom took a strap to me.'

'Your behaviour was beyond reproach and you gave him no reason to chastise you?'

Will laughed. 'I got into as many scrapes as the next boy, but I was careful to keep my exploits from my father's ears. The pater had a way of looking down his nose if he was disappointed.' He shook his head. 'He didn't need to say a word. *The look* was enough to make me aware I had not lived up to his expectations.'

'I hope he gave you praise as was due.'

'Actually no.' Will shrugged, a little too casually. 'He was not one to show emotion.'

Lizzy's heart went out to her highly complex, very conflicted husband. It was apparent he had not enjoyed the carefree childhood he deserved because he had spent his days endeavouring to live up to his father's high standards. He seldom spoke about old Mr. Darcy, but whenever he did reveal something about his character, it made it easier for Lizzy to forgive the cold nature of Will's first proposal to her — the one which infuriated her and which she had experienced little difficulty in declining. Since the cradle he had been made aware of his position as one of the wealthiest landowners in the country — a person of substance and consequence to be revered and respected. He had assumed anyone invited to share in that lifestyle would grasp the opportunity with gratitude.

Lizzy was, she suspected, one of the few women in England who saw beyond his wealth and splendour. In declining him, she had unwittingly increased his determination to have her. That, in turn, forced Will to question all his most cherished principals, releasing the true Fitzwilliam Darcy from an emotional wasteland. Lizzy happily accepted credit for being the making of the man she loved with such a fierce passion it sometimes scared her.

'If our children don't fight with one another, skin their knees, fall from trees, and get entangled in all the scrapes children are supposed to embrace, I shall feel I have failed as a mother.'

Will laughed. 'There are plenty of trees at Pemberley for them to fall from. Don't imagine I don't know which ones are the best. I just took care to hide the resulting injuries from disapproving eyes.'

Lizzy leaned up and placed a gentle kiss on Will's lips. 'I am very pleased to hear it.'

Simpson interrupted them to announce Mr. Sanford.

'Show him in, Simpson,' Will said, removing his arm from around Lizzy's shoulders and sitting up straight.

'That was quick,' Lizzy remarked. 'I did not anticipate seeing our new neighbour again so soon. Georgie will be sorry to have missed him.'

'And perhaps we will discover what Sanford's been doing with himself all these years, and what brings him back to Derbyshire so unexpectedly.'

'He caused quite a stir at the wedding yesterday, especially amongst the single ladies. He's remarkably handsome.'

'You are not supposed to notice such things, Mrs. Darcy.'

'I am married, Mr. Darcy,' she replied, laughing. 'Not dead.'

The young gentleman who had made such an impression upon Georgiana walked into the room before Will could respond. Mr. Sanford was impeccably attired, if a little windswept. Hardly surprising since presumably he had come on horseback. It was perishing cold and a sharp north wind prevailed.

'Darcy, Mrs. Darcy.'

Will and Mr. Sanford shook hands. He then turned to Lizzy. She offered him her hand but didn't stand.

'Please excuse me if I don't get up, Mr. Sanford,' she said. 'In my condition, getting out of a chair is not so easily accomplished.'

'I would not have you do so, and I apologise for intruding. I am sure you have been advised to keep off your feet as much as possible.'

Ha.' Will barked a laugh. 'For all the notice she takes.'

Lizzy wondered what had caused Mr. Sanford to make what some might consider to be an indelicate remark. As though sensing the nature of her thoughts, Mr. Sanford spoke again.

'Forgive me if you think I spoke out of turn. I am a doctor, you see, and sometimes cannot seem to help giving professional advice, even when it has not been requested.'

'Then you are especially welcome home,' Will said.

'Simpson, some tea, please,' Lizzy said as Mr. Sanford seated himself across from them.

'At once, ma'am.'

They made polite conversation about the weather, about the wedding, about nothing of consequence, until tea was brought in.

'You have business to discuss with my husband,' Lizzy said, once she had drunk a cup. 'I ought to leave the two of you alone.'

'If you can spare the time, ma'am, I would appreciate your advice on domestic matters.'

'Then you shall have it, although I should warn you that I have not long been married and am not terribly familiar with the area yet. This house ran like clockwork before my arrival, and I know better than to interfere.'

Mr. Sanford smiled politely. 'I have chosen the wrong time of year to return, I quite realise that now. The house is barely habitable, and certainly not fit for me to receive visitors.'

Lizzy nodded. 'I feel persuaded you will receive more invitations than you can manage to honour. No one will expect you to return them until your house is restored to order.'

'That is a relief. None of the upstairs rooms are habitable because of the leaking roof, you see. I have made arrangements for it to be patched. Then we can dry out and redecorate the bedrooms, and in the spring I shall arrange for the roof to be completely replaced.'

'It seems as though you have everything in hand, Mr. Sanford.' Lizzy smiled at him. 'So how can I be of help?'

A frown creased his brow. 'I understood my uncle had made arrangements for the property to be cared for all these years, but that doesn't seem to have been the case.'

'We have seen no one there,' Will replied. 'Other than Mrs. Gibson, but then we can barely see your estate, especially in summer when the trees are in full leaf.'

'I had no idea it had been neglected so badly, but my uncle is dead so I can't ask him what went wrong.'

'I am sorry to hear that,' Will said politely.

'Thank you. My uncle was an excellent man, and could be exceedingly generous. But he was also Scottish to the bone, with a Scotsman's parsimonious instincts, and took a dim view of wasting money.'

'You think,' Will mused, 'that because the property was closed up and likely to remain so, he thought it unnecessary to keep it in good repair.'

'I cannot think of any other explanation. He probably thought it wouldn't cost me much more to put it right if and when I returned, than constantly keeping up with repairs. However, I shall never know the answer now.'

'Is the death of your uncle the reason for your return?' Lizzy asked.

'In part, yes, but I will come to that. Firstly, I need to employ some domestic staff, but they won't be able to live in until the roof is repaired and the attics made habitable. I wondered if you would have the goodness to point me in the right direction, ma'am.'

'Certainly. I am sure our housekeeper will know of girls in the village keen for work.'

'Thank you.'

'You will need someone to attend to the outdoor work, too,' Will pointed out.

'Yes, speaking of which, I was in the woods yesterday. Do I have your keepers to thank for maintaining a clear track through them?'

Will shook his head. 'Not to my knowledge.'

'Oh, that's strange. Everything else outside is totally overgrown, but the long track through the woods is not, and there are signs of people having used it recently. I assumed you had taken them as a shortcut, as we used to when we were boys.'

'No, even if it had occurred to me, I would not have done so without your permission.'

'How strange.' Mr. Sanford's frown intensified. 'No matter. I'm sure there is a perfectly reasonable explanation.'

'I will ask my steward if he knows anything about it,' Will said.

'Thank you.'

'I am not surprised to learn you have taken to the medical profession,' Will remarked after a short pause. 'You had an interest in the sciences, even as a boy, if memory serves.'

'Quite, and my uncle encouraged that interest and I followed him into his profession. I obtained a medical degree at Edinburgh University and was recently admitted to the London Company of Surgeons.'

Lizzy and Will exchanged a glance, aware such a prestigious appointment would ensure Mr. Sanford a comfortable future. Lizzy admired the casual modesty with which he admitted to his achievements.

'I was in Egypt, learning something of their ways with medicine, when I heard of my uncle's death. Naturally, I returned to Scotland, but my aunt died some years ago and my uncle's children all have their own establishments. There is nothing left for me north of the border, and so I am considering setting up as a doctor in this locality — '

'Someone with your qualifications will be a welcome addition to our community,' Darcy said. 'Although not everyone will be able to afford you.'

'I shall adapt my charges in accordance with the patient's ability to pay. I cannot turn a person who is seriously ill away simply because they are unable to pay me.'

'That is very noble of you,' Lizzy said, impressed by his compassionate nature. A man with his abilities could set up in London as surgeon to the aristocracy and make a small fortune. Instead, even though he no longer had strong ties to the community, he chose to return to the district where he was born and help those most in need.

'Thank you, but before I look to my career,

I must first restore my home to good order, and more importantly, delve into the business that brought me back to Derbyshire.'

'Which, I surmise, is what you wished to consult me about,' Will said.

'Quite.' Mr. Sanford momentarily lost himself in thought. He really was a most remarkably handsome man, Lizzy thought, as well as being intelligent and compassionate. 'When my uncle died a few months ago, we discovered papers in his study relating to my family. Specifically my father's diaries.'

'They must have made for distressing reading,' Lizzy said softly.

'Distressing enough, but less so than if I had read them at the time of my parent's demise. Time is a great healer, and far cheaper than consulting me.'

Lizzy and Will smiled at his attempt to lighten the mood.

'I can't imagine why my uncle did not pass them on to me when he was still alive, but that is another question I will never know the answer to.' He paused, as though collecting his thoughts. 'My father was the local magistrate, you will recall, Darcy.'

Will nodded. 'My father thought highly of him.'

'It's kind of you to say so, and it is his duties as a Justice of the Peace that have engaged my attention. He was taken up by a case a short time before his death. Something to do with a gang of highwaymen operating in the locality.'

Will shook his head. 'I don't recall, but I was still a boy myself at the time and, like you, away at school for most of the year.'

'The ringleaders were brought before a jury at the quarter sessions. My father was the presiding magistrate. The jury found them guilty, but they escaped the death penalty and were transported instead. They got off lightly because, according to my father's diaries, they didn't merely stop coaches and rob them, but took pleasure in terrorising the people travelling in them, which was cruel and unnecessary.'

'Perhaps they had been unfairly treated by a person of consequence,' Lizzy suggested, 'and were taking their revenge where they could get it.'

'Possibly. Not much of the contraband was recovered, but the parish constable received intelligence that led him to the culprits, and he found enough loot in their possession to condemn them.' Mr. Sanford seemed especially sombre. 'Once it became apparent that my father would be hearing the case, he received threats against himself, my mother, and me. If the miscreants were not acquitted, none of us would be safe.'

'Good God!' Will said.

'Quite so, and the pater took those threats seriously enough to ensure I didn't come home from school for the summer. Instead, I was sent to Scotland, and he and my mother decided to take a long trip after the case was heard.' Mr. Sanford swallowed. 'Unfortunately, they did not live long enough to do so.'

'You think their accident was no accident?' Will asked.

'It is a strong possibility. My father did not panic needlessly but was clearly very worried about the threats. I know he spoke with your father about them because he refers to the fact in his diaries. I wondered if there was anything in your father's papers that would shed more light on the matter. I can't let it rest, you see. Not until I know the truth. I was deprived of my excellent parents well before I ought to have been, and I need to know what really happened to them.'

'That is entirely understandable, Mr. Sanford,' Lizzy said, feeling very sorry for him. With no siblings, and no family other than his Scottish relations, she wondered if he had thrown himself so wholeheartedly into his education because . . . well, because it helped him to conquer his grief. 'In your situation, I would feel the same way.'

'I can certainly look at my own father's diaries,' Will said. 'But it will take some time to read through them all. He kept copious notes upon every little occurrence in his life.'

'There is no particular hurry. It has waited this long.'

'Do you know the names of the perpetrators?'

'Jordan, father and son. That's all I know. I applied to the presiding magistrate in Newcastle who has control of the parish records, but it seems that those for the period in question have mysteriously disappeared.'

Will sat a little straighter. 'How peculiar.'

'Precisely. It feels as though someone deliberately destroyed all records of the crime. I can't help wondering why. But if they did have accomplices who carried out the threat against my parents after the villains were transported, then I would very much like to know who they are.'

Will frowned. 'You do realise, Sanford, that even if you discover their identity, there's almost no hope of your being able to prove anything to their detriment.'

Mr. Sanford fixed Will with a probing look. 'In my situation, what would you do?'

'Just like you, I would want to know the truth. I simply don't want you to get your hopes up only to have them dashed.' Will paused. 'If my memory doesn't play me false, a man called Ventnor was the parish constable at the time. He is still alive and lives in Lambton. I can provide you with his direction. He might remember something.'

'I'm obliged to you, Darcy.' Mr. Sanford smiled, and Lizzy compulsively followed suit, thinking if Georgie had been there to see how the gesture transformed Mr. Sanford's face, illuminating his eyes and banishing the sadness from them, she would very likely have swooned. 'That is a possibility that had not occurred to me.'

'Come to dinner tomorrow night, if you are not already engaged, Mr. Sanford,' Lizzy said. 'By then, I shall have had an opportunity to consult Mrs. Reynolds and might have news regarding your requirement for servants.'

'Thank you. I shall be delighted.'

Mr. Sanford took his leave a short time after, and Will and Lizzy were at leisure to discuss his rather unusual request.

'What did you make of all that?' Lizzy asked.

'After fifteen years it will be next to impossible for him to prove his parents were the victims of anything other than an unfortunate carriage accident.'

Lizzy wrinkled her brow. 'But yesterday you

told me it occurred in the height of summer on a quiet country lane, and that Mr. Sanford's father was a first-rate whip.'

'Even the most proficient driver can't always maintain control if his horse is spooked say, by a bird flapping unexpectedly from a bush . . . by a rabbit running across his path, or something of that nature. If that horse leaves the road in its fright, it stands to reason the conveyance it is harnessed to will finish up overturned in a ditch, especially on a narrow lane. That is what happened to Sanford's parents.'

'Even so, in his position, I would want to ask questions.'

'And I shall do everything I can to help him, even if it gets him nowhere.'

'Why not ask Georgie to help you with your father's diaries?' Lizzy thought how much of Will's life had been lived trying to please a man he didn't understand. Georgie must know even less about him. 'It will be good for you both.'

'I'm not sure about that. I have hardly looked at them myself. She might find it distressing.'

'She's stronger than you think. And she will love it if you ask for her help, especially since it might benefit Mr. Sanford.'

'Well, if you think so. I shall be guided by

you, my love, as always.'

'And I shall be happy to take the credit if you and your sister gain something from the experience. If you do not then I shall remind you that I carry your son and cannot, under any circumstances, be scolded.'

Will laughed, returned his arm to her shoulders and pulled her head against his chest. 'I shall try to remember that.'

'I wonder if the highway robberies stopped after Jordan was convicted, or if his fellow highwaymen continued with their thievery.'

'Don't get ideas about investigating this yourself, Mrs. Darcy. I will not have you even thinking about highwaymen.'

'What highwaymen?' Georgiana asked, entering the room with Kitty.

'You just missed your Mr. Sanford,' Lizzy replied.

'Oh, did I?'

Lizzy shared an *I-told-you-so* smile with Will. Her rather too casual response, and the fact that her face coloured, showed more than a neighbourly interest in Mr. Sanford. And, unlike Major Halstead, there was nothing about Mr. Sanford that even Will, the most protective of brothers, could take exception to. He was educated, had his own property, and was charm personified.

'Never mind. He is coming to dinner

tomorrow evening.' Lizzy looked at Georgiana as she spoke. 'Mr. Sanford is a surgeon.'

'Oh.' Georgiana executed a casual shrug. 'Does he plan to use his skills in this locality?'

Lizzy quelled a smile. 'I believe so.'

Georgiana sat beside the fire. 'You did not tell us why you were speaking of highwaymen. Ought we to be concerned?'

'Not in the least.' It was Will who replied. 'But you can be of help to me, if you feel inclined to read some of our father's diaries.'

'By all means.' Georgiana looked confused, but at the same time pleased to be asked. 'But why?'

5

Fitzwilliam had never asked for Georgiana's help with any of his duties, and she felt very adult to be deferred to on this occasion, especially if it enabled her to be of service to Mr. Sanford.

'You must excuse me,' Lizzy said after luncheon. 'If I am not needed, I shall rest for a while.'

'I am very pleased you have decided to be sensible,' Fitzwilliam replied.

'When am I anything other than the epitome of good sense?'

Fitzwilliam looked exasperated. 'I do hope that was a rhetorical question.'

'Make of it what you will,' Lizzy replied with a teasing smile. 'Don't let him keep you at it for too long, Georgie.'

Georgiana couldn't remember what Pemberley had been like when her parents were both alive, but it had never felt more alive for her than it did now that Lizzy was here and Fitzwilliam was so very much in love with her. She watched him following his wife with his eyes until she disappeared around the curve in the staircase and was hard pressed not to sigh.

Georgiana was determined only to marry if she felt the same deep oneness with a gentleman that Fitzwilliam enjoyed with Lizzy. At one time, she imagined she might find that close bond with Major Halstead. When they had been introduced, he quite swept her off her feet with his rugged good looks and the intensity of his attentions. But something had changed since then, and it seemed as though it was too much effort for him to keep up the pretence that his affections were engaged. Either that, or he had decided she was too dull to be worth the effort of courting her, in spite of her money. The bored expression she sometimes saw before the major managed to conceal it, and some of the things he had said recently at unguarded moments, caused her to have doubts about his constancy. She had learned from her mistakes, and would not be rushed into any commitment, even if she persuaded herself she was in love. When she first met George Wickham, she was convinced she loved him, and look at the dreadful scandal that had almost caused.

Now Mr. Sanford occupied her thoughts. Dear God, did she not have a constant bone in her body? Lizzy had assured her she would know when she met the gentleman who was right for her, but given her frequent changes of mind, how could she be absolutely sure, she wondered, as she followed Fitzwilliam into the library.

'Goodness. I had no idea Papa recorded his thoughts and activities quite so conscientiously,' she said, feeling rather daunted by the large pile of leather-bound journals her brother had already removed from a break-fronted cabinet.

'If you find it uncomfortable, I can manage without you.'

'No, I shall be glad to help. It just seems a little intrusive to read something that wasn't intended for our eyes.'

Fitzwilliam's lips firmed. 'If our father didn't wish us to read his journals, you can take it from me, he would have destroyed them.'

'Yes, I expect he would.' She picked up the first journal from the pile in front of her. 'What am I looking for?'

'Any references to Sanford applying to our father for advice on highwaymen named Jordan. The books I have given you are from approximately the right time. Also, anything Sanford might have told him about threats made against Sanford and his family.'

Georgiana sighed. 'Very well.'

They settled down and started to read,

with only the sound of logs crackling in the grate and the turning of pages to break the silence. Georgiana was curious about the innermost thoughts of a father she barely remembered. If Fitzwilliam spoke about him at all, he referred to him as being rigidly correct and difficult to please. She gasped when she read a reference to herself, which painted him in a very different light. Papa described her as his miraculous angel, expressing in touching detail his pleasure at having such a beautiful daughter.

Georgiana wiped her eye, overcome with sentiment as she wondered why she was considered to be such a miracle. Presumably Mama and Papa had despaired of having more children. Her father had great hopes of her making an advantageous marriage. She blushed when several pages later he made reference to George Wickham, and how patient and kind he was with her, Georgiana, when she doggedly followed him everywhere on what her papa described as chubby little legs.

'What is it?'

Georgiana gasped. She hadn't realised Fitzwilliam had stopped reading and was watching her with open concern. She wanted to tell him it was nothing, but it occurred to her then that she had never had a frank

66

discussion with Fitzwilliam about anything. He had always been more of a father figure to her than an actual brother, and she only ever said what she thought he wanted to hear. Lizzy had shown Georgiana there was another way. Recklessly, she decided to put that theory to the test.

'We have never spoken of Mr. Wickham,' she said, stuttering in her anxiety but finding the courage to lift her chin, meet her brother's eye, and speak the forbidden name. 'And yet, I sometimes feel he is still in this house, stalking our thoughts.'

'Go on,' Fitzwilliam said, his bland expression giving nothing away.

'Now, as I read Papa's diaries, I come across praise for him on almost every page.'

Fitzwilliam's jaw was rigid with tension. 'You know as well as I do that Wickham is perfectly capable of making himself agreeable if it's worth his while. I'm glad Father didn't live to see the true nature of his character.'

'That isn't what I meant precisely. I was thinking of the shame, the scandal, I almost visited upon you all.' She swallowed and shook her head, not bothering to check her tears this time. 'The guilt eats away at me each time I think about the trouble I caused you.'

'You were lonely and neglected.' The harsh

expression in Fitzwilliam's eyes softened. 'You talk of guilt, but the load you bear is nothing to the blame I myself must shoulder.'

Georgiana's head shot up. 'You! It was not your fault.'

'Our father died and left me with the responsibility for Pemberley when I wasn't ready to take it on. More importantly, he left me with responsibility for you, and I had absolutely no idea how to care for a child ten years my junior. I was terrified, if you want to know the truth.'

Georgiana widened her eyes. 'Of me!'

'Absolutely. What did I know of young girls? And so, I followed our father's example and remained as remote, unreachable and severe as he had been. You probably didn't feel you could approach me, and yet George Wickham was everything I was not — charming, agreeable, available, and with all the time in the world to devote to you.'

'Even so, I ought not to have been swayed by those considerations. Papa talks in this journal about his hopes of my making a good marriage. I am very glad he was not alive when I agreed to an elopement.'

'If he had been, it would not have been suggested. Wickham always supposed our father would provide handsomely for him, and if he had lived longer, he might well have charmed him into doing so.'

'Mr. Wickham looked upon himself as a member of the family. He was always here, making himself useful, especially when you were not, which was frequently.'

'I ought to have realised what he was about and banned him from Pemberley.' Fitzwilliam ground his jaw. 'He was cultivating you, in case our father disappointed him.'

'He listened to me, and never laughed at my childish aspirations, so I suppose I looked up to him.'

'He caught you when you felt lonely and vulnerable. You were unaware how to gauge the sincerity of a man's affections because your life had been so sheltered, and you had no one to compare Mr. Wickham with.' Fitzwilliam flashed the ghost of a smile. 'I can easily imagine how sophisticated he must have appeared. A man of his experience would have no difficulty in turning your head. You believed he was in love with you because you trusted him. He made sure of that, and I was too preoccupied with my inherited responsibilities to notice.' Fitzwilliam came round to her side of the desk, and placed a reassuring hand on her shoulders. 'He knew exactly what he was doing, but you did not.'

'I knew what he persuaded me to do was wrong.' Georgiana lowered her eyes. 'There's no evading that particular truth.'

'He did not succeed in his ambition, which is all that signifies. It is better not to speak of these things, if it upsets you.'

'Actually, I *want* to talk about it. I want to make you understand. Perhaps that way I shall feel less guilty. When Mr. Sanford mentioned his name at the wedding breakfast, I wanted the floor to open up and swallow me whole, not because I felt uncomfortable, but because I was consumed by guilt for what I almost did to you. I saw how you looked at me, you see — '

'I didn't want you to be overset, but didn't know how to defuse the situation.'

Georgiana widened her eyes. 'But you always know how to do everything.'

'Not always, apparently.' He smiled, weariness etched around his eyes. 'But by all means, let us talk about it. If we discuss that terrible time it might help us both to feel less culpable.'

'Mr. Wickham repeatedly told me he had been treated unfairly.' Georgiana blinked back more guilty tears and met Fitzwilliam's gaze. 'That you had not honoured Papa's wishes. I felt conflicted, caught in the middle of a spiral of accusations I did not understand. I was sure you would not have wilfully ignored any verbal instructions Papa

70

had given you, and yet I also didn't think Mr. Wickham would lie to me. I said there must be some simple misunderstanding and that I would speak to you about it. He adamantly refused, saying it wasn't for me to get involved.' Georgiana nervously folded and unfolded her hands. 'I thought he was being gallant, protecting my finer feelings. Now I realise he didn't want you to know just how close the two of us had become, or that he had discussed his disappointment with me.'

'Especially when, by the time the elopement was planned, so many years had elapsed since our father's death.'

'Yes, although that did not occur to me at the time.'

'Our father intended the living in Kympton for Mr. Wickham. When it fell vacant, he told me he had decided against going into the church and received generous financial recompense instead. Because he led me to believe he fully intended to take the living, I continued to allow him to come here until it was within my gift. I wasn't altogether happy about his frequent visits to Pemberley, but thought it was what our father would have wanted. That proved to be a grave error of judgement on my part, since it gave Wickham more time to cultivate your trust.' Fitzwilliam shook his head. 'I was fully aware of his rapacious nature and should have known the money I gave him would soon slip through his fingers. With pressing debts and a grudge against me, he was hell bent on revenge.'

'And would have achieved it if I had eloped with him?'

'Precisely.'

The full force of Georgiana's stupidity, her gullibility, struck her when she absorbed her brother's savage expression. 'You did stop him coming here several years before . . . well, before I agreed to go away with him. I only met him again by chance when in Ramsgate.'

'That wasn't chance.' Fitzwilliam made a scoffing sound at the back of his throat. 'It was deliberately contrived.'

'Oh.' Georgiana blinked back her surprise. 'I didn't realise. It seems obvious, now that I know.'

'Wickham and I were very close as boys, but I saw his true colours at university and never liked or trusted him much after that. And yet . . . yet, I still allowed him to come here and influence you.' Georgiana had never seen Fitzwilliam so discomposed before and the sight rather frightened her. Her brother was always in control, always knew best, never showed any sign of weakness or uncertainty. 'I shall never forgive myself for that. Never!'

'Don't say that.' She reached out and touched his arm. 'You will make me feel even worse than I already do.'

He looked up, smiled at her, and the torment slowly faded from his eyes. 'No, my dear sister, this conversation will make us both feel better. I am quite sure of that.'

Georgiana sighed. 'You saved me from my own folly, and generously never referred to the incident again.'

'I didn't speak of it to save you from embarrassment, and me from facing up to my own failings as your surrogate father. That was an error of judgement, and now that we have discussed the unfortunate episode, Mr. Wickham will never cast a shadow between us again.'

'Then I'm glad I found the courage to mention his name.'

'You can mention anything you like in my hearing, Georgiana. I also hope you weren't too distressed when Lydia Wickham descended upon us earlier this year. She was not invited, but as Lizzy's sister, I could hardly turn her away.'

'I did feel embarrassed at first, but then it hardly seemed to matter since no one other than you, Lizzy, and the colonel know of my history with Mr. Wickham. But I was astonished to see Mr. Wickham, though. That was quite a shock.'

Fitzwilliam's head shot up. 'When did you see him?'

'In a carriage with Mrs. Wickham and Mr. and Mrs. Gardiner. He waved to me, all smiles and good humour, as though I didn't now know him for the scoundrel he is. Insufferable man!'

'You were not supposed to see him. I thought you were engaged elsewhere when appointing a time for Wickham to call.'

'Actually, I'm glad I saw him. It helped me to appreciate my narrow escape.'

'Well then, I am glad, too.'

Georgiana wanted to ask Fitzwilliam why Wickham had come to Pemberley, and if it had been a terrible shock when Mr. Wickham came into their lives again and married Lizzy's youngest sister. She didn't quite have the courage to ask how he had been involved in ensuring the marriage actually took place, but was sure he had been. She had heard snatched snippets of conversation that made her believe it was Fitzwilliam who had ensured Lizzy's family was not disgraced because Lydia lived with Mr. Wickham before they were man and wife. It probably cost him a lot of money, because that was the only language George Wickham understood.

Georgiana felt as though a great weight of guilt had been lifted from her shoulders. She smiled at her brother and returned her attention to the journal she had been perusing with a much lighter heart.

'How are you getting along?' Fitzwilliam asked after a prolonged period of silence.

'Nothing yet, and I keep getting side-tracked by the things Papa wrote. I think I am more of a hindrance than a help to you.'

'It is time you knew our father better. I should have thought of this before now.'

'If we do find anything, will it actually help Mr. Sanford?'

'Probably not, and he's well aware of that.'

'Then I wonder what makes him bother. He must have more important things to concern himself with.'

'In his position, I would feel the same way.'

'Yes, I suppose . . . oh, listen to this.' Georgiana cleared her throat. '*Today, Fitzwilliam surprised me by reciting Homer's* Odyssey *with great feeling and without once referring to the text. He did so in Greek, and I was much impressed with his improvement in that tongue.*'

'I recall the occasion. Our father merely grunted, but didn't offer his opinion.'

'He may not have known how to express his feelings in words, but he had no difficulty doing so in writing.'

Fitzwilliam lowered his head to the journal he was reading rather quickly. Georgiana could not be absolutely certain, but she was fairly sure his eyes were moist.

An hour later, when neither of them had discovered anything that might help Mr. Sanford, Fitzwilliam called a halt.

'That's quite enough for one day,' he said.

Georgiana stood up and stretched. 'My eyes are starting to feel the strain. Sometimes, Papa's handwriting becomes almost illegible.'

'Go and rest before dinner. You have been a great help.'

'Very well.' Georgiana smiled at her brother. 'I'm not sure I have . . . helped, that is, but I have enjoyed myself, and I am very glad we talked about things.'

Fitzwilliam smiled and placed an arm around her shoulders. 'Then I am glad too,' he said.

6

It occurred to Dominic halfway through the evening that reading the rather musty, water-damaged papers his father had left at Sanford House was probably a waste of time. Anything of value and interest had been included in the boxful of possessions taken to Scotland. A systematic search of the documents remaining in Derbyshire confirmed the fact. With a legitimate excuse to abandon them, he put aside his father's old, meticulously-kept accounts. He had learned nothing from them, other than that the pater suspected he had been overcharged for repairs to his carriage.

'Right then, Hamish,' he told his dog with a heavy sigh. The two of them had settled as close to the kitchen range as possible without actually singeing themselves. 'I suppose I had better examine the diaries in more detail, just in case I've overlooked something important.'

But Dominic had read the relevant passages so often that he almost knew them by heart. He found his mind wandering and wondered if it had it been a mistake to return to Derbyshire. Nothing could be as it once was. But then, the same could be said of Scotland. He had been made to feel perfectly welcome by his aunt and uncle. Yet at the same time, he was never completely accepted by the clannish Scots who were suspicious of all Englishmen, perhaps with good reason. He had countered his unhappiness by burying himself in his education and interest in the advances being made with modern medicine. It completely occupied his mind and saved him from dwelling upon his devastating loss.

Now the time had come to settle down and use that medical knowledge to help those less fortunate than himself. He did not wish to be in a big city. He had little interest in society, where he would doubtless have endless eligible females pushed in his direction simply because he was single and a man of property. Matrimony did not interest him either, so Derbyshire was as good a place as anywhere to avoid it.

The wind howled around the chimneys and rattled the windows, disturbing Dominic's tangled reflections. Hamish lifted his head and whined.

'I seem to remember Derbyshire being a very agreeable place in the summer,' he told Hamish with a wry twist to his lips, trying to convince himself as much as his dog that he had made the right decision in coming back.

He retired early and was up again at first light. Not a moment too soon since the range was on the point of expiry. Mrs. Gibson had given him precise instructions on how to keep it going, and he had failed to adhere to them. The curmudgeonly Mrs. Gibson scared the life out of him, and he had no wish to get on her wrong side. He let Hamish out, riddled the range, and concentrated upon coaxing it back to life. Not accustomed to such menial tasks, he felt mildly euphoric when he succeeded.

Just as he did so, Mrs. Gibson pushed through the kitchen door, bundled up in a weird array of clothing, her nose and plump cheeks red from the cold. She drove herself to and from his house, every day except Sunday, in a dilapidated gig pulled by an ancient cob. The accident, if that's what it was that had killed his parents, occurred in the middle of a clear summer day while driving a modern, roadworthy conveyance. Fearing for Mrs. Gibson's safety, Dominic had offered to have her collected and returned daily by a carriage supplied by the Lambton inn, but she had seemed insulted by the suggestion.

'I am well able to drive myself, thank you all the same, sir.'

And there the matter rested.

'Good morning, Mrs. Gibson. It looks colder than ever out today.'

'Warmer than in here,' she replied with a suspicious sniff that told him she knew he had failed to bank up the range before retiring.

And that was the sum total of their conversation. Mrs. Gibson was conscientious in the execution of her duties, and appeared grateful for the extra hours she now worked since Dominic's return. But she showed no inclination to engage in gossip and spoke only when she had something to say, which was seldom. Dominic had grown accustomed to her taciturn character and no longer tried to engage her in conversation.

While Mrs. Gibson set about making his breakfast, Dominic took himself off and attended to his ablutions. There was no hot water, and so they did not delay him for long. When he had partaken of coddled eggs, fried bacon, and fresh bread most probably made by Mrs. Gibson's own hand before she set out for Sanford House, Dominic decided to make another effort at inspecting the cottage in the grounds. He briefly stopped at his makeshift stable to wish Midnight a good morning. He was greeted with a whinny of recognition. Dominic patted his horse's neck, refilled his manger with fresh hay, and broke the ice on the surface of his water bucket. He threw in a small feed of oats and sliced carrots, then left the beast to his breakfast.

'I know you want to stretch your legs,' he told the stallion. 'And so you shall, in a little while.'

With Hamish dashing ahead of him, Dominic covered the same ground as the previous day, feeling a little less cold. The day was clearer, with no hail or snow in prospect, and the wind seemed less severe. He threw back his head and breathed deeply of the frigid air, filling his lungs with its fresh purity and feeling completely content, in spite of the massive task he had ahead of him in restoring his house to a habitable state.

He noticed things he had not seen the last time he made this journey which definitely indicated the path had been in regular and recent use. Indentations in the mud made by more than one pair of feet and ruts made by the wheels of a cart. It made absolutely no sense, and Dominic reminded himself to ask Mrs. Gibson if she had seen anyone in his woods.

As they approached the cottage, Hamish became obsessed with a particular tree, barking and clawing at its trunk. Dominic could see no special reason for his interest — squirrels probably — and left him to it.

Instead, he turned his attention to the cottage, relieved to see the roof indeed appeared to be intact. The rest of the outside looked a little neglected, but was in a much better state than the main house.

'Everything's relative,' he said to himself as he produced the key from his pocket and inserted it into the front door lock.

To his considerable surprise, that proved to be unnecessary since the place was unlocked. A feeling of unease gripped him, and he wished he had thought to come armed with a weapon. Someone had used the track through his woods often enough to take the trouble to keep it clear. Now he found the door to his cottage unlocked. Could someone be living here? Well, if they were, they could damned well explain themselves to him. He wasn't about to cower here on the threshold as though *he* was the trespasser. Even so, he called Hamish to his side before picking up a stout piece of wood he could use as a club, if necessary. He then squared his shoulders, pushed the door wide open, and called out a warning. Hamish's hackles were raised, causing Dominic further concern, but the musty stillness of a cold, empty house quickly reassured Dominic no one was there at that precise moment.

The cottage had a small entrance lobby, off

which there were three doors. Most of the space was taken up by one good-sized salon. The second door led to the only bedchamber, the third to a scullery. Dominic remembered it from his childhood and, with light spilling from the open doorway, was able to quickly open the shutters and allow further light to penetrate the dusty interior.

The windows were warped, he noticed. He would need to do something about that. A quick check of the bedroom and scullery confirmed he and Hamish definitely had the place to themselves. The furniture was shrouded in sheets but the dust on the boarded floor had been disturbed by feet other than his own. Dominic removed his hat and scratched his head, wondering what the devil was going on.

'I think this might do for us very well, Hamish,' he told his dog when he had made a quick examination of the walls. Unlike in the main house, there were no signs of dampness or mildew. He pictured the cottage in his mind's eye, cleaned up, with a roaring fire heating the entire place. Perfect for his current requirements. 'We shall live in the woods like hermits until the winter comes to an end and you can chase squirrels to your heart's content.'

Woof!

'Good, then we are agreed.'

Dominic lifted one of the sheets from a sofa and winced. The stuffing tumbled onto the floor, and he heard the scurry of tiny feet somewhere deep inside the furniture.

'This lot will all have to be burned,' he said aloud, wondering why he felt the need to articulate his thoughts. He concluded he must still be jittery at finding his property had been occupied, and not only by the mice that had destroyed his furniture. 'But the furniture at the main house has survived intact. I shall simply have enough for my needs moved down here at once.'

He closed up the shutters and made a point of locking the door, wondering if he would find it unlocked again when he next returned. He and Hamish made their way back to the house and sought out Mrs. Gibson. She listened when he told her of his plans, as usual not saying a word until he asked her a question.

'I need a chimney sweep, a strong man to help remove and burn the furniture and replace it with items from this house. Oh, and the windows need to be rubbed down and rehung. And I need a couple of girls to give the place a good clean. Can you recommend anyone, Mrs. Gibson?'

'I'll tell the chimney sweep to call

tomorrow. I pass his cottage on the way home. My grandson can help with the heavy work, and I'll see what I can do about some girls.'

It was the longest speech Mrs. Gibson had made in his hearing.

'Thank you. I shall still need you to come in here daily and prepare my meals for me, if you would be so kind.'

'Ain't no kindness involved. I do it 'cause you pay me.'

'That I do, Mrs. Gibson.' Dominic suppressed a smile, suspecting all the money in the world would not tempt her if her employer did not enjoy at least a modicum of her respect. 'Right, I shall leave you to your duties. I have business in the village.'

Dominic ventured back outside. Midnight had finished his breakfast and whickered when he heard Dominic approaching. He took a brush to his horse and vigorously strapped his black coat until it shone. Dominic was actually warm by the time he was satisfied with his handiwork. He might be prepared to live rough himself, but there was a limit to the number of indignities he would expect his stallion to endure. He fetched saddle and bridle, urging Midnight to stand still while he set them in place. The horse was keen for exercise, and Dominic was in the mood to oblige him. He swung up into his saddle and, with Hamish running alongside, headed for Lambton at a brisk trot. The ground underfoot was solid and icy in places. Dominic didn't intend to risk Midnight by moving any faster, but Midnight had other ideas and Dominic had the devil's own job holding the lively beast in check.

He reached the village and asked at the inn for directions to Ventnor's dwelling. He found himself outside of a neat cottage a short time later. Smoke belching from the chimney indicated someone was at home. He tethered Midnight to the gatepost, and told Hamish to wait there with him. Dominic knocked at the cottage's front door, waited a moment, and then knocked for a second time, but there were no sounds from within. Disappointed, he was at the point of giving up when the door opened. An old man with snow-white hair leaned heavily on a stick, his body bent double with age. If this was Ventnor, then he must have been at the point of retiring from his position as local constable when Jordan was arrested fifteen years previously.

'Mr. Ventnor?' Dominic asked.

The old man screwed up his eyes and peered myopically up at Dominic. 'Who are you?'

'My name is Sanford, sir. I wondered if you could spare me a few minutes of your time.'

'Sanford's dead. The idiot turned his carriage over.'

Dominic swallowed. 'I am Dominic Sanford, the son.'

'Why didn't you say so?' Ventnor shuffled backwards and opened the door wider. 'Hurry up inside, man. You're letting the heat out.'

Dominic removed his hat, stooped to walk beneath the low lintel, and taking the door from Ventnor's hand, closed it behind them both.

'In here.'

The parlour was small, mercifully warm, and spotlessly clean. Ventnor either had a wife or an efficient housekeeper. His hands were claws, Dominic noticed, and clearly caused him pain. Arthritis. Dominic had seen effective relief for such symptoms while in Egypt — a clever mixture of willowbark and alfalfa — but it would be necessary to overcome the suspicions he had met at every turn before a man of Ventnor's age could be persuaded to try something so unorthodox.

'Can't offer you refreshment,' Ventnor said gruffly. 'I'm here on my own.'

'That's perfectly all right, sir. I am sorry to intrude and won't take up much of your time.' Dominic tried to find a comfortable position on the lumpy chair he had been directed to. Realising he was unlikely to achieve that ambition, he made the best of things and came to the point. 'I believe you were responsible for arresting the highwaymen named Jordan.'

'Ah, that's what I thought you must want to know about.' Ventnor suddenly didn't seem quite so doddery. His body might be frail but his eyes had come alive and there was clearly little at fault with his cognitive powers. 'That was a right caper, and no mistake.'

'You remember the case?'

'As plain as day. It caused quite a rumpus in these parts. Half the populace understood why the Jordans did what they did, what with honest work being so hard to come by. The other half wanted to see them swing for their crimes.'

'Did my father discuss their plight with you?'

'Not specifically. That wouldn't have been right, and your father was a stickler for procedures.'

'Quite so.' Dominic rubbed the back of his neck, wondering how to word his next question without influencing Ventnor's response. Before he could think of a way, Ventnor spoke again.

'It's the threats you'll be wanting to know about, I expect.'

Dominic didn't need to pretend surprise. 'You knew about them?'

'I was on the receiving end of 'em. So was everyone else involved in the case including, I suspect, half the jury. That's why they found them guilty but recommended transportation as opposed to hanging, I've always thought. Stands to reason your father must have been threatened, an' all. When he and your mother died, I did wonder about that.'

'But did nothing about it.'

'What could I do?' Ventnor's rheumy old eyes flashed with indignation. 'There was no evidence it was anything other than an accident.'

'Of course you did your duty to the best of your ability.' But Dominic still thought Ventnor could have expressed his suspicions to a higher authority.

'They were right villains those Jordans, and I'm not afraid to admit they intimidated me. I was mighty glad when they were taken from these shores.'

'Were there other members of the gang?'

'There must have been. Who could have issued all them threats while Jordan and his son were locked up else?' The same question had occurred to Dominic. 'But the robberies stopped after the Jordans were arrested.'

'Did they have any other family?'

'Jordan had a wife. She died shortly after her husband was transported. She swore on her deathbed that her heart had been broken.' Ventnor sniffed. 'Anyway, there were no other children.'

Frustration clouded Dominic's thinking. Darcy had been right. This really was a waste of effort. But he couldn't seem to let it go. There had to be something — some recollection, some clue — that had thus far been overlooked. He remained with Ventnor for another ten minutes, but it was evident the man could tell him nothing more. He thanked him for his time and left.

On a whim he stopped at the inn, left Midnight and Hamish with the ostlers, and walked into the taproom. It was half-full of merchants and traders wetting their whistles. They paused in their conversations and looked at Dominic with varying degrees of curiosity and suspicion as he strode into their midst.

'Good afternoon, gentlemen. Drinks all round, if you please, landlord.'

The gesture had the desired effect. Suspicion evaporated and Dominic spent a pleasant hour, fielding questions about himself and the reasons for his return, not yet ready to announce his medical qualifications. Mostly he just listened, quickly discovering the names of the leading families within Lambton, still hopeful of discovering something more about the Jordans. Unfortunately, their name was not mentioned; nor were those of Dominic's parents. If anyone here recalled their accident, they were too well-mannered to speak about it.

Mutton stew had been prepared by the landlady, and Dominic managed two servings. He praised Mrs. Parker on the quality of the dish, making her blush. He was on the point of finishing his ale and heading home when Major Halstead walked in, in full regimentals. He was on his own, probably on the way to Pemberley to call upon Miss Darcy. Surely, he didn't intend to sup ale before visiting a lady and risk breathing alcoholic fumes all over her? Evidently he did, since a foaming tankard was placed before him as soon as he reached the bar. Obviously, he was no stranger to this establishment.

'Afternoon, Major,' the landlord said.

'I was lured here by the thought of your excellent ale, Parker.' Halstead's smile faltered when he noticed Dominic in the midst of his new friends. 'Sanford,' he said politely.

'Major,' Dominic replied with equal verbal economy.

Dominic made a second attempt to leave but the major detained him, quizzing him about the reasons for his return and the intended length of his stay. Dominic wondered why. Did he imagine he was a rival for Miss Darcy's affections? He didn't like Halstead and prevaricated, making his responses short to the point of rudeness.

Finally able to escape, he rode home slowly, trying to decide why he had taken the major in such dislike. He had only met him once before, at the wedding, and they hadn't exchanged more than a dozen words on that occasion. If Darcy thought he was a suitable man to court his sister, what was that to Dominic? For his part, Dominic thought the man vain and untrustworthy. Just the way he had flirted with the buxom barmaid was evidence of that fact.

Back at Stamford House, Dominic stabled Midnight and saw to his needs. Then he turned his attention to his wardrobe. He had an engagement to dine at Pemberley.

7

Lizzy was awakened from a deep afternoon sleep by the distinctive, highly addictive masculine aroma that told her Will had crept into her chamber to check on her. Her heart soared, even though her condition precluded him from employing his preferred method of waking her. She had tried to persuade him that nothing he did was likely to harm her or the baby, but he wouldn't listen. Foolish, over-protective man! She opened her eyes and found herself looking directly up at his ruggedly handsome features, hair flopping across his brow as he dealt her one of his heart-stopping, intimately enticing smiles.

'I didn't mean to wake you.' He sat himself on the side of the bed and brushed the hair away from her face. 'You looked so peaceful.'

'I am glad you did.' She stretched and smiled up at the man she loved more than life itself. She still had nightmares when she thought of how close Miss Bingley had come to spoiling everything with her vindictive spite.

'How are you feeling?'

'Uncomfortable.' She took his hand and

placed it on her swollen belly. 'Your son is full of himself this afternoon.'

'My goodness. He moved!' Lizzy laughed at his incredulous expression. 'Did you feel that? He actually moved.'

'I certainly felt it,' she replied, wincing. 'And you have just proved my point. You actually want a son.'

'Not in the least. You referred to our child as *he*, and I followed your example.'

'Have it your way.' But Lizzy knew better. Of course he wanted a boy. 'What have you been doing with yourself since luncheon?'

'Georgiana and I have read through more of our father's journals.'

'Do you make any progress?'

'Yes, but not in the manner Sanford hopes for.'

Lizzy propped herself awkwardly on one elbow. 'Then how?'

'We . . . er, discussed Wickham.'

'Ah, I hoped you might.'

'When suggesting Georgiana helped me with the task, you imagined it would lead to a discussion on Wickham?' Will frowned. 'How did you reach that conclusion?'

'You have to admit it was a distinct possibility.' Lizzy reached up and traced the line of his jaw, trying to eradicate some of the rigidness, the tight vertical lines beside his mouth that deepened when he was angry or upset. 'You have often remarked that your father thought well of Wickham, so his name was bound to feature in his journals.'

'And yet the possibility had not occurred to me. You ought to have warned me, Lizzy, then I might have handled the situation better.'

'If I had, you would not have asked for Georgie's help. She needed to find the courage to speak to you about Wickham without you having time to consider your responses.' Lizzy paused. 'You will never be free of him until you stop blaming your-selves.'

'I would not have agreed with you beforehand, but I know now that you were right.' His expression was full of admiration. 'As usual.'

Lizzy smiled. 'You blame yourself for what happened, and Georgie blames herself. Worse, she has never forgiven herself because she thinks she failed you and did not live up to your expectations. I hope you told her the fault was not hers.'

'Yes, I did.' Will lowered his head and gently covered her lips with his own. 'What a very wise woman I had the good sense to marry. What would I be without you?'

'Well, naturally I have an opinion on that subject.'

'Oh, naturally.' Will laughed and rolled onto the bed, lying flat on his back next to her. 'Shall I ring and have Jessie bring you up some tea?'

'Ring the bell, but Jessie can help me dress and I shall go down for tea.'

'If you insist.'

Lizzy gritted her teeth when the baby kicked especially hard. She wasn't sure if he should be so lively this far in advance of her time but had no one to consult on the subject. If Will knew she had the slightest concern a physician would be sent for, and Will would insist she remained in bed. What could a physician do, other than to remind her that a little discomfort was an inevitable result of her condition?

A short time later, she joined Georgiana and Kitty in the drawing room, and they enjoyed taking tea together. Before they were finished, Major Halstead was announced.

'Were you expecting him, Georgie?' Lizzy asked.

'I wonder if Captain Turner is with him,' Kitty said at the same time.

'The major is alone, ma'am,' Simpson replied.

Lizzy noticed that Georgiana didn't look especially thrilled by the visit. 'I suppose now the regiment is quartered so close by, we must expect our acquaintances to call more frequently.'

'If you don't wish to see him, I shall have Simpson say we are not at home.'

'No, show him in please, Simpson,' Georgiana replied. 'Next time, he might bring the captain with him, and I would not spoil Kitty's pleasure, but stay with us, Lizzy. I don't want to be alone with him.'

Lizzy raised a brow and made a mental note to ask Georgie at a more appropriate time if she had decided against the major. Will would be pleased if that was the case. Lizzy, who had once liked and approved of him, found she was now in agreement with her husband. She could not say why, precisely. The major was handsome, charming and entertaining company. He had no money of his own, it was true, but he was a gentleman and did appear to be genuinely fond of Georgie. But if she no longer returned his feelings, that put a very different emphasis on matters.

'Of course, if you wish,' she said.

★   ★   ★

James was not in the best of humours before making his visit to Pemberley. That situation didn't improve when he was kept waiting for

97

so long he wondered if the ladies would actually decline to receive him. Simpson, the stately butler at Pemberley who liked to imagine he was intimidating, finally deigned to return.

'The ladies will receive you in the drawing room, Major Halstead.'

Simpson preceded James in that direction, his gait measured and precise, forcing James to adapt his own pace accordingly. James wanted to scream that he knew the way very well and didn't need to be escorted. He had twice been a guest in this magnificent house and had thought the servants in it liked and approved of him. He had gone out of his way to ensure they did — aware that winning the approval of senior servants was vital if one wished to ingratiate oneself with the family they served. For that reason, he had left generous gratuities he could ill afford at the end of each visit.

But Simpson still treated him like a stranger, which was a cause for concern. If Georgiana *had* decided against him, Simpson would know it, and his loyalties would be with her. Damnation, could Sanford have turned her head already? The blasted man had only been in the district for five minutes and had created havoc with James's carefully laid plans. He had patiently cultivated

Georgiana Darcy, and charmed the rest of her family. He'd done a pretty fine job of winning Mrs. Darcy around, but Darcy was a harder nut to crack. Everyone knew he was fiercely protective when it came to his sister's interests.

Even so, if Georgiana set her heart on him, Mrs. Darcy would make her husband see reason. He could tell by the way he looked at his wife that he adored her, listened to her advice, and respected her opinion. James had to stop himself looking at Rose in precisely the same way. Rose was the love of his life, but he could not marry her, even if there was the remotest possibility of her accepting him. Rose was fiercely independent and refused to lean on any man. Sharing her bed with James, bearing his children, she was willing to do. James accepted that the only way to keep her was to take as much of her as she was willing to give. Free spirits such as Rose were as rare and precious as they were impossible to tame.

It was just as well really. James had good reasons for wanting to remain on good terms with his socially acceptable but impoverished family. If he married Rose they would cut him dead. In marrying Georgiana Darcy, on the other hand, he would enjoy his family's approval *and* be in a position to continue his relationship with Rose. Breaking it off had never been an option. Rose was more addictive than opium, as was involvement in the dubious activities that added an element of danger to their partnership. Rose was never more aggressive in the bedchamber than when she had been taking risks, or was being outrageous in her on-going quest for revenge.

When James had seen Sanford at the inn earlier, it seemed like an ideal opportunity to find out more about his plans. Unfortunately, the man had been most unforthcoming. What the devil was he being so secretive about? God forbid he had heard of Rose's activities. If he had, it would be the worse for him. There was nothing he would not do to protect the woman he worshipped — the mother of his child, the guardian of his heart.

James shook away thoughts of Rose for fear of the physical reaction they would engender. That was simply the way it was between them. Rose embraced the physical side of their relationship in the same forthright manner she did everything else, making no attempt to dissemble or pretend she didn't thoroughly enjoy their activities. Her wild abandonment and total disregard for propriety was a refreshing trait, typical of her independent nature. Put simply, Rose didn't give two figs for what people thought of her, and lived her life on her own terms.

It took a supreme effort of will for James to return his mind to the question of Georgiana. During his last visit he had convinced himself she was ready to receive his declaration. A number of them had put on a play, which brought them constantly into one another's company. Georgiana had blossomed as rehearsals continued, relying heavily on James to help her learn her lines. It would have been the ideal time to propose, but he thought of Rose and foolishly hesitated. It wasn't as if Rose didn't know of his plans. They had discussed them endlessly and Rose encouraged him to pursue Miss Darcy. She would benefit from the union every bit as much as James would. Put simply, Georgiana's dowry would ensure Rose and her child's future — together with any further children they might have — would be secure. Not that Rose would allow herself to be supported by him, she was far too independent for that, but what sort of man would James be if he could not take care of his heart's desire?

Damn it. He had miscalculated with Georgiana and missed his chance. No matter, he could recover lost ground easily enough. In spite of her wealth and consequence, she had seen little of the world and was easy to impress. He simply needed to be additionally charming and attentive today. It was unfortunate about the weather, which precluded intimate walks in the grounds. Still, Mrs. Darcy was fairly relaxed about his being alone with Georgiana. Hopefully, an opportunity would present itself.

'Major Halstead, ma'am,' Simpson announced rather pompously, James thought, as he walked past him into the drawing room.

'Mrs. Darcy.' James bowed over her hand. 'I hope I am not intruding.'

'It is always a pleasure to see you, Major, although I am surprised you made the journey in such bad weather.'

James smiled. 'I am a soldier. I think nothing of a little adverse weather, especially with the prospect of calling at Pemberley and enjoying the pleasure of your society to spur me on.' He turned towards Georgiana and Kitty Bennet, seated together on a settee beside the fire, and greeted each of them, fixing Georgiana with an especially intimate smile. 'I trust I find you well, ladies.'

'Thank you, yes,' Georgiana replied, perfectly politely, but her smile seemed a little strained.

'Captain Turner sends his compliments to you all,' James said, focusing on Miss Bennet as he spoke. 'Unfortunately his duties prevented him from joining me today.'

'I am surprised you could be spared yourself, Major, so soon after Colonel Fitzwilliam's removal,' Mrs. Darcy remarked, pouring tea for him and handing him the cup. 'Presumably your own duties have increased as a consequence.'

'At the present time, the regiment is not on active duty, ma'am. In fact, we are hoping to winter here very peacefully, which will allow us time to become more closely acquainted with our friends in the district.'

'Colonel Fitzwilliam promised us a ball,' Miss Bennet remarked. 'I hope the new colonel will honour that promise.'

'I shall take it upon myself to remind him of the commitment when he takes up his duties.'

The conversation became more general and it took James a moment to realise Georgiana had made almost no contribution to it. She had always been quiet, but had become less reserved in his company since they had performed together in the infamous play. She must be preoccupied about something. The alternative — that she was tired of his company — was unthinkable.

'Do you look forward to the regimental ball, Miss Darcy?' he asked.

'When it becomes a fixed engagement, I certainly shall.'

'When does the new colonel join the regiment?' Miss Bennet asked.

'Not for another few weeks. Perhaps not until after Christmas, is my understanding.'

Which, James supposed, would coincide with Mrs. Darcy's confinement. And if she did not attend the ball, there was every chance Georgiana would not do so either.

'How is your new neighbour settling in?' he asked.

Miss Bennet opened her mouth to reply, but Georgiana spoke first.

'Mr. Sanford seems very agreeable. He and my brother were acquainted as boys, but I do not remember him.'

James felt a flash of jealousy because that was the longest speech Miss Darcy had volunteered since his arrival. He was not in love with Georgiana, but still resented her speaking of another man in what, for her, was glowing terms. 'Does he plan to remain in the district long?'

'He didn't say.'

This time it was Mrs. Darcy who spoke. Neither she nor Georgiana were telling him everything they knew. James was sure of that, and their reticence made him uneasy. It was also obvious he wouldn't get the opportunity to converse with Georgiana alone unless Mrs. Darcy issued an invitation for him to stay to dinner. James stretched the visit out to its lengthiest extreme, but no further information was forthcoming regarding Sanford, nor was an invitation to dine. James had no choice but to take his leave. He lingered over Georgiana's hand, but couldn't get her to look at him. She didn't walk with him to the door as she had often done in the past. Instead, the bell was rung, and Simpson did the honours.

He rode back to Kympton in a disgruntled mood, reluctantly accepting that Georgiana's affections were on the wane. James was still confident he could win Georgiana around, if only he could manage some time alone with her. Easier said than done at this time of year, he conceded with a wry smile.

He left his horse with the ostlers at the inn and walked back to Rose's cottage, at which point his mood immediately improved. He ought not to come here so often, but now that he was so close by, he simply couldn't stay away.

8

As soon as the major left them, Georgiana excused herself and went to her room, in need of a moment's solitude. Not so many weeks ago, a visit from the major would have set her heart fluttering and her mind drifting towards the possibility of receiving his proposal. Today his presence had felt like an inconvenience, leaving Georgiana struggling to understand what such inconsistency said about her character. She had been fascinated by Mr. Sanford even before they were introduced, but he was not responsible for her oscillating affections. Her feelings for the major had been in decline before they met.

It was during the rehearsals for the play they had performed that Georgiana first entertained doubts about Major Halstead. The weather had been inclement, they spent many hours in rehearsal together, and most of the time he was his usual charming self. But she had also observed him at unguarded moments, when he hadn't known she was there. His expression seemed to imply that the proceedings were beneath him, and he would have much preferred to be elsewhere.

Given the effort he had made to ingratiate himself with everyone at Pemberley, especially her, that seemed rather extraordinary. His boredom appeared transitory and, at first, Georgiana thought she must have imagined it, until she happened to see him alone in the rehearsal room. He hadn't noticed her and was walking back and forth, talking aloud. She stifled a startled gasp when she realised he was cursing so violently she felt her ears burn. He railed against the unfairness of life, against her brother, even against her. It was quite astonishing. Georgiana beat a hasty retreat as that astonishment quickly turned to anger. If he caught sight of her, he would know she had heard him, and she had no idea what she ought to say to him.

Or rather, she did know. She ought to inform her brother and have the major removed from Pemberley. But how could she do something that would create so much awkwardness? Besides, given the way she had behaved with Wickham, perhaps Fitzwilliam would think she had said or done something to make him resent her. The incident had taught her that the major was not the man she thought he was. Certainly not a man she would be willing to spend the rest of her life with. She would tolerate his presence, rather than make any protests, and give him no further encouragement.

Ever since the unfortunate episode with Mr. Wickham, she had been plagued by guilt for disappointing her brother. She had wanted to explain, to apologise, but he had always seemed so remote, so unapproachable. Now they had not only discussed the matter, but Fitzwilliam had admitted *he* felt guilty. How ridiculous. She was the one at fault. Still, at least now they understood one another, he was treating her like an adult, and she knew she could speak to him about absolutely anything.

Georgiana wished she *had* told Lizzy about the major's strange behaviour. Then, she would not have to tolerate his frequent visits to Pemberley now that his regiment was quartered so close by. But if the major was no longer welcome, Captain Turner might feel he was also excluded and that would be unfair to Kitty. And so Georgiana would be civil and polite to the major, but nothing more than that, and he would soon understand his attentions were no longer welcome.

Thus resolved, Georgiana turned her thoughts to the evening to come which, of course, would see the welcome addition of Mr. Sanford to their family party. She fully intended to continue perusing her father's journals in the hope of finding something that would be of help to him. Fitzwilliam had so many other duties that claimed his time, but he had encouraged her to continue her efforts whenever the fancy took her. And that, she would most certainly do. Papa kept copious accounts of every little happenstance, both within the family and the district, and so if Mr. Sanford's father had spoken with him about the Jordans, there was sure to be mention of it somewhere. The only problem was, Georgiana got so interested in her father's account of life at Pemberley before she was born, and when she was a little girl, that she got constantly sidetracked and was making slow progress.

'It's time to dress for dinner, miss.'

Georgiana's maid's voice snapped her out of her reverie. 'Ah, so it is.'

'Which gown would you like to wear?'

Georgiana bit her lips with indecision. It was an ordinary family dinner, with only the addition of Mr. Sanford. But his presence meant it was not ordinary at all. She wanted to look her best, but didn't want it to appear as though she had made too much effort.

'The damask rose muslin, I think, Sally.'

'A good idea, miss. You look lovely in that gown.'

Georgiana had to agree that the gown was inspired. The neckline was low, displaying her décolletage to its best advantage. The short sleeves were trimmed with white lace, and there were unusual silver sliders on the breast and shoulders which caught the eye. She sat still while Sally dressed her hair, leaving loose curls falling around her face. She examined her reflection and thought her eyes seemed exceptionally large and bright. She was no raving beauty, but she looked fresh and her complexion glowed. Perhaps that was because she felt less reserved than usual, thanks in part to Lizzy's influence and to her recent conversation with Fitzwilliam.

With a flimsy silver shawl over her arms she made her way downstairs and found the others already in the drawing room.

'You look very pretty,' Lizzy remarked, smiling at her.

'Oh, do I? Thank you. I am fond of this gown.'

'It's pouring with rain,' Kitty said, looking out of the window.

Fitzwilliam followed the direction of Kitty's gaze. 'I shouldn't be surprised if it turned to snow later.'

'I hope that doesn't deter Mr. Sanford,' Lizzy said.

'The weather didn't deter the major, and he had much further to come,' Kitty pointed out.

'I was surprised he called so soon after we saw him at Fitzwilliam's wedding,' her brother remarked. 'What did he want?'

Lizzy sent her husband an exasperated look. 'To admire Georgie, of course.'

'Well,' Fitzwilliam replied, his glowering expression softening. 'I can't fault his good taste, I suppose, but I should have thought he would have duties to attend to.'

'Evidently not,' Lizzy said, sharing a playful smile with Georgiana.

'I would think less of Mr. Sanford if a little inclement weather prevented him from keeping his engagement,' Georgiana said. 'But if he is used to Scottish weather, I expect we shall see him.'

Lizzy glanced at Georgiana and smiled, looking as though she wanted to make some capricious remark but then thought better of it.

'Did you have any success with the journals this afternoon, Georgiana?' Fitzwilliam asked.

Georgiana wrinkled her nose. 'Unfortunately not. But I have learned a great deal more about the way Papa managed Pemberley, if that helps.'

'It helps you, Georgie,' Lizzy replied, 'which is all that signifies. You ought to know as much as you can about your parents. Much as my own mother vexes me, it would have been hard to grow up not knowing her.'

'Yes, but what you've never had, you don't really miss.'

'I suppose not.' Lizzy turned to Kitty. 'How is your portrait of the cat coming along?'

Kitty grimaced. 'It might go better if the wretched creature would sit still long enough for me to capture its likeness. It either curls up into a tight ball and sleeps, or chases anything that moves.'

The conversation turned to sketching, and the ill-obliging cat, and Georgiana had little contribution to make to it. Instead, she listened for signs of arrival, hoping Mr. Sanford would not get too wet on his short ride from Sanford House.

★　★　★

Dominic had never enjoyed the services of a valet. Provided there was someone available to launder his linens, he was well able to take care of his own wardrobe. He supposed he had his Scottish uncle to thank for that. His parsimonious tendencies made him baulk at the expense of employing a person simply to ensure he was well turned out.

One of the advantages of living in a freezing house was that one didn't loiter over one's toilet, Dominic was fast discovering. He stood in front of a blistered mirror and tied his neckcloth in a fashionable knot, working quickly and efficiently. Satisfied with his first attempt, he secured the resulting arrangement with a sapphire pin and shrugged into his deep blue coat.

'Sorry, Hamish,' he said when his dog, recognising that his master was dressed to go out, stirred in anticipation of going too. 'You will be better off in front of the range, and don't dare to let it go out or Mrs. Gibson will skin me alive.'

Hamish turned in several tight circles and settled back down to his slumbers with a martyred sigh. Dominic laughed. He took one more glance at his reflection, ran a hand through his hair and decided he would do. Just the short ride to Pemberley in this foul weather would see him soaked and dishevelled by the time he arrived so there seemed little point in worrying about his appearance. He donned his greatcoat and hat, threw Hamish a beef bone by way of compensation and headed outside. Midnight wasn't a fastidious horse that took exception to adverse weather, which was just as well. Dominic quickly had him tacked up, swung up into the saddle, still beneath the protection of the shed roof.

'Right, my friend. Let's brave the elements.'

In the dwindling light, Dominic and Midnight cut across the back of Pemberley Park. He and Darcy had often taken the same route in their youth, and he wasn't surprised to discover that Darcy's gardeners had kept the tracks clear of undergrowth. The shortcut saved a good fifteen minutes, but Dominic would have to take the long way back by road since even he wouldn't risk crossing the park in the pitch dark.

His greatcoat was soaked, and so was Midnight, when he reached Pemberley's mews ten minutes later.

'Please to step this way, sir,' the head groom said. 'The family is expecting you.'

Satisfied his horse would receive the best of care in the hands of Darcy's grooms, he followed behind the man and was handed over to the butler, who opened the side door for them.

'A filthy night, sir,' Simpson said, taking Dominic's hat and coat.

'It's certainly that, Simpson.'

Once again Dominic ran his hand through his hair, which felt damp, but his clothing had come through more or less unscathed.

'Mr. Sanford, sir,' Simpson said from the open doorway to the drawing room.

'Glad you made it through this weather, Sanford,' Darcy said, hand extended.

'I took the short cut,' he replied.

'I rather thought you would.'

Dominic greeted the ladies.

'Shall we go straight through?' Mrs. Darcy asked when pleasantries had been exchanged. 'I dare say you are sharp set, Mr. Sanford, after your cold ride.'

'Dining out trumps a damp ride, especially when invited to Pemberley.'

Mrs. Darcy smiled. 'I am sure you will not want for invitations.'

'None that will offer such congenial company.'

'I have some good news for you,' Mrs. Darcy said as they took their places at table. 'Mrs. Reynolds knows of two girls in the village who are keen to find work. I have taken the liberty of asking her to have them report to you in the morning. I hope that's all right.'

'Actually, that fits very well with my plans,' he replied, lifting his soup spoon. 'I have decided to live in the cottage until the main house is habitable, you see.'

'The cottage in the woods, Mr. Sanford?' Miss Darcy appeared interested. 'I have seen it from a distance. I sometimes walk in that area of Pemberley Park. My brother tells me one of your relatives once lived in it. Was he not welcome in the main house?'

'He was a taciturn fellow, given to quarrelling with everyone. That became quite tiresome, and no one wanted him in the house, but he was too important to be ignored. The suggestion of the cottage was raised when my relations were on the point of coming to blows. It was built quickly and the arrangement suited all parties.'

'Goodness, is that what you shall do with me when I become a burden, Fitzwilliam?' Miss Darcy asked. 'Farm me out into the grounds so I can complain about everything and make myself as disagreeable as possible, but at a distance from you all.'

Everyone laughed, including Miss Darcy herself. Dominic, who had not taken much notice of her at the wedding, looked at her more closely now. Her eyes sparkled, her mind appeared quick, her wit lively. Dominic had met more than his fair share of ladies without an opinion or original thought in their heads. He tired of them very quickly. Miss Darcy, it seemed, was not quite the church mouse he had supposed, nor was she as plain as he had thought when he saw her at the wedding. At home, relaxed in the bosom of her family, those eyes of her, a deep, arresting brown, gave her face character. There was something about her this evening — a newfound awareness perhaps? — that held his attention. Miss Darcy, unless he missed his guess, had moved from beneath her brother's shadow to become a vivacious young lady in her own right. He had heard her spoken of as quiet and reserved — some said haughty, others shy. Dominic saw none of that.

'I examined the place today,' Dominic said, returning to the subject of his cottage. 'Mrs. Gibson has arranged for the chimney sweep to call and for her grandson to help me turn out the old furniture and replace it with items from the main house. All I need are maids to give the place a good clean, and you have resolved that problem for me, Mrs. Darcy. Thank you so very much.'

'It's entire my pleasure, Mr. Sanford.'

'Is the cottage large enough for you, Mr. Sanford?' Miss Bennet asked.

'My requirements are simple. I shall be quite cosy on cold winter nights in my small abode, with a stack of books, and my dog for company. Quite apart from anything else, one large fire will heat the entire place.'

Miss Darcy smiled. 'A very important consideration.'

'Quite so. I was accustomed to Scottish winters, but these past few years I have been travelling. After Egypt I am having a hard time readapting to an English climate.'

'I would imagine so,' Darcy said. 'What were you doing in Egypt?'

'Their knowledge of medicine is more advanced than ours, and quite fascinating.'

'You will meet opposition if you use what many will consider foreign remedies,' Darcy warned. 'You know how narrow-minded country folk can be.'

'Well, that rather depends.' Dominic shared a smile between them. 'If I work in this area and people are unable to pay me, I don't suppose they will complain too vociferously about my experimental methods.'

'Especially not if they are effective,' Miss Darcy said. 'Do tell us more.'

'I have no wish to bore you.'

'We are not in the least bored, Mr. Sanford,' Mrs. Darcy assured him.

'I spent some time in Egypt,' Darcy remarked. 'I seem to recall some of the oldest bronze and copper surgical tools in the world were discovered in an Egyptian tomb.'

'Why would people be buried with such implements?' Miss Bennet asked with a shudder.

'They believe they move on to the next world and require possessions from this one to see them through the transition — food, jewels, and more practical objects, such as pots and pans, too.' Dominic paused to sip his wine. 'The extensive use of surgery, mummification practices, and autopsy as a religious exercise has given the Egyptians a vast knowledge of the body's morphology, and an advanced understanding of organ functions.'

'I should love to see Egypt,' Miss Darcy said. 'Did you see the pyramids, and ride a camel?'

Dominic smiled at her enthusiasm. 'Yes to both questions. And before you ask, I have absolutely no idea how the pyramids were constructed. Labour is cheap and plentiful — '

'And expendable,' Darcy added.

'Yes, that too, unfortunately. The influence of magic and religion upon everyday life in ancient Egypt is also fascinating. Evil gods and demons were thought to be responsible for many ailments, so often the treatments involved a supernatural element, such as beginning that treatment with an appeal to a deity.'

'Rather as though we might pray for a loved one to recover.'

Dominic nodded. 'Quite so, Miss Darcy.'

'There doesn't appear to be a clear distinction between the callings of priest and physician. In fact, the healers, many of them priests, often used incantations and magic as part of their treatment.' Dominic smiled. 'Personally, I prefer a more practical approach.'

'I am relieved to hear you say so,' Mrs. Darcy replied. 'Tell me, do you look at a person and decide what ailments plague them, rather as a writer would enter a room and notice all the details of its decorations, or the mannerisms of the people in it?'

Dominic laughed. 'Unfortunately, I am sometimes guilty of that habit.'

'Will and Georgie have been hard at work, trawling through their father's journals in the hope of finding a reference to the Jordans,' Mrs. Darcy said after a short break in the conversation.

'I'm much obliged, but I did not mean to inconvenience you on the matter, Miss Darcy.'

'I am rather enjoying learning more about my family.'

'We have nothing for you yet, Sanford, but we shall keep at it.'

'That's good of you. Thank you.'

Darcy and Dominic stood when the ladies withdrew. Alone with Darcy, Dominic explained about the cottage being unlocked.

'The track has definitely been kept cut back for regular use. It's deuced odd.'

'Well, if someone was making use of it in your absence, I don't suppose they will come back now. If nothing was taken, then you have no cause for concern.'

'Damned peculiar though.'

'We don't often get that sort of thing around here. Vagabonds taking over vacant property, I mean. We're too isolated for that. Still, word of your return will spread and whoever was responsible will keep well clear.'

'I expect you're right.' But Dominic still felt uncomfortable.

'Come along, Sanford.' Darcy stood. 'Let's rejoin the ladies. We keep country hours here at present, especially with my wife in — '

'I understand perfectly.'

Dominic, mindful of Darcy's wish for his wife to retire early, did not linger. He donned his greatcoat half an hour later and rode back through the frigid night, grateful that at least the rain had stopped. As soon as he had seen to Midnight's requirements, allowed Hamish out and riddled the range, he lost no time in diving beneath the covers and sleeping like a baby until first light.

9

The following morning dawned bright yet freezing cold, the muddy ground frozen solid and slick with ice. In spite of the weather, Sanford House was awash with people at an early hour — Mrs. Gibson and her burly grandson, together with the two maids Mrs. Darcy had sent.

'Send the sweep down to the cottage the moment he arrives, Mrs. Gibson.' Dominic turned to the others. 'Right, come this way. You girls can make a start on the cleaning while Gibson and I break up the furniture. It will make useful fuel for the fire.'

'We can use me grandma's horse and cart to move more furniture down this track.' Gibson, as sparing with his vocabulary as the grand-mother in question, kicked at the frozen, rutted track with the toe of a worn boot.

'A good suggestion, Gibson. I had not stopped to consider how we would remove it. Shall your grandmother mind?'

He shrugged massive shoulders. 'It were her suggestion.'

'We'll wait a bit. See if the sun thaws the ground out.'

Gibson grunted.

By the time they reached the cottage, a large individual was already camped out on the doorstep. Dominic tensed, wondering if it could be his phantom resident. He realised his mistake when he saw a dilapidated cart belonging to the sweep parked in the clearing in front of the cottage. Dominic greeted him and unlocked the door, relieved to discover no one had been near the place since he locked it up the previous day. Dominic had left several small pieces of furniture directly inside the door. It would have been necessary for anyone entering the place to move them in order to gain access. They were still exactly where he had placed them.

Gibson pumped water from the well, the sweep set to work, and the girls started their efforts in the scullery, out of the sweep's way. They seemed obliging enough, but were wary of Gibson, who kept a weather eye on them. Dominic idly wondered if they were part of the extended Gibson family. If he intended to employ them permanently then he would have some responsibility for them and ought to find out.

Dominic and Gibson started hauling the furniture outside and set about it with axes. It was hard, physical work that Dominic found strangely satisfying. Better yet, it got the blood circulating through his body and warmed him to the extent he needed to strip off his coat. He breathed deeply of the crisp morning air, taking it deep into his lungs. He exhaled slowly as he leaned on his axe and took a good look at the isolated spot that would be his home for the winter, already feeling in tune with his surroundings.

By the end of the morning, they had a good-sized pile of rotted timber ready for the fire.

'Won't last for long,' Gibson said, rubbing his chin. 'You'll need me to chop more to keep you going. The weather will get worse before it gets better.'

Dominic rather liked the idea of chopping logs himself. Gibson would be of more use in other areas.

'You would be better employed dealing with the windows, Gibson, and making sure they open and close properly.'

Gibson sniffed. 'If you like,' he said, trundling off to do as Dominic asked.

'The sweep's finished, sir,' one of the girls said. 'Shall we start on the main room now?'

'If you please.'

Now that he had taken on the girls and employed the services of the sweep, Dominic's plans to remain in the district would become common knowledge before the end of the day. In which case perhaps, on his next visit to Lambton Inn — an establishment he fully intended to frequent on a regular basis — he ought to mention he would be setting up as a doctor. It would give the villagers time to get used to the notion. Country folk were notoriously slow to trust, suspicious of modern methods and new ideas. Not that many of the local populace could afford the services of a doctor, and probably fell back on remedies that had been passed down through families for generations. Dominic was a firm believer in the use of herbal potions, but they had their limitations. He could do so much more for any number of previously untreatable ailments, if he could win the people's trust.

So perhaps it would be better to keep his plans to himself for the time being. He wouldn't be ready to receive patients until the main house was habitable, and he could use the interim period to get to know the villagers better.

Dominic thanked the sweep and sent him on his way. As he did so, he saw Mrs. Gibson, bundled up in her weird array of clothing, lumbering down the track with a loaded basket. Dominic automatically moved forward to take it from her, but she frowned and he held back.

'Thought you might want some luncheon,' she said gruffly.

'That is very thoughtful of you, Mrs. Gibson, and we're more than ready for it.' He slapped Gibson's massive shoulders. It was like striking a rock.

Mrs. Gibson grunted and disappeared into the now pristine scullery. A short time later they were all tucking into fresh bread, ham and cheese. The fact that Dominic was perfectly willing to eat with his servants appeared to find favour with Mrs. Gibson, who served him with a slice of lard cake and actually told him she had made it especially for him.

'You are very kind,' he said, eating every morsel of the cake. 'And this is delicious.'

Gibson looked at the girls and raised a brow. They immediately jumped up and scurried to collect up the plates. They washed them in a bowl of warm water they had heated on the range — a smaller edition of the one in the large house — that Gibson had managed to coax into life.

'Right, Gibson,' Dominic said. 'Let's get back to the big house and decide what furniture we shall bring down here.'

They made three trips with the cart, managing large pieces of furniture between them — sofas, a bed, tables, writing

126

materials, a whole box of wax candles, bookcases and, of course, books to fill them. Mrs. Gibson had taken it upon herself to pack up Dominic's clothes into two large valises. She had also bundled up bedding, cushions, towels and other small touches he would not have thought of that would make his cottage more homely.

'I found these curtains,' she said. 'They will do very well. I'll come down and hang them myself.'

That was when Dominic realised by working beside her grandson and proving he was perfectly willing to get his hands dirty, he had earned Mrs. Gibson's respect.

By the time the sun set, the cottage was spick and span, with the furniture in place and a roaring fire dancing up the chimney.

'Did you know my parents, Mrs. Gibson?' he asked as they stood together admiring the results of their labours.

'Aye, that I did. A fair man, your father was. Always listened and took notice of what was said to him.' Her gaze raked Dominic from head to foot. 'I had my doubts about you at first, but I reckon you're cut from the same cloth.'

'Thank you. If your grandson doesn't have other work, then there is plenty he can do up at the house.' Gibson was reliable, but clearly a little simple-minded. Not everyone would trust such a person.

'I reckon so,' Mrs. Gibson agreed, from which Dominic inferred a bargain had been struck.

'The girls, too. They were very obliging today. They could start cleaning up there,' he said, waving his hands in the direction of the main house. 'Under your supervision, of course. I rely upon you to know what needs doing, and in what order.'

Mrs. Gibson nodded, setting her multiple chins wobbling. 'Good enough.'

'Thank you so very much, all of you. Mrs. Gibson, would you kindly take the girls back to the village with you.'

'Well, I'll hardly let them walk, will I now?'

Dominic waved them off, glad of their help, but pleased to be left alone.

'Come along, Hamish,' he said to his dog. 'Let's go and check on Midnight. Then Mrs. Gibson has left some supper for us at the big house.'

★　★　★

James Halstead relied upon his enveloping greatcoat to cover his regimentals, preventing them from showing up like a beacon between the bare trees on this dull November day. He

128

concealed himself behind a sturdy oak and watched the activity around the cottage in Sanford's grounds with growing despair. It looked as though Sanford planned to live in the place, a suspicion that was confirmed when the sweep left and smoke puffed from the chimney very soon thereafter. God's beard, they were tearing the place apart! They were bound to find the loot before the day was out, then there would be hell to pay.

In which case, James could not afford to linger. His hiding place was far from secure, and he would have a hard time explaining himself if he was discovered here. He moved slowly and carefully back to the spot where he had left his horse and rode not to Kympton but to Lambton. With all this activity, someone at the inn would know what was going on, and he needed to get his facts straight before he faced Rose.

Sure enough, it was now common knowledge that Sanford intended to remain permanently in Derbyshire and would live in the cottage until the large house was made habitable. The sweep was in the centre of a group of locals, pleased to pass on this interesting piece of gossip.

'Nice gent, so he is,' the sweep said. 'Not too high in the instep, if you get my meaning.'

James wanted to ask what they had found

inside the cottage, but couldn't risk drawing attention to himself. Besides, if the loot *had* been found while the sweep had been there, he wouldn't have kept quiet about it. Now James was thinking more rationally, it occurred to him that the hiding place was very secure, unlikely to be found by accident, even if furniture was being move around. He relaxed for the first time that day, drained his tankard, and quietly left the inn.

James groaned when he arrived in Kympton and saw Patrick, Rose's brother, in the garden of her cottage. He and Patrick did not see eye to eye.

'What are you doing here?' Patrick asked belligerently.

'I have news for Rose.'

Patrick scoffed. 'Is that what they're calling it this week?'

'Mind your tongue!'

James pushed past Patrick into the cottage. Patrick followed him and closed the door behind them both.

'Did you get it?' Rose asked by way of greeting.

'Not precisely.'

'See, I told you he was worse than useless,' Patrick complained. 'Too high and mighty to get his hands dirty. You should have let me go.'

'Sanford's here to stay, and he's living in the cottage for the time being. The place is swarming with people, cleaning it up.'

Rose took the news with surprising calm. 'Did they find it?'

'Not that I could tell.'

'You would have known if they had. The parish constable would have been summoned at the very least.'

'Unless Sanford decides to keep it for himself.'

'Unlikely,' Rose replied. 'From what I hear, he's as righteous as his dratted father was.'

'Lot of good that did him,' Patrick said, turning his head and spitting on the boarded floor.

'What shall we do now?' James asked.

'We can't leave it there,' Patrick replied. 'I'll watch the place, wait for him to go out, then retrieve it.'

He and James both turned towards Rose, aware the decision was hers. She was pensive and didn't immediately respond.

'No,' she eventually said slowly. 'Don't do that.'

'I know that calculating look,' James said, smiling. 'What thoughts are going through your lovely head?'

'Why would a gentleman of Sanford's ilk want to live in little more than a workman's

131

cottage when he has a whole house at his disposal?'

'The roof leaks,' Patrick reminded them.

'Yes, it does,' Rose agreed. 'But the lower floor is habitable. It seems to me only a man with secrets to keep would live so inconveniently.'

'Perhaps he simply requires privacy. I heard tell plenty of writing materials were taken to the cottage,' James remarked. 'He might wish to write his memoirs.'

'A man of his age?' Patrick scoffed.

'But,' Rose persisted, a vindictive smile playing about her lips, 'if he did have something to hide . . .'

James responded with a smile of his own. 'I know what you are thinking, but it would mean sacrificing the loot.'

'If someone were to anonymously inform the constable about what's hidden beneath the floorboards, suspicion would fall on Sanford.'

'Our revenge would be complete,' Patrick said, grinning. 'We must do it, sis.'

'I rather think we must. Now run along home, Patrick. I need to think about this.'

'What about him?'

'He needs to help me think.' Rose clapped her hands. 'Just go. I shall send for you when I have decided what's to be done.'

'See that you do.'

James sent Patrick an impassive look, his excitement building as he watched Rose's brother grudgingly take his leave. Thoughts of revenge upon the Sanford family never failed to arouse Rose, and when she was in that frame of mind she was delightfully demanding in bed.

She glanced at the baby, still sleeping peacefully in his crib, and then beckoned James to follow her into the bedchamber.

10

Georgiana spent the following morning ensconced in Will's library, pouring over their father's journals. Lizzy and Kitty sat together in the small salon. The sky was clear, but a strong northerly wind whistled through the bare tree branches beyond their window and rattled around the chimneys. Kitty was frowning over her sketch of the disobliging kitchen feline, while Lizzy tried and failed to find a comfortable position. She was fairly sure the baby shouldn't be so active this far in advance of her time, but would compare symptoms with Jane before mentioning it to Will.

'Are you all right, Lizzy?' Kitty glanced up at her. 'You keep fidgeting.'

'I am very well.' She smiled, keen to change the subject. 'Are you expecting to see Captain Turner soon?'

Kitty pulled a wry face. 'I have no expectations of seeing him at all.'

'Why not?' Lizzy frowned. 'Is there something you have not told me?'

'If only it were that simple.' She sighed. 'Captain Turner's attitude has changed.'

'Changed in what respect?'

Kitty looked ready to burst into tears. 'I don't think he likes me anymore.'

'Nonsense!' Lizzy ignored her discomfort, moved closer to Kitty and threw an arm awkwardly around her shoulders. 'He adores you, and doesn't seem to mind who knows it.'

'*I* do not know it.'

'That's because you are too closely involved. I did not believe Mr. Darcy liked me.' Lizzy patted Kitty's hand. 'Tell me what has changed about the captain's behaviour and perhaps, between us, we can account for it.'

'It was at the wedding, he seemed preoccupied. More than preoccupied,' Kitty amended. 'He appeared angry and upset. I thought that might be because he had just visited his father. They do not get on and seeing him always makes the captain uneasy. But when I asked him if something was wrong, he warned me there might be some unpleasantness, and to be on my guard.'

'Good heavens!' Lizzy elevated both brows. 'Whatever did he mean by that?'

'I have absolutely no idea. I tried to make him tell me, but Major Halstead joined us and he changed the subject.'

'But you think it concerns his father?'

Kitty shrugged. 'Whatever else can I think?

135

It makes me so angry, Lizzy. He does not think highly of his son, in spite of everything the captain has done to earn his respect, and yet he will meddle in his life.'

'It might have nothing to do with his father. He did not actually say it had, did he?'

'Well no, but he could hardly tell me if it was.'

'The captain is a serving soldier, and these are uncertain times. Has it occurred to you that his regiment might be sent somewhere less safe than Derbyshire?'

'Of course I have considered that possibility, but if that was the case, he would have told me so.'

'Perhaps he is not at liberty to speak about it.'

'No, I don't think that's what it is.' Kitty looked so crestfallen Lizzy impulsively hugged her. 'He *does* admire me,' she said, her voice muffled against Lizzy's shoulder. 'But his father's opinion is too important for him to go against his wishes.'

'Then he is not the gentleman we thought he was, and you ought to forget all about him.' Lizzy spoke with more hope than conviction in her tone. 'You can do a great deal better.'

Kitty sniffed. 'He seemed so severe at the wedding. So brooding, so ... well, so everything I never thought he could be.'

'I expect there is a reasonable explanation.'

Kitty ran to the window when they heard wheels on gravel. 'Oh, it's Jane and Mr. Bingley.'

Lizzy hauled herself to her feet. 'I am not in the least surprised to see them again so soon. Jane and little Emma would be coming to stay while Mr. Bingley visits his sisters in London.'

'Why does he wish to leave them at such a time?'

'He has duties that cannot be put off indefinitely,' Lizzy replied as she and Kitty made their way to the front door. Kitty and Georgiana did not know the reason for Mr. Bingley's separation from his sisters, nor would they learn of it could be avoided.

'Gentlemen of property always seems to have so much to do with their time.'

The sisters greeted Jane affectionately and made a big fuss over the precious baby.

'I hope you don't mind us coming so soon,' Mr. Bingley said as he shook Lizzy's hand. 'I have exchanged express letters with Louisa and my sisters are anxious to see me.'

'We are very glad you are here,' Lizzy replied, meaning it. 'I hope you intend to spend the night, Mr. Bingley, and start your journey in the morning. Will is out all day on

Pemberley business, but he will be back for dinner.'

'That was my intention, if it's no trouble.'

'None whatsoever.'

Kitty stole the baby from Jane's arms and sat by the fire, cooing at the little girl.

'It seems an unnecessary expense to employ a nursemaid for our daughter,' Mr. Bingley said, smiling. 'Between Jane and me, and now her aunts, the baby scarcely knows her nurse.'

'That is just how it should be,' Lizzy replied. 'Your daughter is as beautiful as her mother and deserves to be indulged.'

'There I must agree with you,' Mr. Bingley replied, sending Jane a devoted smile.

After luncheon, Lizzy managed to snatch a few minutes alone with Jane.

'How does Mr. Bingley feel about Caroline, now he has had time to consider the situation?' Lizzy asked. 'He seems his usual affable self, but I observed strain around his eyes, and his thoughts seemed miles away at times.'

'He is still very upset, as am I.' Jane clasped Lizzy's hand, looking truly distressed. 'Only to think the damage she might have done with her wickedness, and the shame she might have heaped upon us as a family by discrediting you. She would have torn

138

Charles and me apart, as well as you and Mr. Darcy, but I don't suppose she stopped to consider that. I should have taken your part, of course.'

'It did not come to that, thank goodness.' *But it so easily could have.* 'What did Mrs. Hurst have to say about Caroline's condition?'

'Not a great deal. I think she was mighty relieved that Charles now knows what she did, which means Louisa no longer has sole responsibility for their sister.'

'Jane!'

'What . . . what did I — '

'That was almost a disparaging remark.' Lizzy smiled. 'Good girl! I never thought you had it in you.'

'Nor did I.' Jane inverted her chin. 'Until Caroline behaved so abominably towards my favourite sister. Even I have my limits, Lizzy.'

'Apparently.' Lizzy smiled. 'All right then, I must contain my curiosity until your Charles has seen his sister for himself. Shall he bring them all back to Derbyshire for Christmas?'

'That depends upon how Caroline seems. He plans to have a frank discussion with her and make her understand what damage her meddling could have caused. I have never seen Charles half so determined about anything before. He blames himself for not keeping better control of Caroline.'

'It is not his fault.'

'That's what I have told him, but he seems determined to shoulder the blame.' Jane sighed. 'Anyway, we shall soon know. Charles does not intend to remain in London for long.'

'Because he can't bear to leave you and Emma?'

Jane's gentle smile illuminated her lovely face. 'That is what he says.'

'Will is the same way with me. He almost did not go into Newcastle today, even though the engagement has been fixed for some time.'

'You do look a little tired, Lizzy.'

'Did you worry that you had no one to turn to for advice each time the baby moved?'

Jane visibly relaxed. 'All the time. That's why I was sorry not to have Mama with me to put my mind at rest.'

Lizzy thought she would probably fuss and make matters worse, but did not say so. 'Did Emma keep you awake by kicking when you still have over a month to go?'

Jane considered the question. 'I can't remember how far ahead she started to get impatient. If you have concerns, you ought to send for the physician.'

'Will has the best man in Newcastle on

standby, but I hesitate to bother him when it's probably nothing. Besides, our new neighbour is a very enlightened doctor, so help is at immediate hand if necessary.'

'Even so, Lizzy — '

'You have reassured me so please don't say anything to Will. If he knew I was worried, he would force me to remain in bed, and that would drive me demented. I am not the first woman to have a child and certainly won't be the last. No fuss is required.'

'Very well, if you're sure.' Jane didn't look convinced. 'But I shall be keeping a close eye on you while I'm here. Mr. Darcy would never forgive me if something went wrong and I was in a position to prevent it.'

'What could possibly go wrong? I am surrounded by every possible luxury. Most women are not so fortunate.'

★   ★   ★

Dominic enjoyed his first night of solitude. With the fire and range joining forces to warm the small cottage, he enjoyed the resulting comforts of an active day. He ate the supper Mrs. Gibson had prepared for him in the kitchen of the big house, attended to Midnight's needs, and then he and Hamish walked through the twilight, back to their

141

new abode. The sun had just disappeared over the horizon, and it was now a bitterly cold night. As darkness fell, the stars put on a show for his personal enjoyment, and he stood at the cottage window trying to identify the various constellations, just as he had once done as a boy. It was strange, but he could almost sense his father's comforting presence at his shoulder, pointing out the bear or the plough, telling him he had done the right thing in returning home.

Seated in front of a roaring fire with a book open on his lap and Hamish spread full length in front of the blaze, he made inroads into the supply of fine single malt whisky that had travelled from Scotland with him. He listened to the wind soaring through the trees that surrounded the cottage and was glad to have had the foresight to move somewhere so manageable.

The moment he read his father's journals the decision to return had been made for him, and he hadn't had to think too deeply about it. Derbyshire was where he belonged. If he could find no obvious clues about the cause of his parents' supposed accident, then he would talk to the locals in the inn's taproom and see what the older ones could recollect about those times. Someone, somewhere had to know something. It was simply a matter of gaining their trust and persuading them to talk to him.

The book didn't hold his attention, and instead he found himself staring into the flames, thinking about the turn his life had taken. Regardless of the outcome of his investigations, Dominic was satisfied he could put his skills as a physician and surgeon to much greater good here rather than pandering to the wealthy, demanding denizens of the *ton*.

'We shall never be rich, Hamish,' he told his dog. 'But we shall be content.'

Hamish opened one eye, flapped his tail, and then and closed it again.

Dominic laughed, stood up, and stretched. He felt the effects of his physical day, to say nothing of the whisky. He whistled to Hamish, who had to be persuaded to leave the fire in order to go outside and attend to his business. He was back again in no time flat, at which point Dominic locked the door, mindful of the possibility of uninvited guests, and retired early to sleep soundly.

Early the next morning he called at Sanford House and found Mrs. Gibson had her grandson and the girls already hard at work. Dominic felt surplus to requirements. Having broken his fast and made sure all the work was proceeding in accordance with his instructions — as though it would dare to do otherwise with Mrs. Gibson in charge — he saddled Midnight and rode into Lambton to attend to a few matters of business.

After taking luncheon at the inn, intent upon furthering his ambition to become a familiar figure amongst the locals, he returned to the cottage in search of occupation. There was no sunshine today. Instead heavy clouds threatened rain, or even snow. He would chop some more logs while he still had an opportunity, he decided, whistling to Hamish as he plunged into the woodland in search of logs to chop.

★　★　★

Georgiana made a fuss of Mrs. Bingley's adorable baby girl. Lizzy and her sisters made her welcome but she felt like an intruder. She envied the close bond that existed between the sisters — especially Lizzy and Jane — never having had a close friend herself until Kitty came to live at Pemberley. She thought of all those lonely years she had spent rattling around the place as a child and tried to tell herself she was fortunate to have the very best of everything. In reality, she would have given up much of that good fortune if she could have had sisters to confide in, to love, worry about, and be loved by in return. If she ever married, she would have a dozen children, and they would never know a moment's loneliness.

Adjuring herself not to feel so downhearted when she had no real reason for regret, she returned to Fitzwilliam's study and continued to trawl through her father's journals, determined to find something that would help Mr. Sanford. She had so enjoyed his society the previous evening. When he walked into the drawing room, his hair damp and dishevelled after his ride, his elegant manners and compelling charm had taken her breath away. His lively discourse about his time in Egypt and his determination to use his medical knowledge to help those less fortunate than himself had moved her tender heart. Such compassion, such intelligence, such magnetism and potent masculinity had agitated her passions in a most unsettling fashion.

Georgiana no longer chastised herself for inconstancy. Lizzy had told her the previous day that her sister Jane had often considered herself to be in love, until she met Mr. Bingley. The moment she met that gentleman she knew it was the real thing, and all those she had liked before him paled in significance. It was the same in her case, Georgiana decided. Her reaction to Mr. Wickham and then to Major Halstead was perfectly natural — passing fancies that thankfully caused no lasting harm. She was still set upon having the reciprocal love that her brother and Lizzy enjoyed. She would rather become an old maid than settle for half measures.

Georgiana's mind wandered, and she almost missed the first reference. With a start, she sat straighter and re-read the entry. Then she read it for a third time and eagerly turned to the next page. She sat back, slowly absorbing the implications of what she had just read, excitement surging through her. Mr. Sanford needed to know, and he needed to know straight away. But Will was gone from Pemberley for the day. Lizzy was engaged with her sisters, and she could hardly ask Mr. Bingley for help. She glanced out of the window. There was a blustery wind and dark clouds, but it wasn't actually raining. Presumably Mr. Sanford would be at his cottage. She knew the way and the walk didn't take long if one cut across Pemberley Park. It probably wasn't seemly for her to call upon him alone — it definitely was not — but this was too urgent to brook delay. She would be gone and back again before anyone missed her.

She ran up to her room, donned a bonnet

and her warmest pelisse and gloves and slid unseen out of the side door, the journals in question secured in a large reticule. Mr. Sanford needed to read the entries for himself, and she did not have time to copy them out.

The wind was stronger than she had realised, and it almost knocked her from her feet. She found it bracing and strode into it, fighting its might as the last of the autumn leaves whirled around her ankles and adhered to her clothing. It took her almost half an hour to reach her destination and she was quite out of breath by the time she walked into the clearing where the cottage stood. Smoke puffed from the chimney, and everything appeared neat and orderly, just as she would imagine Mr. Sanford's life to be. She tried to quell her disappointment when she observed a man, in shirtsleeves, energetically chopping logs. She had not admitted it to herself, but she had badly wanted Mr. Sanford to be alone when she arrived.

'Shame on you!' she muttered aloud, unable to quell a nervous giggle.

She stopped where she was, aware the man had not yet seen her, wondering whether to call out or return home. Mr. Sanford might not want to discuss his business in front of strangers, and there was the small matter of her being there unchaperoned. Her eyes were drawn to the man again while she tried to make up her mind. He was sideways on to her and she had a clear view of rippling muscles flexing and contracting as he wielded the axe with considerable vigour. Oh my! Georgiana's throat felt inexplicably dry, but not because her walk had made her thirsty. His stance conveyed a sense of power and strength that she found both fascinating and unsettling. All that flowing masculine power appealed to her on a level she appeared to have no control over, and she couldn't seem to stop drinking in the sight of him.

In a white billowing shirt, the sleeves rolled back and open and the throat, his torso was clearly visible through the thin fabric. Georgiana had never seen a man anything other than properly dressed before and found it difficult to look away as she admired this unexpected display of muscle, sinew and raw, unharnessed power.

He turned his head sideways, giving her a better view of his profile, obliging her to clap a hand over her mouth and smother a gasp. Her feminine side had recognised what her eyes had not immediately comprehended. This was no stranger, but Mr. Sanford, chopping the logs himself. With a careless shrug, she continued to drink in the sight of him, all lithe muscle and graceful coordination as he continued with his labours.

Her fascination was interrupted when a huge black and white beast — a wolf of some sort — saw her, barked and loped towards her. Georgiana was terrified, unsure whether to run or stand her ground.

'Hamish, what the devil . . . '

The dog, for that's what it was, not a wolf, continued straight for her, massive teeth barred. It was too late to run, and so Georgiana remained rooted to the spot, heart pounding, too petrified to move. The dog reached her, threw back his head and sniffed, then pushed his huge head under her hand, panting. Georgiana released a long breath, her legs trembling as she patted his massive head.

'Hamish, where on earth are you?' Mr. Sanford strode into view and stopped dead at the sight of her. 'Miss Darcy?' he said, his eyes widening with surprise. 'Whatever brings you here?'

⋆ ⋆ ⋆

James hid himself behind another tree, further back than the one he had utilised the previous day. Sanford's savage dog had already taken a lump out of his thigh, damn him. He shouldn't really be here. His battalion was on training manoeuvres. He had delegated his responsibilities but couldn't stay away for much longer without questions being asked. Thankfully, with Fitzwilliam gone and his replacement not yet with the regiment, he could virtually do as he pleased since there was no one with the authority to question him.

He understood Rose's decision to leave the loot where it was and then alert the constable as to its location. Revenge against the Sanford's had always been Rose's *raison d'être*, and this opportunity to exact it was irresistible. By helping her, James would see Sanford's reputation besmirched and it would leave the pitch clear for him with Miss Darcy.

Regardless of Sanford's influence or otherwise with Miss Darcy, James had taken an extreme dislike to him and would happily orchestrate his downfall. Even if the theft of the jewels could not be directly attributed to Sanford, doubt would be cast upon his integrity when they were discovered in the cottage he had chosen to live in, in preference to the main house. People were bound to scratch their heads about that decision, even before the loot was found. James managed a brief smile as he tried to ignore the cold seeping through his bones, well able to imagine the court according to the taproom at Lambton Inn discussing the matter and declaring him guilty by association. The gentry would turn their collective backs on him also, and he would have no choice but to sell up and leave the district.

James wrinkled his nose when he watched the man chopping his own logs. That was what servants were for. He clearly wasn't as wealthy as James had supposed. He wished he could think of a way to drop that delicious piece of information into conversation the next time he was at Pemberley.

He would let Rose do her worst, but there was something of his inside the cottage that he would need to retrieve before she did so, which was the reason for his return visit. He hadn't told Rose about it, not wanting to show himself as anything other than her avenging hero, lover, protector and heart's desire. It had been stupid and careless of him to leave his property behind, but he hadn't missed it until he was halfway back to the garrison and how was he supposed to know that Sanford would come back in the meantime and choose to live in this hovel? No matter, he was bound to leave here this afternoon, if only to see to his horse — something else that he appeared to do for himself because he was too tight-fisted to employ servants. It would only take James five minutes to pop into the cottage, retrieve the offending item, and no one would be any the wiser.

Damnation, the dog was staring intently at his hiding place. Even from a distance, James could see its hackles were raised and hear it growling.

'Hamish?' Sanford put the axe aside and stared right at James's hiding place, as though he could see him through the solidity of the tree trunk that protected him. James remained stock still, wishing his heart would stop beating so violently. He most emphatically was not afraid of Sanford, but it would be deuced awkward if he was found here, hiding behind a tree. *That* was the only reason for his palpitations. 'What is it, boy?'

James crept sideways until he was downwind of the dog.

'Seeing squirrels where none exist again?'

Sanford tugged the stupid beast's ears and went back to his logs. James was about to give up and retreat altogether when the beast let forth with a volley of barks and loped off in the opposite direction. James lingered to see what had attracted his attention, surprised to see a young woman had appeared.

Perdition, it was Miss Darcy. And she was alone.

Jealousy surged through James. His instincts had been right about her attraction towards Sanford, but he would never have imagined the fastidious Miss Darcy calling upon a single gentleman unchaperoned. He watched them exchange a few words and then go inside. Part of him wanted to creep closer and listen to what they were saying. But there was the dog to consider, and also the trifling matter of returning to the battalion he was supposed to be commanding.

With murderous thoughts surging through his brain, James backtracked until he reached his horse and rode rapidly away.

11

'I'm sorry about Hamish,' Dominic said, as he joined Miss Darcy. 'I hope he didn't frighten you. He can seem intimidating just because of his size, but he's really quite a gentle chap. Unless he thinks you are a threat, which obviously you are not.'

'He did give me quite a start, but I can see he's just a big baby.' She smiled at Hamish, sending him into a state of near ecstasy by tugging his ears. 'He obviously thinks it's his job to protect you.'

'Quite so.'

Dominic put from his mind the uneasy feeling he'd had over the past couple of days; an intuitive sense that someone had been watching him, accounting for Hamish's unusually alert state.

'I apologise for arriving unannounced, Mr. Sanford.'

'It is a pleasure to see you, Miss Darcy.' And it was. Her eyes were sparkling, her face flushed from exercise and exposure to the wind. He no longer looked upon her as being plain, but did wonder about the wisdom of her calling upon him alone. This was the country, and he was no threat to her reputation but, even so . . . 'You have given me a legitimate excuse to abandon my labours,' he said, smiling at her. 'Please come inside and take some tea.'

'I would not have come, but Fitzwilliam is out for the day, and I discovered something in my father's journals that I thought you should know about.'

Dominic jerked his head backwards, snapping his attention away from the rather pleasant, albeit inappropriate, thoughts that occupied his head when he considered being alone with Miss Darcy in his cottage. This simply would not do! Darcy was an old friend, and Dominic was supposed to be a gentleman. Gentlemen did not have such thoughts about a neighbour's sister, especially one who had struck Dominic as being fragile and vulnerable, with limited knowledge about . . . well, about the subjects plaguing Dominic's mind. Georgina Darcy was loved and admired locally and was expected to make an advantageous marriage. He would not succeed in his ambition to remain in the district and build a reputation for himself as a philanthropic doctor if he besmirched the reputation of their local darling.

'Then I am very much obliged to you for walking all the way here in such weather. But if you had sent word by a servant I would gladly have saved you the trouble and called at Pemberley.'

Her face fell. 'You think I should not have come.'

'Just so long as your brother won't object, I am very glad you did. Besides, I confess to a great curiosity about your findings.' He placed his hand on the small of her back and steered her towards the front door. 'I ought to warn you my cottage is very small and unpretentious, but I think we can manage tea and some of Mrs. Gibson's rather good lard cake.'

'That would be very welcome.'

Hamish stayed beside her as they walked towards the cottage, rubbing his head against her skirts.

'He likes you.'

'He's adorable,' she replied, leaning down to pat his body. The dog was so large she did not need to lean very far.

Dominic guffawed. 'Hardly the way I would describe him.'

'Don't pretend you are not fond of him. He's walking beside me, it's true, but he keeps looking up at you to make sure you are there. The bond between you must be very strong.'

'He's still little more than a puppy, believe

it or not. I found him during one of my walks on the moors shortly after my return to Scotland following my uncle's death. He had a lame paw and was all skin and bone.'

'So you took him in and nursed him back to health?' Dominic nodded. 'I think that shows great compassion.'

'Well, I could hardly leave him to die.' Dominic shrugged. 'I should not think well of anyone who could ignore a helpless creature in distress.'

'No, nor I.'

'It transpired he had a huge thorn in his paw, so deeply embedded that he couldn't pull it out with his teeth. I did it for him and haven't been able to get rid of the hound since.'

Miss Darcy laughed. 'I can see that situation causes you considerable distress.'

'He is good enough company in that he listens to me articulate my thoughts and never disagrees with me or tells me I'm being an idiot.'

'Yes, I have one-sided conversations with our cat all the time.'

'Shall we?'

He opened the door to the sitting room and stepped back to allow Miss Darcy to step through it ahead of him.

'It is very cosy,' she said, looking about

with evident interest as a wall of warmth hit them.

'One of the advantages of a small cottage and an efficient chimney,' he replied. 'May I take your pelisse?'

She removed the garment and handed it to him, still taking in her surroundings. The entire cottage was probably smaller than her suite of rooms at Pemberley. He belatedly recalled his own state of undress and looked at his coat, hung negligently across the back of a chair. He reached for it, then thought better of it and, shrugging, left it where it was. Presumably she wouldn't swoon because he was in his shirtsleeves.

'Please take a seat. The tea will be but a moment.'

But she didn't sit. Instead, she followed him into the scullery.

'I would offer to help but, to my great mortification, I have never made tea in my life.'

'There is absolutely no reason why you should have.' He sent her a smile as he set water to boil. 'You have an army of servants at Pemberley who would probably take exception to you assuming their duties. I do so myself only out of necessity. This cottage is too small to accommodate me, Hamish *and* a maid.'

'You did not have servants in your uncle's house?'

'Oh yes, we had people there, but I learned to take care of myself early on in my travels. I once took tea in a Bedouin tent in the middle of the Egyptian desert, you know.'

'Gosh, how exciting.' She pulled a face. 'I have never done anything the least bit daring . . . well, nothing like that anyway.'

Dominic glanced at her, surprised by the guilt in her tone, more surprised still to see her blushing furiously. She had lowered her head and was concealing her face beneath the brim of her bonnet but her ears, burning red, gave her away.

'I would dearly love to know what excitement you *have* enjoyed,' he said with a wicked smile that was as inappropriate as his comment. But somehow, being in his shirtsleeves and making tea for a pampered young woman who was just starting to discover the power of her own femininity made him reckless.

'Really, Mr. Sanford, what a thing to say.' She briefly raised her head, biting her lower lip in a very compelling manner. 'Tell me more about the Bedouins.'

'It wasn't nearly as romantic as you probably suppose,' he replied, pouring boiling water over tea leaves and leaving them to steep. 'Imagine children and goats running everywhere, while you sit cross-legged on a mat, trying to remain cool in the stifling heat and avoid being eaten to death by the bugs.'

'Now you have completely ruined the picture I had conjured up in my mind.'

'Perhaps I have done you a favour.' Dominic fought against a grin. She really had no idea of life beyond Derbyshire. 'Imagination is usually more pleasurable than the reality of most situations, Miss Darcy.'

A short time later, Dominic had assembled all the required items on a tray and carried it through to the other room.

'Mrs. Gibson has her standards,' he explained when Miss Darcy was unable to hide her surprise at the good quality china in which he served her tea. 'She insisted I brought the very best with me, which I thought was unnecessary because I did not anticipate entertaining visitors. Now I am grateful to her since at least I don't have to be ashamed of my china. Left to myself, you see, I would have made do with earthenware mugs.'

She laughed. 'I dare say I would have survived the experience.'

'Can I persuade you to take some cake? Mrs. Gibson's efforts are well worth tasting.'

'Thank you. Yes.'

Dominic sliced her a generous serving and passed it to her on a plate, complete with cake fork. She scooped a little into her mouth, chewed slowly, and sighed.

'You are right, Mr. Sanford. It is quite delicious.'

Hamish watched her hopefully, huge head tilted to one side, tongue protruding. At a command from Dominic, he reluctantly lay flat on the rug in front of the fire, still watching the distribution of the cake as though he hadn't eaten for a month.

'Now then, perhaps you would care to tell me what you discovered in your father's journals,' Dominic said when she had eaten and drunk her fill.

★　★　★

Georgiana's first impressions of Mr. Sanford's living arrangements had been favourable. Although impossibly small, the inside of the cottage was immaculately clean and fresh curtains hung at the sparkling windows. The furniture shone, and the aroma of beeswax polish competed with the sweet, pungent scent given off by the logs crackling in the grate. There were books — lots of them on a myriad of subjects — and a desk with a neat pile of papers in one corner.

A door led to another room, presumably

161

his bedchamber. Georgiana's cheeks warmed at the thought of being in such close proximity to a gentleman's bedroom. Everywhere she looked, there was something to remind her of the unorthodox nature of her situation. Most notably, Mr. Sanford in his shirtsleeves, a dusting of curling chest hair peeping from the opening at his throat where his neckcloth ought to have sat.

She had enjoyed the sight of his strong forearms, roped with muscles, as he attended to the delicate and, to her, alien business of making tea. It really was shocking she had no idea how to go about such a simple task herself. She could play complicated concertos on the pianoforte, embroider well enough to earn a living from it if the need ever arose, sketched quite well, spoke several languages, and could point to Patagonia on a map — yet she didn't have the first idea how to make a pot of tea. Mr. Sanford, on the other hand, appeared capable of doing absolutely anything he set his mind to.

She watched, fascinated by his long fingers as they delicately arranging china on a tray. Just a few minutes ago those same hands had been wielding an axe as though it was made of matchwood. He was so very competent that being with him only increased her feelings of inadequacy. She sensed he was fiercely intelligent. That much was evident in his discourse and manner of expressing himself. Well, he must be to have been admitted to the Company of Surgeons, and she did so admire intelligence in a gentleman.

'Miss Darcy?'

Oh lud, she had been staring at him, thinking just how beautiful he was. Once again, she was conscious of her face flooding with colour. How gauche and unworldly he must think her, but Georgiana simply couldn't stop looking at him and admiring what she saw. He seemed elegantly relaxed, his limbs casually draped in the chair he occupied beside his own hearth, his chocolate-brown eyes glinting as he fixed her with a penetrating, focused gaze.

She found the courage to return his look, and hold it, conscious of an indefinable something filling the silence that stretched taut and expectantly between them. Her body warmed as he continued to hold her captive with his eyes, his expression speculative. A pleasant sensation settled in the pit of her stomach, her pulse skittered in her veins, and she felt as though she was on the brink of discovering . . . discovering what, precisely? Georgiana wasn't entirely sure, but was convinced they had just experienced a moment of shared awareness that surprised him almost as much as it did her.

'Oh, pray excuse me,' she said, pulling herself together with an extreme effort of will. 'I was wool-gathering there, just for a moment.' She reached for her reticule, removed the journals from it and cleared her throat. 'Your father did call to see mine on several occasions during the Jordans' trial. I saw several references to it but none of them surrendered information that would be of help to you, until I came across these particular ones.' She paused to open a journal at the page she had marked. 'Your father, it seems, watched all the people who came to the trial very carefully, hoping to identify some of the Jordans' partners in crime, none of whom they were prepared to give up.'

Mr. Sanford sat forward expectantly, hair flopping across his brow, a hint of anxiety in his facial lines. 'Such is the code of honour amongst thieves,' he said with a wry twist to his lips.

'Mrs. Jordan did not once show herself, which your father thought was rather odd, given that her husband and only son were on trial for their lives. It subsequently transpired that she was too unwell, close to death, in fact.'

'Then I am very sorry for her,' Mr. Sanford replied quietly. 'I had no quarrel with her.'

'Do you suppose her husband and son's capture made her condition worse?'

'It would not have helped, but without knowing what was wrong with her, it's hard to be sure what effect it would have had.'

'Yes, I can see that.' Georgiana returned her attention to the journal. 'There were a number of villagers, and people from the surrounding district, watching proceedings every day. Your father mentioned he seldom saw the same faces twice, although he got the impression most of the spectators had sympathy for the Jordans.'

'If they had been the victims they might have felt differently.'

'That is what I thought, too. However, your father gradually became aware of a woman who attended the trial every day, with two children in tow. She stood out because she was very beautiful, clearly had a connection to Jordan senior, and didn't try to conceal the fact she supported him. For his part, he never once looked at her. Your father said his determination to ignore a woman whom all the rest of the men in the room couldn't stop admiring made him suspicious. No one knew who she was, and my father advised yours to try and discover her identity.'

Mr. Sanford quirked a brow. 'Mr. Darcy thought she was connected to Jordan?'

'Quite so.' Georgiana swallowed. 'Your own father also mentioned that the woman made him feel uncomfortable, because when she was not looking at the Jordans she held him, your father that is, in what he described as a death stare.'

'She held him responsible for the Jordans' arrest?'

'That is the impression he got. However, she could not have had anything to do with their accident because two days after the Jordans were found guilty, the woman was found dead outside the gaol where they were being held.'

Mr. Sanford blinked. 'Dead?'

'She had drunk poison. When Jordan senior heard of it, he became demented, ranting and raving and issuing all manner of threats. Finally, he had to be restrained.'

'Did they identify her?'

'Yes, her name was Isobel Watkins, and she lived in Newcastle.'

'Did they find out anything more about her?'

'No, but it was generally assumed she was Jordan's mistress. The children were his.'

'What became of the children?'

Georgiana shrugged. 'That's all I know, unfortunately. But I shall keep reading, see if there is more. Would you like to see what my

166

father wrote for yourself?'

'Yes, please.'

Mr. Sanford leaned on his elbows as he studied the journal entries intently, which gave her an opportunity to study him without his being aware. His expression was a combination of curiosity, anger, and sadness. Georgiana was unsure whether the information she had unearthed would put an end to his quest to discover what happened to his parents, or whether it would increase his determination to get to the truth. Whatever he decided, she was quite determined to be included in it. She had earned the right.

'Thank you,' he said, looking up again and closing the journal. 'I am very much obliged to you. I wonder how old those children were.'

'Oh, I saw reference to that in an earlier entry. Your father thought between the ages of eight and ten. There was a boy and a girl. He thought they might even have been twins.'

'I expect they would have finished up in the workhouse.' Mr. Sanford stood up. 'Thank you, Miss Darcy. You have given me something to work with.'

'You will try to trace the children?' she asked, standing also, as did Hamish.

'They must keep records. We know the approximate date and the surname of the children.'

'But they could not have caused your parents' accident. They were too young.'

'Children from that walk of life grow up quickly.' He frowned. 'I don't think they were involved, but they might lead me to whoever was.'

'Perhaps.'

'I can't thank you enough for what you have done, Miss Darcy.'

'Actually I was very glad to help.'

'Oh, why so?' He leaned against the wall, arms folded across his chest. 'How did this situation benefit you?'

Why had she said that? He was looking at her expectantly, as though he was interested in her affairs. He was probably being polite, but she felt an irrational urge to confide in him, to talk about . . . well, the subject which she never talked about. Except that was no longer true. Since speaking about it with Fitzwilliam she knew the blame was not hers alone.

'You asked about Mr. Wickham and why he was not at the colonel's wedding. You probably also wonder why he is no longer welcome at Pemberley.'

'Miss Darcy, this is obviously a subject which distresses you, and is really none of my business.'

'Actually,' she replied, finally finding the

courage to meet his gaze, 'I want to tell you. Something happened, you see. There is no excuse for my behaviour, other than I was lonely, but that is not really an excuse at all. Most girls would give a very great deal to be in my position.'

'Let me guess,' he replied, scowling. 'Wickham exploited your vulnerability.'

Georgiana couldn't hide her surprise. 'Whatever makes you suppose that?'

'You forget, I know Wickham well.' Mr. Sanford curled his upper lip disdainfully. 'I had nothing to offer him to his advantage so he saw no reason to hide his true character from me.'

'It took a long time for Fitzwilliam to discover the true nature of his character.'

'Your father indulged him. Wickham misunderstood his intentions.'

'Yes.' Georgiana shook her head. 'I know that now, having read his journals, which is why I am obliged to you. Mr. Wickham persuaded me I was in love with him, you see.' She lowered her eyes. 'We were to elope. It was the purest chance that Fitzwilliam prevented it.'

'Ye gods.' Mr. Sanford looked truly shocked.

'I had a terrible fit of conscience afterwards, and Fitzwilliam and I never spoke his name.' She paused. 'Until we read my father's journals, and he was mentioned so often in them that we couldn't help discussing him.' Georgiana fixed Mr. Sanford with a wide-eyed expression. 'Only imagine. Fitzwilliam blamed himself, and I blamed myself. Now we both understand neither of us was responsible.'

'Certainly you were not.' He shook his head. 'I won't offend your sensibilities by telling you some of the cruel and spiteful things Wickham did when he was a boy, but even though I was young myself, younger than him, I knew his character was bad. He was also very artful, careful not to show his true colours around your brother and father.'

'Yes, I know that now.' Georgiana looked directly at Mr. Sanford. 'There, now you are one of the few people who knows my secret.'

'Which I will never repeat.' He reached out a hand and gently touched her face. 'It was very brave of you to tell me. It cannot have been easy.'

She smiled, acutely conscious of his fingers searing into her face. 'It gets easier with each telling.'

'Wickham is now married to one of Lizzy's sisters.'

Mr. Sanford flexed his brows. 'Is he indeed. That cannot be easy for you.'

'I think he tried to compromise her as well, and Fitzwilliam somehow ensured they married to protect Lizzy and the rest of her family.' She shook her head. 'My poor brother bears it all with his customary stoicism, but it must have been a terrible time for him. Anyway, Mr. and Mrs. Wickham now live in London, and we don't see them.'

'I should hope not.'

Her mouth curved into an uncertain smiled. 'And now you know I am not quite the sheltered little innocent you imagined me to be.'

'I am impressed by your courage.' He returned her smile with an infectious one of his own. 'Now come, the daylight is fading fast. Hamish and I will walk you back to Pemberley.'

'If you don't mind my saying so, Mr. Sanford,' Georgiana said as he helped her into her pelisse, 'your desk is in the darkest corner of this room. I imagine you spend a lot of time at it so you might be better advised to move it beneath the window, where you will gain the full benefit of the light, and put the sideboard where the desk now is.'

He glanced around the room, as though seeing it through her eyes. He was so quiet that she thought he might take exception to her interference. Then he sent her such a dazzling smile that she felt weak at the knees. 'I think you might have a point. I knew something wasn't quite right with the arrangements but couldn't decide what it was. Thank you for the suggestion. You obviously have an eye for such things.'

She shrugged, embarrassed by the praise. 'It just seems like the sensible thing to do.'

'And I shall certainly do it, just as soon as I have seen you home.'

'There is no need for you to walk with me. I am perfectly safe here, and I expect you have more important things to do.'

'On the contrary, there is every need.' He pulled his greatcoat on directly over his shirt, turned the collar up so his hair spilled over it, and offered her his arm. 'Now come.'

12

Dominic locked the door behind them, unsure if he was more surprised by Miss Darcy's discoveries in her father's journals, or by her frank revelations regarding her relationship with Wickham. He was baffled by her decision to make such a potentially ruinous confession to a comparative stranger. It was evident after speaking with her brother about her narrow escape, Miss Darcy was now on much better terms with her own conscience. Perhaps that explained why she appeared more mature all of a sudden, less inhibited, and infinitely more intriguing.

The nature of Dominic's interest in a neighbour who no longer felt any need to suppress her inquisitive nature or spirited personality was diametrically opposed to his initial impression of her, and entirely inappropriate. He would need to be on his guard. He had no thoughts of matrimony at present, and if he showed too much interest in Miss Darcy his intentions might be misconstrued. Even if he *was* predisposed to find himself a wife, Darcy would expect more for his beloved sister than a relatively impoverished surgeon more interested in new methods and research than in immersing himself in society.

'Let us go this way,' he said, guiding her towards the track, Hamish loping ahead of them. 'I assume you came the long way around.'

'I didn't want to pass your house, just in case . . . well, you know.'

Dominic did know, and thought it charming that she blushed so readily. If she had been seen heading towards his cottage alone, tongues would have wagged. 'There will be no one at the house now, and this track will take us to Pemberley much quicker.'

They reached the outhouse where Dominic stabled Midnight. The stallion heard their approach and whickered a greeting.

'Later, Midnight,' Dominic said, pausing to pat his horse's neck. 'As soon as I have escorted Miss Darcy home you shall have my undivided attention.'

'He's beautiful.' Miss Darcy reached out a hand to touch Midnight's neck also.

'Beautiful certainly, but temperamental. Be careful.'

But it seemed Midnight was as affably disposed towards Miss Darcy as Hamish was, and graciously allowed her to smooth his neck.

'Midnight is an unusual name,' she remarked, feeding the stallion the carrot that Dominic produced from the adjacent shed he was using as a feed store. 'But it suits him. He has something of the night about him.'

'Midnight is the time he entered this world. I should know, I delivered him myself.'

'You doctor animals as well as people, Mr. Sanford.' She glanced at him, flexing a brow in evident surprise. Midnight snorted into her gloved palm, hopeful for more treats. 'Your talents run deep.'

'It's the same principal.' Dominic shrugged. 'Midnight's mother belonged to my uncle. She got into difficulties with her labour, I happened to be there and helped the process along. My uncle was so grateful he gave Midnight to me.'

'How very generous of him.'

Not so very generous, Dominic thought with a wry smile. What his uncle actually did was *sell* Midnight to Dominic at a reasonable rate and then deduct the cost of his keep from Dominic's inheritance.

'Yes indeed, most generous.'

They continued on their way and reached the edge of Pemberley Park very soon thereafter. They spoke little, but Dominic was acutely aware of his fair companion's close proximity and his growing attraction toward her. Perdition, he ought to ride into Newcastle, where he could remain anonymous, and find a light-skirt to take the edge off his growing need. Then perhaps he would see things more clearly.

They skirted the magnificent Pemberley lake, and Dominic delivered Miss Darcy safely to the terrace directly in front of the house.

'Once again, you have my thanks.'

'It was a pleasure to be of use.'

'Should I come here tomorrow and ask Darcy if he has made progress? I don't want to land you in trouble.'

She shot him a look of alarm, as though she had not previously considered the question. Then her expression settled into one of stubborn determination. 'There is no reason why I should not tell him that I called upon you.'

Dominic could think of several, but remained silent on the point. 'It is always better to be honest,' he said instead, smiling at her. 'Shall I come in, just to ensure no blame attaches to you?'

'You are very welcome to come in, but Fitzwilliam had an engagement in Newcastle today. He is probably not back yet.'

Darcy was fiercely protective when it came to his sister's interests. Now Dominic knew of her history with Wickham he better understood why. However, he was not Wickham and she had been perfectly safe in his care, but for the lascivious nature of his thoughts. Still, if a man could be prosecuted for his thoughts then the gaols would be overflowing.

'In that case, please tell Darcy I shall call here tomorrow afternoon. There are a few things I need to discuss with him about your discoveries.'

'I hope you will include me in those discussions.' This time he was the beneficiary of her determined look. 'I was the one to uncover the information, and I'm now almost as intrigued as you are about the Jordans, and the cause of your parents' accident.'

'Certainly, I shall include you, if your brother does not object.'

'I should like to see him attempt it,' she replied, squaring her shoulders and jutting her small chin pugnaciously.

Dominic laughed as he took her hand and kissed the back of it, holding it for a little longer than was strictly necessary. 'You have a natural talent for sleuthing, Miss Darcy. It would be a shame not to exploit it.'

'I can read, Mr. Sanford, and that was all I was required to do.'

'Until tomorrow then,' he said, waving as she turned to enter the house.

He waited until he saw a servant open the front door to admit her and then retraced his steps. Walking quickly to ward off the cold, he mulled over the revelations her father's journals had given up. The possibility of Jordan having *another* family had not occurred to Dominic, and he would make it a priority to discover what had happened to those children.

He dealt quickly with Midnight, then he and Hamish returned to the cottage.

'Well, Hamish,' he said as he unlocked the door, pleased to discover there had been no invited guests in his absence. 'What do you think? Shall we follow Miss Darcy's advice and move the desk to a different position?'

Hamish was more interested in the fire than in Dominic's dilemma. Dominic rolled his eyes, threw off his coat, and added a couple of logs to the dwindling blaze. Then he set to and pushed and pulled the furniture into different positions. The desk was deuced heavy, and he was sweating by the time he had almost manoeuvred it into place. Really, this was a two-man job. He ought to have waited until the morning and got Gibson to help him. But, having decided the desk needed to be moved, moved it would damned well be.

He cursed as one of its legs caught on an

uneven piece of floor, bringing the desk to an abrupt halt. Dominic, pushing from behind with all his strength, was jerked sideways when it stopped moving, and he fell heavily on one knee, out of breath, muscles protesting. As he did so, he felt the board beneath that knee spring upwards against the force of his weight.

'Damnation, now I've damaged the floor.' He moved off the offending board and it sprang completely upwards, smoothly, like it was supposed to act that way. 'What the devil?'

He moved to one side and took a closer look. The floor had appeared perfectly sound when the girls set about washing and scrubbing it. His heart rate quickened when he saw this was not a damaged board after all, but a manmade hiding place. The spring that kept the board in place was so cleverly hidden it would have been almost impossible to find by accident. Only by falling hard on that particular board had Dominic caused it to open. He could see the board was shorter than its fellows, as though it had been deliberately cut to that size to make it distinguishable.

Dominic sat back on his haunches, scratching his head. He held onto the hope that he had chanced upon an old hiding place

— something to do with the relative who had initially inhabited this cottage — but knew in his heart that was not the case.

'This must be the reason for my mystery visitors,' he said aloud, feeling a terrible sense of foreboding as he lifted the board completely clear. 'Right, what do we have here?'

He stared down into a dark void stuffed almost completely full. His hands were unsteady as he reached into the hole and pulled out a heavy bundle. He suspected what might be inside, but placed it on the table and hesitated, waiting for his breathing and heart rate to slow. When they had done so he slowly removed several layers of cloth and was confronted with a dazzling array of jewellery — gold, precious stones, rings, gold sovereigns.

Dominic fell into a chair and simply stared at the brilliant haul spread across his table. He ploughed a hand through his hair and sighed, wondering how the devil it came to be in his cottage. He assumed it must have been stolen and hidden where no one would think to look for it. But the coincidence — his father being involved with bringing the most notorious highwaymen to plague the district to justice — and now loot similar to their hauls hidden on Sanford property. It could not possibly be happenstance. His cottage had been chosen for a particular reason. Was it supposed to be ironic; a symbol of some sort, or were more sinister forces at play?

Dominic shook his head, still too stunned to think coherently.

Why? Who? Could the gang that Jordan started still be operating without their activities having come to the notice of the authorities? Once again, Dominic thought of those children, who would now be fully grown. No, it couldn't be. If highway robbery was again taking place in this corner of Derbyshire, Darcy would have known about it. There must be some other explanation. Part of him wanted to believe these items had been left behind in all the confusion after the Jordans had been captured. It was a convenient explanation that had no basis in fact. This cottage had been occupied at the time by his reclusive relative who seldom left the premises and was famed for frightening away anyone brave enough to approach it by discharging his blunderbuss.

No nearer to finding an explanation that made sense, Dominic left his find where it was, spread out on the table, but replaced the floorboard and managed to push his desk into its new position. Miss Darcy was right, he thought absently, it looked so much better where it now was.

The energy required helped to calm his raging anger. He threw himself into the chair by the fire when everything was set straight and made a calmer effort to reason the matter through. The haul had to be worth a small fortune and whoever had stolen it would not be prepared to leave it where it was once they knew Dominic was living in the cottage. He could handle himself in a one-to-one fight, but what if there were several of them? If these were the people who organised his parents' accident, they wouldn't think twice about doing away with Dominic also.

He poured himself a generous measure of whisky to help his thought process along. His discovery explained why the track had been kept clear, but there was so much more he did not understand. Perhaps there were more clues in the hiding place. He got up, but only needed to move the desk a few feet in order to access the corner of the short board. He pressed firmly down and it sprang open. Dominic took a closer look, holding a candle over the space, but there was nothing to help him. He felt about with one hand anyway, and on the point of giving up, his fingers closed about something hard.

'What do we have here?' he asked aloud,

thinking it must be another jewel that had fallen from the bundle when he removed it.

He hunkered back and opened his hand to confirm that suspicion, only to discover he had got it wrong. It was not a jewel, but something of far greater value. It was a button. Not just any button, but one torn from the sleeve of an officer's uniform, still attached to a fragment of red material.

One of his majesty's soldiers had turned thief.

★ ★ ★

Lizzy was getting worried about Will. It was time to dress for dinner and he had still not returned from his day's business. The weather was bitterly cold; everyone said it would snow overnight, and she wanted him safely home while the roads were still passable. He burst into her room just as Jessie was putting the finishing touches to her hair.

'There you are at last,' she said, looking up and smiling.

'I'm sorry, my dear. My business took longer than anticipated.'

'Did it go well?'

'Tediously, but Fenton and I managed to negotiate good terms for the sale of our excess harvest next year.'

'Then I am glad.'

Jessie bobbed a curtsey and left them, at which point Will bent to kiss her long and deep. 'How are you, my love? I missed you today.'

'I am very well,' Lizzy replied, even though that was not precisely true. She would have actually admitted as much and allowed Will to summon the physician, except that with Mr. Bingley here for just one night, she didn't want to spoil Will's pleasure in spending the evening with his closest friend. What she felt was probably normal. 'Jane and Mr. Bingley arrived earlier.'

'So I understand. I am glad you have had your sister's company today.'

Lizzy grinned. 'And we have had the added pleasure of fussing over Emma. She is an absolute delight, and I have yet to hear her cry.'

Will smiled as he stripped off his shirt. 'Probably because she is never left to her own devices for long enough.'

'Kitty is the worst offender.' Lizzy wrinkled her brow. 'Do you think it is a transference of her affections?'

'What do you mean?'

Lizzy frowned. 'I am worried about Kitty. She thinks Captain Turner no longer admires her, and it's breaking her heart, which of course breaks mine. I don't know how to reassure her.'

'There is nothing you *can* say, other than to try and keep Kitty's spirits up. Don't forget that Turner has his military duties to occupy him. These are uncertain times.'

'That is what I tried to tell Kitty.'

'Excuse me for one moment.'

Will disappeared through the door that connected their two chambers and returned a commendably short time later, impeccably attired in pristine evening clothes.

'How do you do that so quickly?' Lizzy asked accusingly.

'The services of an efficient valet and the added incentive of returning to your company.'

'Not much of an incentive when I resemble a beached whale.'

Will kissed the top of her head. 'A beached whale carrying my child. Besides,' he added with a raffish smile, 'I have a great affection for whales.'

'You wretch!' She tilted her head backwards so he could lean over and cover her lips with his own. 'That's better. You are forgiven.'

Will wiped imaginary perspiration from his brow.

'By the way, Georgie found something interesting in your father's journals today.'

'What did she find?'

Lizzy explained. 'Mr. Sanford wants to consult with you about her findings.'

Will, in the process of adjusting his neck cloth, half-turned to face her, frowning. 'Georgiana went to see him?'

'Yes.'

His scowl intensified. 'Alone?'

Lizzy shrugged. 'Sorry. Jane, Kitty, and I were caught up with the baby. We thought Georgie was in your library, and we had no idea she had gone out until I asked Simpson where she was when she didn't appear for tea. He said he had seen her leave the house and . . . well, I guessed where she must have gone. Don't be angry, Will. I can imagine how excited she must have felt. She so wanted to make herself useful. She *likes* Mr. Sanford very much, even though she would deny it if asked. She has learned from her mistakes and knows how to behave.'

'I beg to differ on that score.'

'Surely not because of — '

'Wickham? No, I would never hold that against her, but why the devil didn't she take her maid along with her?'

'She has blossomed these past few days. I don't know if it's because you and she have cleared the air regarding Wickham, or if we

186

have Mr. Sanford to thank for the transformation. Either way, she has developed a mind of her own, for which you will no doubt blame me. I am not exactly an ideal example; that much I readily admit.'

'Again I must disagree with you, my love.' Will exhaled slowly. 'And I don't suppose any real harm came of Georgiana's visit. I trust Sanford to behave honourably.'

'Well, there you are then.' Lizzy bit her lip to prevent a smile from escaping, relieved Will had taken the news of his sister's behaviour so calmly. Georgie, for all her newfound defiance, had been worried about his reaction and asked Lizzy to break the news to him. 'Georgie is determined not to be left out of the discussions.'

'I suppose there is no reason why she should not be a party to them, providing Sanford can get here. The weather's closing in.'

'You think we shall have snow?'

'I'm sure of it.' Will held out a hand and helped her to her feet. 'Come now, let us entertain our sisters and Bingley to a comfortable family dinner.'

13

The discovery of the button put a very different complexion on matters. Dominic reasoned if someone in the military was involved, it vindicated Jordan's illegitimate children, if that was indeed who they were. Unless, of course, the boy had taken the king's shilling, but if he was predisposed to villainy, Dominic doubted whether he would have chosen a career that required discipline.

He wondered what he supposed to do now. He couldn't leave the haul here, nor could he conceal it anywhere else on his property. He thought of asking Darcy to care for it but as quickly dismissed the idea. This situation could become dangerous.

It *was* dangerous.

Mrs. Darcy was close to her time, and he would not have her or Georgiana implicated by association.

He threw more logs on the fire, ate the supper of cold meats that Mrs. Gibson had left in the scullery for him, and washed it down with liberal amounts of whisky. By the time he was replete, he had also reached a decision. He sat at his newly-positioned desk and reached for pen and ink, and took a moment to assemble his thoughts before writing a long missive outlining his discovery and the circumstances that led up to it. He read it through and, satisfied he had got it right, sanded and sealed the document.

Tomorrow he would ride into Lambton and call upon the country solicitor who resided there. Chandler had served his parents, and Dominic had recently engaged him to handle his own affairs. The loot and his explanation as to its discovery would remain in his keeping until Dominic could discover who had used his cottage as a hiding place. His instincts told him the wait would not be a long one.

All that was left to do was to decide where to put the stolen property until morning. He settled for wrapping it up again and putting it in the bed with him. Anyone wishing to get to it, would have to get past him, the dagger he had secreted beneath his pillow, and Hamish. Satisfied with the arrangement, Dominic opened the door to let Hamish out and smelt the threat of snow in the air. Damnation, that was a complication he could do without, at least until he had rid himself of his unwelcome windfall. Hamish didn't linger outside and brushed his wet coat against Dominic's breeches in his haste to return to the warmth.

'You're supposed to be Scottish, accustomed to inclement weather,' Dominic told him.

Dominic spent a restless night. The howling wind soaring through the trees surrounding the cottage caused all sorts of noises to disturb him, every one of which made it sound as though someone was forcing their way into the cottage. Common sense told him that Hamish would warn him if intruders came calling, but that knowledge was scant comfort. One man and a dog were hardly likely to deter the ruthless individuals behind the thefts when the alternative was to hang for their crimes, or be transported, which some said was a worse fate.

At first light, Dominic gave up on sleep altogether and pushed back the covers.

'Sleep is overrated,' he told Hamish as he washed quickly and threw on his warmest clothes. He glanced out of the window and noticed it was snowing, albeit lightly, but the clouds were heavy, implying there was plenty more to come.

He and Hamish trudged up the track. Dominic paused to give Midnight his breakfast and then quickly moved on to the main house. Rubbing his hands together to restore the circulation, he walked into the warm kitchen. Naturally, Mrs. Gibson had already arrived. It would take more than a dusting of snow to deter her from her duties.

'Good morning, Mrs. Gibson,' he said, his nose twitching at the appetising smell of frying bacon.

'Good morning, sir. Breakfast is ready.'

'And I am ready to do it justice,' he replied, sitting down and nodding his thanks for the large mug of tea she placed in front of him.

'Can't start the roof repairs in this weather,' Mrs. Gibson said as she smacked a plate of food in front of him.

'That is what I supposed.' Since he fully intended to remain in the cottage until the spring, it was no longer so important.

Leaving the organisation of indoor work in Mrs. Gibson's capable hands, Dominic braved the conditions and quickly tacked up Midnight. His saddlebags were bursting with the loot he had retrieved from the cottage, and he was anxious to offload it into Chandler's temporary care.

He didn't have an appointment but was only required to wait a short time before Chandler was able to receive him. The solicitor listened in frank astonishment to Dominic's explanation of his find and his request to lodge it with him for safe keeping.

'A commendable notion, Mr. Sanford,' he

said, nodding emphatically. 'But would you not be better advised to consult with the parish constable on the matter?'

'That was my initial intention, but I decided against it. I mean no offence, but I am unsure who is involved and whom to trust.'

Chandler rubbed his chin. 'Yes, I quite see your difficulty. In some parts of the country highway robbery, if that's what this is about, is considered to be a legitimate pursuit. Given the very large divide between rich and poor, I suppose one can understand that attitude. Not that I approve of it, mind. There can be no justification for stealing.'

'When you have nothing to lose, you have no reason to abide by the laws of the land.'

Chandler steepled his fingers beneath his chin and nodded approvingly. 'Precisely so.'

'Whoever hid this haul will soon learn of my occupation of the cottage, if they don't already know about it. If they do not, they very soon will since my next stop will be the taproom, where I shall make a point of speaking openly about it.'

Chandler smiled. 'That means of communication is as efficient as it has ever been.'

'I imagine the thieves will wish to recover their goods sooner rather than later.' Dominic flexed his jaw. 'And when they do, I shall be ready to confront them.'

'I must urge you to exercise caution, sir.' Chandler looked rather alarmed. 'I dare say they are desperate fellows, and I should not like you to come to any harm so soon after your return to Derbyshire.'

Dominic smothered a smile, deducing it would be all right for him to be harmed when he had re-established himself. 'Thank you, Chandler, but I am well able to take care of myself, especially if I am prepared. I shall let you know what happens. But now, you must excuse me.'

'It is a pleasure to see a Sanford back in the district, sir. Your father was a fine gentleman, and I can see you are cut from the same cloth.'

'Thank you.' Dominic stood and shook the man's hand. 'It's good of you to say so. Oh, by the way, does the name Watkins mean anything to you?'

Chandler stood also, creasing his brow as he considered the question. 'I cannot say that it does. Do you have a particular reason for asking?'

'No, it was just a thought.' He was not ready to share everything he had learned with Chandler, although for his own protection, he had detailed it all in the sealed and dated missive now in Chandler's safe. 'Good day to you, Chandler. I shall be in touch.'

Dominic and Hamish strode into the taproom a short time later, nodding to people whom he already recognised, some of whom were the men who ought to have been working on his roof that day. He talked openly about his occupation of the cottage and knew that by the end of the day, everyone in Lambton would know his business. He washed down a large portion of beef pie with a tankard of excellent local ale. Hamish also took a slice of pie, but not the ale.

By the time he set Midnight on the road to Pemberley, Hamish running alongside them, the snow was so thick he had a hard time seeing where he was going. He was very glad to arrive without coming to grief. Grooms ran to take Midnight from Dominic when he rode into Pemberley's mews.

'Dreadful day, sir,' the head groom told him. 'Mr. Darcy told us to expect you, but we thought the weather would keep you at home.'

'I'm used to living in Scotland, Marshall,' Dominic replied, stamping his feet and clapping his hands together to restore the circulation to his extremities. 'This seems like a fine afternoon compared to some of the squalls we get up there.'

'I dare say so, sir. Would you like to come this way?'

'Stay here with Midnight, Hamish.'

'Er, Miss Darcy said the dog was welcome in the house, should you bring him with you.'

'How very thoughtful of her. Come along then, hound, but make sure you're on your best behaviour.'

Woof!

Hamish wagged and preceded both men to the door, as anxious to be out of the cold as his master was. Simpson materialised to take Dominic's outdoor garments. A momentary flicker of one eyebrow was his only reaction to Hamish. Poor Simpson! His dignity would never recover from having a nondescript dog given the run of Pemberley.

'Mr. and Mrs. Darcy are in the drawing room, if you would care to follow me, sir.'

Georgiana Darcy was there also and Hamish, still wet from the snow, made straight for her and shook vigorously all over her. She laughed and tugged Hamish's ears.

'We did not imagine you would venture out in such conditions, Mr. Sanford,' she said, looking up sending him an aware smile that caused an inappropriate reaction in Dominic.

'Oh dear!' Dominic tried not to smile as Hamish stretched full length on what was probably a very expensive rug, directly in front of the blazing fire, and rolled about on his back to dry himself off. 'I apologise. I really should have left him in the stables.'

'Nonsense,' Mrs. Darcy replied. 'He is as welcome as you are.'

'Thank you.' He shook her hand and then Darcy's. 'I hope you do not live to regret your generosity. My advice, for what it's worth, is to keep food well clear of the beast.'

'Mrs. Darcy smiled. 'I'm sure cook can find him a beef bone if he gets hungry.'

'Ah, but he is always hungry, that's the problem.' Hamish righted himself on the rug, canted his big head and gave a gentle woof, much to the collective amusement of his audience. 'Did I also mention he is impossibly pretentious?'

'Well,' Darcy said, when they were all seated and tea had been served. 'I hear my sister made some interesting discoveries in my father's journals. I have now read the entries myself but the question is, what do you plan to do about them?'

'Before addressing that problem, you ought to know of something that happened subsequently. I am obliged to you for that discovery also, Miss Darcy, since it only happened because I followed your advice and rearranged my furniture.'

'Really?' She looked intrigued.

Dominic explained to his astonished neighbours the nature of his discovery. He went on to explain about his visit to Chandler, and the reason for it.

'That was sensible,' Darcy said, rubbing his chin and looking very sombre. 'Chandler is a reliable man. This is a rum affair, and no mistake. I agree the jewels must be stolen, and recently too, but I have heard nothing of highway robberies occurring in the district.'

'I can't get past them being hidden on my property.'

'You think there is a connection between the Jordans and these latest robberies and they are somehow trying to implicate you?' Mrs. Darcy asked.

'Not implicate me, ma'am. No one knew I was coming back until recently. Too recently for the arrangements to have been put in place. I gave no one advance warning of my arrival, and once I was here, they could not risk going to the cottage. People have been brought in to work on the house, and anyone going to the cottage has to pass by it. They would be seen.'

'Except at night,' Darcy pointed out.

'Precisely.' He shared a look between them. 'That hiding place had been specially made by a skilled carpenter. It could not have been done in a hurry, so the cottage must have been used as a storeroom for some time.'

'You think the use of your property is some

way symbolic?' Darcy asked.

'Yes, I do.' Dominic scratched his head. 'But I fail to understand how or why, and therein lies my difficulty.'

'Unless the children that might be Jordan's offspring are somehow involved,' Miss Darcy said. 'Do you still plan to try and find out more about them?'

'I shall make enquiries in local parishes as far afield as Newcastle, if only to satisfy my own curiosity.'

'You don't have much information to work with, Sanford,' Darcy remarked.

'I'm aware of that.' He paused, wondering how much of his thoughts he ought to articulate in front of the ladies. In the end, he settled for candour. 'But I shall do nothing until I have neutralised the threat to my privacy at the cottage.'

'You can't stay there alone, Sanford,' Darcy said decisively. 'You have no idea how many of them there are, or how desperate they might be.'

'There isn't room for more than one person to live there. Besides, I'm not alone.' He nodded towards Hamish. 'He isn't so good-natured if he thinks I am under threat, and is a very good early-warning system.'

'Even so . . . '

Lizzy followed the discussion between Will and Mr. Sanford, but her attention was all for Georgiana, a convenient means of ignoring her increasing discomfort. Georgie's gaze seldom left Mr. Sanford, and she seemed totally absorbed by every word he spoke, every gesture he made. He really was a very handsome man. He was also charming and intelligent, with beautiful manners and a certain boyish attraction that even she, who was totally and completely in love with her husband, could not fail to admire.

'I could lend you some of my men to patrol the woods around your cottage,' Will offered.

'Thank you, but that won't serve. They will find it hard to conceal themselves at this time of the year. Anyway, they would freeze to death, standing about doing nothing in these conditions.'

'True, but even so — '

'The villains won't just walk up to the front door. They will wait until they think I am not at home, and when there is no one at the big house either, because they will need to use the track. The only other approach is from Pemberley's park and they can't gain access to that. That being so, it limits their options since there is activity in the main house all day now, even in this weather.'

'And so they will have to come at night,' Lizzy suggested.

'Very likely, ma'am, and soon, too. They cannot risk the possibility of my discovering their haul.' He paused. 'It's funny, but recently I have had a feeling that I am being watched. Hamish felt it too, but I assumed he had got the scent of rabbits or squirrels.'

'Not too many of those about in this weather,' Will remarked.

'Quite so. However, you have not heard the best of it yet.'

Lizzy's mouth fell open rather inelegantly when Mr. Sanford told them about the military button. Georgie and Will looked equally shocked.

'Fitzwilliam's regiment was only quartered here fairly recently, but there have been troops at the garrison in Newcastle for decades,' Will said, recovering first. 'But I agree with you, Sanford. That puts a very different complexion on matters.'

Lizzy was glad Kitty was upstairs on the nursery floor with Jane. She would not like to hear anything that reflected badly upon the local battalion.

'Soldiers can move around the country unchallenged,' Will said distractedly. 'If one is involved, or was coerced into being so, he

200

could easily carry stolen goods from point to point without raising suspicion.'

'Yes,' Georgie replied. 'But how would he know about the cottage? It is hidden in the woods, not easily accessible.'

'Which makes it an ideal hiding place in many respects,' Will replied.

'I suppose so, but . . . oh, here's little Emma.'

Kitty and Jane came into the room, Kitty with baby Emma in her arms, bringing their discussion to an end.

'Have you seen the weather?' Kitty asked. 'It's snowing so hard, it's impossible to see . . . oh, excuse me, Mr. Sanford, I did not realise you were here.'

'Good afternoon Miss Bennet, Mrs. Bingley.' He stood and inclined his head to both ladies. 'And I assume this is Miss Bingley.'

'My, how strange that sounds,' Jane replied, smiling broadly. 'Yes, this is my daughter.'

'She is fortunate in that she favours her mother,' Mr. Sanford said, dutifully peeping at the peacefully sleeping infant.

Jane smiled. 'It is kind of you to say so, but she is still too young to look like anything other than a wrinkled prune. Naturally I am biased, but even I must admit that much. Besides, I am sure I was not nearly so well behaved as Emma is.'

'You have always been well behaved, Jane,' Kitty said, making it sound like an accusation. 'It was very hard for the rest of us to live up to your good example.'

'Some of us didn't even try,' Lizzy said, thinking of Lydia.

Mr. Sanford was now watching the falling snow also. 'It's getting thicker,' he remarked.

'Then please stay and dine with us,' Lizzy invited. 'You cannot possibly ride home under such conditions. In fact, it might be better if you were to stay the night. No one will go near your cottage in such atrocious conditions.'

Mr. Sanford hesitated, then glanced at Georgie, who just happened to look up and smile at him, which appeared to settle the matter.

'Thank you, Mrs. Darcy,' he said. 'I should be delighted, although I would not have you think I called at such an hour in the expectation of receiving an invitation.'

'You will be doing my husband a favour. He will feel a little less outnumbered with your support.'

Will laughed. 'I am not afraid of you ladies.'

'Which is very unwise of you.' Lizzy suddenly felt hot and cold at the same time, and her head span. 'You will stay to dinner, Mr. Sanford?'

'Lizzy?' Will looked at her with concern. 'You just invited Sanford and he accepted.'

'Did I?' Lizzy was sure she had only thought about inviting him. 'I well then, I . . . argh!'

'Lizzy, what is it?'

Lizzy was conscious of Will and Jane crouching on either side of her, but the pain ripping through her abdomen was so debilitating that she was unable to speak.

'Lizzy, look at me!' Will sounded so frantic that Lizzy forced herself to lift her head. 'Tell us what's wrong.'

'The baby,' she gasped. 'Something's happening.'

'It's too soon.' Will glanced frantically around, as though expecting the eminent consultant he had engaged to appear from behind the furniture. 'We need to send for the physician.'

'He will never get through the snow,' Jane replied anxiously. 'Whatever shall we do?'

'It's all right.' Lizzy forced herself upright again, feeling perspiration trickling down her brow. 'The pain has eased a little.'

'You are fearful pale, Lizzy,' Kitty said.

'If I may?' Mr. Sanford asked.

Will, who had appeared on the point of

literally tearing his hair out, turned to him with a grateful expression. 'Please, Sanford, whatever you can do. This is disastrous. Now, of all times. I thought I had everything organised — '

'Babies make up their own minds about these things,' Mr. Sanford said with such quiet competence as to make even Will seem less anxious. 'My advice is for you to carry your wife up to her chamber, Darcy. I have a feeling this particular baby is in a hurry to join his or her cousin.'

'But it's too soon,' Will said for a second time.

'Please,' Lizzy said, lifting her arms, almost delirious with pain. 'I should like to go to my room. I shall be more comfortable there.'

'Take Emma back to the nursery, Kitty,' Jane said. 'I shall stay with Lizzy.'

Will bent his knees and, with infinite care, scooped Lizzy into his arms. Mr. Sanford and Jane followed them up the stairs. Lizzy's head was woozy, the severity of the pain in her stomach only superseded by her fear of losing the baby.

'Something is wrong,' she heard Will say in a terse undertone. 'Whatever you do, Sanford, if there is a choice to be made, save my wife.'

14

Mrs. Darcy was in a state of extreme agitation. It could be that she had gone into early labour, but Dominic's instincts told him otherwise. He kept his thoughts to himself, remaining calm as Darcy carried his wife into her sumptuous chamber and deposited her with infinite tenderness onto her bed.

'What now?' Darcy asked, almost aggressively. 'You have to help her, Sanford.'

'I shall do everything I can.'

'You don't understand.' Darcy ran a hand abstractedly through his hair. 'Lizzy isn't one to make an almighty fuss when she's unwell, quite the opposite, in fact.'

'This is her first confinement. She does not know what to expect.' Dominic spoke with calm authority. 'Childbirth is a very painful business.'

'If Lizzy actually admits to being in pain, then you can be sure she isn't exaggerating. Something isn't right.' Darcy clenched his fist and pummelled it against his thigh. 'Damnation, why did this have to happen now, right in the middle of a snowstorm?'

'Send someone across the park to my

cottage,' Dominic said, imbuing his tone with competency designed to reassure. He pulled the key from his pocket and handed it to Darcy. 'There is a black bag in my bedchamber with my medical equipment in it. I shall need it brought here as quickly as possible.'

Darcy looked towards the bell rope, clearly reluctant to leave his wife. Dominic knew he would be more of a hindrance than help if he remained.

'See to it yourself,' he said. 'You will only be in the way here. But you could send your housekeeper up. There are certain arrangements that need to be made.'

'All right, but you will tell me . . . ' His voice caught. He noisily cleared his throat and tried again. 'You will tell me if there's anything . . . anything I can . . . anything I need to know.'

'Of course. But for now, if you want to help, make immediate arrangements for the bag to be delivered.' Dominic glanced through the window. 'A man on foot should have no difficulty getting across the park, even though the snow is falling hard.'

Darcy leaned over his wife, and brushed the hair from her face. He looked deeply into her pain-filled eyes and kissed her brow. 'I will see you very soon,' he said, almost as though he could make it so by the sheer force of his determination. 'Enough of this lingering about in bed all day and having us all running around after you.'

Mrs. Darcy managed a wan smile that was clearly an almighty effort for her. 'I never could deceive you.'

'Nor shall you, my love. Not ever.'

Darcy lingered at the door, deep lines etched on his forehead as he watched his wife's suffering. Then, looking close to the breaking point, he slipped through the door, closing it quietly behind him. It must be hard for a man of his wealth and consequence, Dominic supposed, to have all that power at his fingertips and yet feel so helpless when those he loved the most were in danger. And it was readily apparent he really did adore his wife. That gave Dominic added incentive to do everything in his power to see her and her unborn child safely through this ordeal.

'Poor Mr. Darcy,' Mrs. Bingley muttered beneath her breath.

Mrs. Reynolds joined them very quickly, presumably because she had been waiting to be summoned.

'Mrs. Bingley,' Dominic said. 'Perhaps you would help Mrs. Darcy out of her clothing and into something less restrictive. A nightgown perhaps.'

'Oh, but — '

'I know the common way is for the mother-to-be to wear something warm, but I don't subscribe to that point of view. It is quite warm enough in this chamber with such a big fire.'

'Very well, Mr. Sanford. I am sure you know best.'

Let us hope so. 'And er . . . Mrs. Darcy, if you could void your bladder, that would help considerably.' Dominic turned to Mrs. Reynolds. 'Do you have something prepared with which to protect the bed?'

Mrs. Reynolds opened the door to the landing and called to Mrs. Darcy's maid. Between them, they made the necessary preparations. When they were finished and the maid had been sent from the room, Mrs. Bingley helped her trembling sister onto the bed.

'Now then, Mrs. Darcy,' Dominic said, removing his coat and tossing it aside. 'Let's see if we can discover what is going on with you. First, I shall need to feel your abdomen.'

'Yes,' she replied weakly. 'Do whatever is necessary, but please make this pain stop.'

'How long have you been feeling uncomfortable?' he asked, gently placing his hands on her swollen belly.

'For two weeks or more.'

Dominic struggled to conceal his disapproval. 'You did not think to mention it to anyone?'

'I — I thought it was normal.'

'She asked me about it,' Mrs. Bingley said in a stricken tone. 'I should not have made so light of her concerns. This is my fault.'

'It's no one's fault,' Dominic replied firmly.

'The baby was moving a lot, and now he isn't,' Mrs. Darcy said, gritting her teeth against the pain. 'Help me, Mr. Sanford. Please help me. I know something isn't right.'

No, Dominic thought, it most definitely was not. 'When is the baby due?'

'Not for another six weeks. This should not be happening yet.'

'Your baby has other ideas. There is nothing so very unusual about that.'

But the degree of pain she was experiencing so early on definitely was out of the ordinary. He felt her brow, concerned because she appeared to be burning up, even though she was deathly pale. Dominic returned his hands to Mrs. Darcy's abdomen and sought to find the position of the baby's head. As he had supposed would be the case, it hadn't fully turned. That could be because he wasn't yet ready to be born, but it did not explain the degree of pain Mrs. Darcy was suffering.

'If your baby is ready to make his debut, Mrs. Darcy, he is in the wrong position.'

'Wh-what do you mean?' She groaned as another pain gripped her.

'Babies are born head first, but this one has his feet where his head ought to be. If we allow him to come into the world that way, he might get the birthing cord caught around his neck and be strangled by it. That is a situation it would be better to avoid, if we possibly can.'

'What if he is not ready to be born yet?' Mrs. Bingley asked.

'I think he will have to be,' Dominic replied, indicating with his eyes that Mrs. Bingley should not ask such questions. It would be better for Mrs. Darcy not to hear the answers.

'What will you do?' Mrs. Darcy asked, screwing her eyes up as another pain gripped her.

What indeed. 'Please bring your knees right up, and try to relax your tummy muscles. I know it's asking a lot, but it will help no end if you put your trust in me.'

Mrs. Darcy bit her lip against the pain. 'I shall try.'

With her legs positioned appropriately, Dominic cautiously applied pressure to Mrs. Darcy's stomach. She cried out and tensed up against him.

'I'm sorry but I have to do this. Please try not to fight me.'

'It's hard to relax when every instinct is urging me to push.'

'Under no circumstances should you do that!'

Dominic spoke harshly, causing Mrs. Bingley, who was holding her sister's hand, to look up at him and blink back her surprise. If Mrs. Darcy pushed at this point, it could prove disastrous. When he felt her relax as much as she was likely to, he applied more pressure but nothing seemed to happen. *Damnation, that should have worked.* He didn't want to exert more force, but there was no alternative. Her screams echoed around the room when he did so.

Mrs. Darcy grunted as her sister wiped perspiration from her brow. 'Be brave, Lizzy,' she whispered. 'It will all be worth it in the end. I promise you that.'

Dominic was becoming more concerned by the minute and desperately tried to remember all he had learned about childbirth during his training. He didn't think it would be an appropriate time to tell either lady that his only previous practical experience at bringing a new life into this world had been with Midnight's mother.

'You're doing well,' he said as he applied

more pressure still, unsure if that was true.

'I think something moved,' Mrs. Darcy cried in delirium, her face twisted with pain.

Dominic touched her stomach again and experienced a moment's euphoria. 'The baby's now pointing in the right direction.'

But Mrs. Darcy was not in a good state. Her pulse was racing, as was her heart, but the baby wasn't moving at all. What to do? What could it mean?

There was a tap at the door and Darcy came in, Dominic's bag in his hand.

'How is she?'

Dominic steered him back into the corridor, not wanting him to see the state of his wife. He pulled the door behind him too so the ladies inside would not hear what he had to say.

'The baby was the wrong way round. I've managed to turn it,' he explained.

Darcy took a moment to digest that information. 'Does that mean it will be born today?'

'Possibly, but we can't wait for nature to take its course. She has a fever and I don't think she has the strength to endure the process, so I shall have to encourage it along. As well as a fever, your wife's heart rate is too fast, and the pain is adversely affecting her already weakened condition. I won't hide that from you.' He met Darcy's desolate expression and grimaced. 'What worries me almost as much as your wife's condition is the baby's sudden inactivity. Mrs. Darcy tells me it moved a great deal — '

'It did.'

'Well, not anymore. For the sake of mother and baby I think I should hurry things up.'

'You can do that?'

Could he? 'There is no alternative.'

Darcy's eyes were moist. 'Save my wife, Sanford, I beg of you. We can have more children but . . . ' His voice broke and he took a moment to compose himself. 'I will never find another Lizzy.'

'Go and wait downstairs. Have a brandy to calm your nerves. I will call you as soon as there is news, but it might take a while.'

Dominic slapped Darcy's shoulder and returned to the bedchamber.

★   ★   ★

'How is Lizzy?' Kitty asked.

Georgiana and Kitty were sitting huddled together on a settee, gripping hands.

Fitzwilliam shook his head. 'Something isn't right,' he said yet again, reaching for the brandy decanter and pouring himself a substantial measure.

'Mr. Sanford will help her,' Georgiana said confidently. 'She could not be in better hands.'

'It was fortunate that he happened to be here,' Kitty added.

'This inactivity is intolerable.' Fitzwilliam paced the length of the room, making steady inroads into his brandy. 'This should be a time for rejoicing; not a living nightmare.'

Georgiana shared a glance with Kitty, unsure what to do or say to comfort her brother. She had never seen him like this before. His face had drained of all colour, his hair looked wild, his clothing dishevelled, and his hands shook.

'I feel so helpless,' he said, over and over again.

Georgiana stood up and grasped his arm as he tried to brush past her. 'This isn't helping. Come and sit down, brother.'

He put up no protest when she steered him to the seat she had just vacated. He was like a little boy, she thought, lost and bewildered. She was suddenly the adult, the one in a position to give solace.

'I should have insisted upon a month nurse, or a midwife, or someone with experience living in before now.'

'No one would be better than Mr. Sanford,' Georgiana replied, taking his hand

214

and keeping a firm grasp on it. 'As Kitty just remarked, we were very lucky he happened to be here when Lizzy was taken unwell. Do try not to worry so.'

The snow was falling steadily outside, meaning no other help could be summoned, even if Fitzwilliam thought it would do any good. Dear God, his shoulders were shaking. He was crying, the tears spilling down his face. Georgiana wasn't sure if he would want them to see him like this, but she didn't think they ought to leave him alone, either. They were suffering, too. After all, Lizzy was Kitty's sister and the kindest, wisest person ever to have graced Georgiana's life. They would be better off staying together and comforting one another. In the end, Georgiana simply wrapped her arms around Fitzwilliam and allowed him to sob on her shoulder.

'If she dies,' he managed to splutter, 'my life will be over.'

'Shush, don't say such things.' Georgiana stroked his back. 'She will not die. Mr. Sanford will make sure she does not.'

'I'm sorry.' Fitzwilliam pulled out of her hold, and appeared to have regained control of himself. He took a large swig of his brandy and managed a wan smile. 'Talk to me, girls. Tell me what you have been doing and take my mind off of things.'

And so they did. Georgiana talked openly about her visit to Mr. Sanford's cottage, and about how much she admired him. She watched her brother carefully, expecting him at any moment to object to her attachment to their neighbour, whom he would probably say was not good enough for her. Instead, he merely smiled and made some remark about Sanford being a good sort of chap.

For her part, Kitty talked about Captain Turner, and how she lived in hope of receiving his proposal. Neither one of them would have spoken to Fitzwilliam so candidly about their hopes and aspirations under normal circumstances. But these circumstances were far from normal. By losing control of his emotions, Fitzwilliam showed himself to be flesh and blood, with fears and vulnerabilities, just like everyone else, and Georgiana no longer felt quite so much in awe of him.

'I wonder if Captain Turner knows anything about the jewels hidden in Mr. Sanford's cottage. Georgie told me all about it,' Kitty explained when Mr. Darcy sent her a surprised look. 'I don't mean to imply he would be involved in stealing, because of course he would not, but perhaps he has his suspicions about who might be tempted to do such a thing.'

'You cannot ask him anything about it, Kitty,' Georgiana said. 'You must promise me you never will. It might put Mr. Sanford in danger if we say something to the wrong person.'

'Yes, I am aware of that. I was simply thinking out loud. Anyway, when could I ask him?' A note of ill-usage entered Kitty's voice. 'He hasn't been anywhere near me since Colonel Fitzwilliam's wedding, and he hardly spoke to me then.'

'He *did* speak to you,' Georgiana protested. 'And the wedding was only a few days ago. He has his duties to keep him busy, and even if he did not, the weather is hardly conducive to riding all the way out to Pemberley.'

'Major Halstead did.'

'Yes, well, the major is more senior than Captain Turner so perhaps he has greater freedom to do as he pleases.'

Kitty shrugged. 'Possibly.'

Their chatter appeared to revive Fitzwilliam. He stood again to refill his glass but did not recommence pacing. Instead, he fell into another chair and concentrated a frown on the logs in the fire, or on Hamish stretched full length in front of it. It was difficult for Georgiana to know which. But at least he appeared calmer now.

Georgiana refused to believe in anything

other than a positive outcome. Mr. Sanford would have the situation under control; she was absolutely sure of that. She had total confidence in his abilities, and he would not permit anything untoward to happen to the mistress of Pemberley.

★　★　★

'Mrs. Darcy, I think it's time your baby came into this world.' Dominic said cheerfully.

'Anything to stop this pain.'

'Quite so.' He felt her forehead, which was hotter than ever. Unfortunately the pain would get worse before it went away, but there seemed little point in saying so. 'Now then, I am going to see how things stand.'

She was still in the early stages of labour, and the pains ought not to be so severe, or so close together. He thought about it for a moment and then pulled Mrs. Bingley aside.

'I don't think your sister has the strength to see this through unaided. She is getting weaker by the moment.'

'What can you do?' Mrs. Bingley asked, looking terrified.

'I shall have to use forceps,' he said, well aware how dangerous that procedure could be.

Mrs. Bingley's entire body trembled but

she appeared to have touching faith in his abilities 'Whatever you think best.'

What Dominic thought best would be to have someone here with greater experience than he had. But he had wanted to become a doctor to help people, and Mrs. Darcy was in desperate need of his help. He would concentrate his efforts on saving his neighbour's wife, and if he failed in that endeavour, at least he would be able to look Darcy directly in the eye and assure him he had done everything within his power.

'Right,' he said to Mrs. Darcy as he returned to the bed. 'The next time you feel the urge to push, please feel free to do so.'

Mrs. Darcy nodded, but Dominic was unsure if she had actually heard what he said. In spite of the pain, she was losing consciousness for increasingly long periods of time. From exhaustion, or the effects of the debilitating fever she had clearly contracted, presumably.

'Stay awake, Mrs. Darcy,' he said firmly. 'There will be plenty of time to sleep when this is over.'

'So tired,' she muttered, thrashing her head from side to side. Then she screamed as a contraction gripped her.

'Now push!'

She did so, but her efforts were so feeble

that they made no discernable difference.

An hour, maybe two, passed with no further progress other than Mrs. Darcy becoming increasingly delirious. Dominic glanced up at Mrs. Bingley's worried face and shook his head. He could not give her false hope.

'Is there nothing more you can do?' she asked bleakly, brushing away tears.

'Unfortunately not,' he replied quietly.

'What about the forceps you mentioned?'

'I can't use them until I can see the baby's head.'

'Dear God, we can't lose her.' Mrs. Bingley's tears intensified. 'Mr. Darcy will never recover if that happens.'

Mrs. Reynolds placed a cool compress on Mrs. Darcy's forehead while Dominic listened to the increasingly frantic beating of her heart, and despaired. What was the point in all that training if he could not even deliver a baby and save its mother from all that suffering?

He was startled out of his despair when Mrs. Darcy's eyes flew open and she gave an almighty scream. Dominic could see her giving way to the urge to push and cried out himself when he saw the crown of the baby's head appear. He sprang into action, feeling the skull carefully to satisfy himself it was sufficiently exposed for him to finish the process with his forceps.

'Well done,' he said. 'Now, can you tilt your pelvis up for me?'

She did so and Dominic carefully applied the forceps to either side of the baby's head. 'Lift a little more, if you can,' he said. 'Now, all your strength into one more push, Mrs. Darcy. Can you manage that?'

She could, barely, but it was enough for Dominic to pull the baby clear of the birth canal and have it slither into his waiting hands.

'It's a boy,' he said jubilantly, astonished that he was actually breathing. A few moments ago he had not thought mother or child would survive. Not that they were clear of danger yet, but their chances of survival had just improved exponentially.

'Lizzy, did you hear that?' Mrs. Bingley cried. 'You have a son, and he is the most beautiful creature on God's earth.'

Mrs. Darcy's eyes were closed, and she probably did not hear. She was totally and completely exhausted, as well as in the grips of a violent fever. Dominic cut the umbilical and slapped the baby's bottom. His cry was pitifully weak, but still the most welcome sound in the world. This tiny creature was alive only thanks to him, and he was breathing unaided. Amazing!

He passed the infant to Mrs. Bingley, the release of tension causing tiredness to seep through his own bones. He watched Mrs. Bingley wash the baby and wrap him in a warm blanket before placing him beside his mother. Dominic was unsure if that was safe or not, given that Mrs. Darcy had a fever. The same thought obviously occurred to Mrs. Bingley, who removed him and carefully laid him in his crib. She and Mrs. Reynolds then turned their attention to Mrs. Darcy, who didn't want to move, but couldn't be left to wallow in the detritus of giving birth.

'Let us make you comfortable, Lizzy,' Mrs. Bingley said. 'Then you can sleep.'

With swift efficiency, the ladies moved the new mother carefully to one side and whipped away the soiled blanket and sheet. Mrs. Bingley bathed her sister's heated face, and then the rest of her. Dominic turned respectfully away.

'Well,' he said, feeling almost as exhausted as the new mother appeared to be, 'I think Darcy needs to know about this.'

'You were remarkable, Mr. Sanford,' Mrs. Bingley replied, tears streaming down her face. 'My sister would have most likely died, had it not been for you. You were so calm, so competent. I don't know how we can ever thank you.'

'I did what I have been trained to do, nothing more.'

'I disagree, you did a very great deal more. However, we shall not argue and keep poor Mr. Darcy waiting in a fervour of agony.'

'No, indeed not. Excuse me for a moment.'

He ran down the stairs two at a time, conscious of servants loitering all over the place. An air of depression fuelled the atmosphere, as though they had all been prepared to expect the worst. If they had heard Mrs. Darcy's agonised screams, he did not blame them, but he could hardly tell them the optimistic news before Darcy knew of it.

Mindless of the fact that he was still in shirtsleeves, and the shirt in question was covered in blood, he bounded into the drawing room. Darcy and the ladies turned to look at him, stopped their conversation, and all stood. Miss Bennet gasped and sat straight back down again when she saw the blood all over him.

'Come and see your wife and son, Darcy,' he said, smiling at them all.

'They are alive?' Darcy blinked repeatedly, as though he thought he was hearing things. 'Both of them?'

'Thank you for the vote of confidence,' Dominic replied, firmly shaking Darcy's hand.

'You have a son, Fitzwilliam,' Georgiana said, grinning. 'I told you Mr. Sanford would not let you down.'

'I am an aunt again,' Miss Bennet said, dazed. 'Is Lizzy all right, Mr. Sanford?'

'She is very tired, and has a fever — '

'A fever?' Darcy asked sharply. 'How? Why?'

'I can't say. The baby was in distress, which would have distressed your wife. How she managed to contract a fever as well is a mystery. But come upstairs and see them, then we shall see what we can do about that.'

'But you can make her better?'

'I hope so. I shall do my very best. As to the baby, however, I can make no promises. He is very small. You ought to be aware that he might not survive.'

But Darcy wasn't listening. He was already dashing up the stairs, taking them three at a time. Dominic picked up the new father's half-full glass of brandy, never having been in greater need of its fortifying properties. He drained it in one and, winking at Georgiana, ran off after Darcy.

15

Even if the snowstorm had not made the roads near impassable for the previous three days, James could not have returned to Lambton anyway. The new colonel had arrived at a most inopportune time. James, along with the rest of the officers, was required to be on hand for collective and individual briefings from a man he immediately pegged as inadequate, inexperienced, and interfering. Damnation, that was all he needed! Fitzwilliam had left him to his own devices, more or less, but it was apparent his replacement would require constant briefings. Colonel Ponsenby was too young to have seen active service and too arrogant to make that admission.

God help them all!

Now, two interminably long days after the storm, at least the roads were clear, and he had the afternoon to himself. He rode towards Lambton in a dire frame of mind. He wanted badly to see Rose, but first he must make another attempt to retrieve his button — an incriminating piece of evidence that could not be left to fall into the wrong hands.

By the time he reached the inn at Lambton, he was frozen to the bone. He left his horse in the mews and strode into the taproom, intent upon wetting his whistle and warming up in front of a good fire. He paused on the threshold, his senses on high alert. Something wasn't right. The place was usually packed with bodies and full of noise and laugher. The bodies were there right enough, but no one was saying much, and a pall of despondency fuelled the atmosphere.

'Thank you, Millie my dear,' James said, treating the barmaid to a winsome smile as she served him a tankard of ale, wondering why the buxom beauty looked ready to burst into tears. 'It's as cold as the grave out there.'

A sharp intake of breath was her only response. Had someone died, making his flippant comment appear insensitive? James turned to the fellow next to him. He couldn't recall his name, but he was a regular and nothing of consequence that occurred in the district escaped his notice.

'Why the long faces?' he asked.

His drinking companion sent him an incredulous look. 'Don't tell me you ain't heard.'

James shrugged. 'Heard what?'

'You're a regular at Pemberley. I thought you might have news to tell us.'

'Pemberley?' *This is about Pemberley.* 'I have been engaged with my duties, and not been to Pemberley for some days. What's happened?'

'Mrs. Darcy had a boy.'

'Oh, I see.' James had not realised her confinement was so imminent. 'But that's a cause for celebration, surely?'

The man sniffed. 'She's right ill, almost died. Would have done so, word is, had not Sanford been there.'

'Sanford?'

'Aye, their neighbour. He's a fancy doctor and happened to be at Pemberley when Mrs. D. got taken ill. Fortunate for them that he was, otherwise . . . well, it don't bear thinking about.' The man paused to take a long draft of his ale, forcing James to wait for more details. 'It's still touch and go if the baby will survive. Same goes for Mrs. Darcy, they say. Mr. Darcy is beside himself.'

'Well, he would be,' said someone else, joining their conversation. 'He dotes on his wife. Took long enough for him to find the right one, so it did, and now this.' The man shook his head. 'Don't seem right.'

'When did all this take place?' James asked.

'The night of the storm,' the first man replied. 'That's why it's so lucky Sanford happened to be at Pemberley. No one else could have reached them.'

What the devil was he doing there? 'Oh, I thought he had been sent for.'

'Heavens, no. Couldn't see yer hand in front of yer face during that storm. Worst we've had around here for years, and we're used to bad weather. A footman managed to get through to one of the cottages on the estate the next morning to fetch a girl who just had a babe. Needed her for a wet nurse, so they did.'

The other man scratched his head. 'The way I heard it, Mr. Darcy was all for trudging through the snow and fetching her his self. Anything to save his son.'

James didn't doubt the validity of this information since it would have come directly from the mouths of Pemberley coachmen when they called at the inn. Besides, gossip picked up from this establishment was almost always accurate, if sometimes exaggerated in the telling.

'So Sanford's still at Pemberley?'

'I reckon Mr. Darcy would hold him there with a shotgun if he tried to leave. Not that he would, of course. He's far too honourable. Right lucky we are to have him in the district.'

Jealousy deprived James of the ability to think rationally. Sanford had been closeted at

Pemberley with Georgiana for three whole days and nights. James had spent longer under that roof with her, but the proprieties had been strictly observed on those occasions, and he had never been alone with her. With the house in uproar, and Georgiana probably upset about Mrs. Darcy and the baby, he could just imagine her turning to Sanford for comfort. Perdition, she had already visited him unaccompanied at his cottage! He had to do something, act immediately to bring her to her senses, and remind her that it was him, James, for whom she had developed a *tendre*.

James did not love Georgiana Darcy. He was deeply and passionately in love with Rose — a woman whom he could never marry, even if she would have him. In order to impress his family, maintain his position in society and support Rose financially, he needed urgently to marry an heiress of Georgiana's ilk. That is why he had gone to so much trouble to cultivate Miss Darcy's good opinion. And he had been making a damned fine job of it, until that cove Sanford came along and turned her silly head. James quietly fumed. He would see Sanford in hell before he allowed him to undo all his good work.

He allowed his companions' desultory

conversation to wash over him, satisfied there was nothing more to learn from it, and turned his mind to the question of Rose. She was a compelling contradiction of single-minded villainy and almost moral compassion. Put simply, before she reached her fifteenth year, her sharp brain had masterminded the continuance of the business that had seen her father transported. However, her methods were so low key, so efficiently contrived, that the authorities had not yet woken up to the fact it was going on beneath their very noses. Rose did not want notoriety.

She thirsted for revenge.

She could be living in the lap of luxury from the proceeds of her criminal activities, but she gave almost all of them away to those less fortunate than herself. She and her brother had lived in appalling conditions after her mother had taken her own life. Her brains had seen Rose rise above all the squalor, but she had never forgotten it. In some respects, James was glad she didn't take much for herself. If she did, she might decide she had no further need of him, despite the fact that they were soul mates. If their relationship was not conducted upon traditional lines . . . well, that was no one's business but their own.

What to do now? If Sanford was at Pemberley, then it would be an ideal opportunity for him to retrieve his button.

'I suppose all work on Sanford's house has been suspended in this weather,' he said to his fellow drinker.

'Nah.' The man gave a contemptuous sniff. 'It only stopped for a couple of days. A bit of snow ain't enough to put Derbyshire men off honest work.'

That was what concerned James. If there was activity at Sanford House, he would never get down the track to the cottage undetected. His only alternative was to wait until nightfall and go back then.

'I must go to Pemberley and see if I can be of service,' he said to his companions.

'Don't suppose they'll be receiving guests,' one of the men replied.

'I feel sure they will receive me,' James replied, not feeling sure of any such thing. He drained his tankard and slammed it down on the bar. 'Until later, gentlemen.'

By the greatest good fortunate it was not Simpson who opened the door when James arrived at Pemberley. He was perfectly sure the austere butler would have refused him admittance. As it was, a relatively junior footman was on duty. Matters clearly were at a tense stage for standards to slip to that extent. The footman recognised James and allowed him into the entrance vestibule.

'Be good enough to wait in here, sir, and I will see if the family is receiving.'

James stepped into the ante-room that adjoined the drawing room. He could hear voices coming from next door and stepped closer to listen. One voice was Georgiana's, the other belonged to Sanford. It didn't seem as though anyone else was in the room. Worse, they were actually laughing about something. The house was supposed to be in a state close to mourning and the two of them were laughing. Did Sanford have no shame? James quietly fumed as he listened to the footman announce James's arrival.

'Oh,' Georgiana replied, not sounding especially delighted. 'Did Mr. Simpson not tell you we are not receiving?'

'Yes, Miss Darcy, but since it's Major Halstead, I wasn't sure what to say.'

'Well, I suppose if he has ridden all this way in these conditions.' There was a long pause. 'Very well. Ask him to come in, Greenway.'

'Very good, miss.'

James could have wished for a warmer welcome, but at least he was not being turned away. He entered the drawing room with a concerned smile for Georgiana, and even managed a civil nod for Sanford. Damnation, that brute of a dog of Sanford's was spread full length in front of the fire. It lifted its head and its hackles when James walked in and a growl rumbled in its throat. At a word from Sanford, he stopped growling and rested his head on his huge front paws, unnerving James by following his every move with his eyes, and salivating.

'Miss Darcy,' he said, taking her out-stretched hand and kissing the back of it. 'I came the moment I heard, hoping I could be of some small service.'

'Thank you, Major, but there is nothing to be done, except to wait and hope.'

'How is Mrs. Darcy and your nephew?'

'Both are weak, but there have been small signs of improvement, and we are hoping they will recover. Mr. Sanford is taking the best possible care of them.'

He seems to be devoting more time to you than to them, damn his eyes. 'How fortunate for you to have him so close by.'

'My thoughts precisely,' she replied, send-ing Mr. Sanford an intimate smile that pointedly excluded James. 'He saved Lizzy's life, and that of the baby. We are all in his debt.'

Sanford sighed with feigned impatience. 'How can I make you understand that you owe me nothing?'

Sanford looked disgustingly sure of himself

233

in these surroundings — surroundings that James quite looked upon as his own territory. It surprised him just how much he had been depending upon persuading Georgiana to marry him and making them so. He had no intention of giving up on that ambition. What was a country doctor when compared to a dashing war hero in a red coat? Sanford might currently enjoy Georgiana's gratitude but James knew she was actually infatuated with him and was not given to whimsical changes of heart. If he could contrive a few minutes alone with her, he wouldn't scruple to remind her of the fact.

The gods appeared to be smiling upon him because shortly after tea had been served, a servant appeared and told Sanford he was needed upstairs.

'Is everything all right?' Georgiana asked anxiously.

'I couldn't say, ma'am,' the servant replied.

'If you will excuse me,' Sanford said, standing.

'By all means,' James replied affably, even though the remark had not been addressed to him.

The door closed behind Sanford, and finally James was alone with her. Unfortunately, she seemed a little uncomfortable with that situation and James racked his brains for something amusing to say that would make her relax. Before he could do so the door opened again and Mrs. Bingley walked through it, looking strained and tired. Damnation!

'Mrs. Bingley,' James said, standing and treating her to his most charming smile. 'How is your sister?'

'Oh, good afternoon, Major. I did not know you were here.'

★   ★   ★

Lizzy felt as though a heavy fog had been lifted from inside her head. She opened her eyes and blinked, recognising her chamber, but wondering what was different about her. It hurt too much to think, and so she closed her eyes again almost immediately, wondering why every bone in her body ached. The baby! Something had happened to the baby. Her hands instinctively covered her stomach — a stomach that was no longer large with child. Her eyes flew open again as panic ricocheted through her.

'Hello, my love.'

She followed the familiar sound of her husband's voice and looked directly into his concerned eyes. He was dishevelled and there were dark circles below those eyes, as though he hadn't slept for days.

'Will, what happened? Where ... the baby?'

'Shush, my love, stay calm.' He caressed her face with a tender touch. 'Welcome back.'

'Where have I been?'

'To the brink of hell and back.' He bent to place a soft kiss on her forehead. 'You gave us all the most terrible scare.'

'I don't remember anything.'

'No, I don't suppose you do.' Will turned and told someone to fetch Sanford. 'Perhaps that is as well.' His beautiful smile was a joy to behold. 'We have a son, my love. The most beautiful son a man could wish for.'

'A son.' Her eyes widened. 'How could I have when I don't remember anything? Are you absolutely sure?'

Will laughed. 'Never more so.'

'I want to see him.'

'In a moment.' He motioned over his shoulder, presumably so the baby could be brought to her. 'I expect you want to know what happened.' Lizzy nodded. 'Were I not so relieved to see you back with us, I would scold you for not telling anyone you were in pain.'

'I didn't know it was out of the ordinary.'

'All your problems came about on the worst night for weather in living memory around these parts. None of the people I had standing by could have reached you, even if I was able to get a message to them.'

'But Mr. Sanford was here. I do remember that, so everything was all right.'

'I thank God for his presence. You have been so very ill. The baby started to come, but you had contracted a fever. Sanford doesn't know what brought it on so suddenly and we . . . ' He choked back his emotion. 'We feared we might lose you both.'

'Oh my poor love.' Lizzy reached for his hand, but even that small effort exhausted her. 'You will not get rid of me that easily.'

'Two days and nights now you have been raving, burning up with fever. We kept the baby away from you, just in case he caught it.'

'And you have been sitting beside me all that time?'

'Where else would I be?' Will bent to kiss her forehead. 'Sanford had to help the baby to be born, and he is very tiny.' Will shook his head. 'He is a fighter, but you must prepare yourself . . . he may not — '

'Don't say what I think you were going to say.' Tears swamped Lizzy's eyes. 'I can't bear it. Not after all we have been through.'

'Of course I want our son to thrive, but you are my first priority. Without you, I could not — perdition, Lizzy.' His voice broke on a sob.

'I thought I had lost you.'

'Hush, Will, I feel weak but lucid. That must be a good sign.'

'I pray you are right.'

'Help me to sit up. I want to hold my son. I think I have earned the right.'

'Unquestionably.'

Will eased her torso forward, plumped up the pillow behind her and helped her into a sitting position. He found a thick shawl and draped it around her shoulders.

'There, is that better?'

'Much.'

The door opened and a girl Lizzy recognised from the estate came in carrying a small bundle in her arms. She smiled awkwardly at Lizzy and passed the baby to Will, who cradled him with surprising gentleness.

'Thank you, Martha,' Will said. 'Leave us now, please.'

'Very good, sir.'

'Please, Will, let me see.' Lizzy peeped into the layers of blankets swaddling the baby. 'Let me hold him.'

'Are you strong enough? You probably still have a fever.' Lizzy merely smiled and used all her strength to lift her arms. 'Very well.'

Will placed the baby in her open arms and sat on the edge of the bed, watching as she took her first look at the child who had almost killed her.

'He is quite the most beautiful baby in the entire world,' she said, tears streaming down her face. 'But, as you say, so very small. Hello, darling,' she said to the sleeping infant.

'What shall we call him?'

'Well, I assumed Fitzwilliam — '

'Heavens no, it's such a mouthful. I have always disliked the name. That's why I am so pleased that you call me Will.'

'I have always liked the name Marcus.'

'Then Marcus it shall be.'

'Are you sure?'

'My love, you could call him Cynthia and I wouldn't object.' He smiled at her. 'That is how relieved I am to have you back with me.'

'That is hardly a fate we can visit upon our poor son.' She returned Will's smile. 'Very well then, Marcus Fitzwilliam Darcy, you just listen to your mama, and listen well. You are going to get completely well and grow big and strong, as befits the son of this grand house. If you do not, then you shall have me to answer to.' She nodded, exhausted by her small speech, but filled with the most comprehensive love for the precious bundle in her arms. The baby briefly opened its eyes, and promptly closed them again. 'You see, Will, we understand one another already.'

'Welcome back, Mrs. Darcy,' said a voice from the doorway. 'You had us all worried there for a moment.'

'Mr. Sanford, I believe I have you to thank for my safe delivery.'

'Seeing you restored to us is all the thanks I require.' He felt her forehead and took her pulse. 'How do you feel?'

16

'Jane, whatever's wrong?' James watched Georgiana as she jumped from her seat, her face deathly pale. 'Why are you crying? Has Lizzy taken a turn for the worse?'

Mrs. Bingley covered her face with her hands, but a torrent of tears spilled over her fingers. Even James was starting to worry. If Mrs. Darcy had died it would play havoc with his plans. Georgiana would be in mourning and her accepting a proposal would be out of the question. Then Mrs. Bingley removed her hands and James was relieved to see a wide smile gracing her features.

'She has woken up! The fever appears to be gone and she is no longer raving.' Mrs. Bingley's smile widened. 'It really is the answer to all our prayers.'

'Oh, I am so relieved!' Georgiana and Mrs. Bingley embraced, laughing and crying at the same time. 'My brother must be ecstatic.'

'Oh yes, but he wants Mr. Sanford to see her, just to be absolutely sure. I can tell just by looking at her she is over the worst, but it's best to be cautious. She is no longer burning up and her eyes are bright.'

Georgiana trembled, presumably with relief. 'I cannot tell you how much — '

'I understand completely.'

'I am very pleased to hear the news, ladies,' James said, wondering if they had forgotten he was there. Wondering too if he was intruding and ought to leave. He decided to remain.

'Thank you, Major,' Mrs. Bingley replied, extracting herself from Georgiana's arms. 'Now, if you will excuse me. I feel as though I have not slept for a week.'

'Oh, Jane, please don't — '

'By all means, Mrs. Bingley,' James said at the same time, opening the door for her.

James closed it again after her and turned to face Georgiana. She was still standing and seemed rather alarmed to be left alone with him — well, alone apart from the damned dog, who was still watching him intently, growling whenever he moved too close. He ignored both the beast and the desire to snarl back at it.

'I am glad things have turned out so well,' he said, treating her to his most engaging smile.

'Yes. We really did fear the worst at one point. We still don't know if the baby will survive, but at least it seems Lizzy will recover. We will never be able to adequately thank Mr. Sanford.'

James knew better than to criticise his despised rival. 'Quite so,' he said. 'Now, shall we sit down again?'

He guided her to the settee furthest from the dog, waited for her to settle herself and then sat beside her. 'I welcome this opportunity to speak with you alone, Miss Darcy. I feel sure you know why.'

Her eyes widened and she looked frightened rather than expectant. 'I don't have the least idea.'

Ah, so she was going to pretend coyness. 'You must be aware how much I admire you,' he said, clasping her hand. 'I have made no effort to hide my feelings, and I flatter myself that they are reciprocated.'

'Major, please — '

'I realise my timing is not ideal, and that you are distracted by family concerns. Be that as it may, I am a solider, dedicated to my duty. As such, I must grasp my opportunities when they arise. I hope you don't think me guilty of disregarding your sensibilities, because nothing could be further from the truth. It is because my own feelings are so very strong I cannot waste this opportunity to tell you how deep they actually run.' Trying not to be discouraged by her shocked expression, he sent her a beguiling smile. 'You must forgive a man who is gripped by the fiercest of loves if he speaks out of turn.'

Her face flushed a deep shade of crimson. 'Major Halstead, I appreciate the compliment, but as you so rightly point out, this is hardly the appropriate time. Besides, I — '

'Of course I must ask your brother's permission to pay court to you, and that was my intention when calling here today. But obviously, he is preoccupied, and I would not think of troubling him at such a time.'

Her lower lip trembled, whether with pleasure or distress, he was unable to decide.

'No, certainly Fitzwilliam cannot receive you today, Major.'

'I shall not always be a soldier, if it is fear for my safety that makes you hesitate. I readily admit I do not have a great deal of money of my own, but my feelings for you have nothing to do with pecuniary concerns. I come from a very good family and — '

'Please, Major Halstead.' She stood and pulled her hand from his grasp, compelling him to stand also. She appeared very agitated. 'I don't know precisely what you are asking of me, nor do I wish to hear it at this juncture.'

At this juncture? 'I apologise. I have been insensitive and allowed my feelings to overcome me without making allowance for yours. I do not get a lot of time away from my duties, and selfishly wanted to make the most of this opportunity to pursue my heart's desire.' He paused, allowing himself what he thought was a very realistic sigh. 'You must forgive me if I assume too much, but I treasure the time we have spent together here at Pemberley, and cannot seem to think about anything else. I had rather hoped you felt the same way. Tell me at once if I am wrong, and I will try to put my disappointment behind me.'

Ye gods, she didn't jump at the opportunity to correct him. Was he losing his touch? No, that was not possible. Damn Sanford to hell and back. This was all his fault.

'If you are saying what I think you — '

'Would that be so very bad?' He placed two fingers beneath her chin and tilted her head backwards until she was forced to meet his gaze.

'Well, I — ' She appeared breathless, her eyes luminous, wary, but he detected a reawakening of interest in the depths of her expression.

'Come, Georgiana,' he said softly, stroking the curve of her face and dropping his voice a persuasive purr. 'I believe you feel the connection between us every bit as much as I do.'

'Oh, excuse me, I am interrupting.'

Damn it, Sanford had chosen the most inconvenient moment to walk into the room. Another few minutes and James would have secured Georgiana's commitment. Once given, he was sure she would not have reneged upon it.

'No, don't go, Mr. Sanford,' Georgiana said when he turned away. 'The major was just leaving.'

I was? 'You are interrupting us, Sanford,' James said at the same time, glaring at him with open dislike. Sanford had the temerity to fix him with a level gaze that implied he would not be easy to intimidate. 'Miss Darcy and I are engaged in a private conversation.'

'Which is now at an end. Thank you for calling, Major,' Georgiana said with great composure as she squared her shoulders and rang the bell. 'I shall be sure to pass on your regards to my brother and sister.'

James was furious. He was being dismissed like a recalcitrant schoolboy. When Simpson rather than a footman answered Georgiana's bell, he had no choice but to take his leave with as much dignity as he could muster, but beneath it all he was smouldering with rage. How dare an insignificant nobody turn the head of a vulnerable young lady such as Georgiana? Now that he was no longer sure of her affection, James had convinced himself he was almost in love with her. Well, as in love as it was possible for a man already committed to another woman to be.

He mounted his horse and, in spite of the icy conditions, rode away at a reckless canter, determined now to convince Rose to take more permanent steps to eradicate Sanford's tiresome presence.

★　★　★

'I apologise,' Dominic said, leaning against the door and folding his arms across his chest. 'Clearly, I interrupted you.'

'No, actually you did not.' Georgiana seemed confused and embarrassed. 'I was glad for your return. How is Lizzy?'

'I am happy to confirm she is over the worst,' he replied. 'I'm confident she will make a full recovery.'

'I am so very glad.' Her smile was spontaneous and uncontrived. 'Fitzwilliam must be very relieved.'

'He is beside himself with joy. Mrs. Darcy will have to remain in bed for a while, but she would have had to do that anyway.'

'And the baby?'

'If a mother's love plays any part in such matters, then he too will be thriving before the week is out.' Dominic shook his head.

'She already has him in her arms, and although she barely has the strength to hold him, she refuses to let him go.'

Georgiana laughed. 'That sounds like Lizzy. Is there any danger of him catching her infection?'

'No, she is beyond the infectious stage.'

'Good. Then when can I see her?'

'Later. I have ordered her to sleep. And your brother, too. Sleep has been in short supply at Pemberley these past few days and everyone is exhausted.'

'And you are anxious to return home, I suppose.'

He elevated one brow. 'You appear very keen to see the back of me.'

'Oh no, not at all. You must never think that. It's just that I know you are anxious to further your enquiries regarding the Jordans. After all you have done for us, it would be a sorry way to repay you if we kept you here when it is no longer necessary.'

Dominic remained where he was, fixing her with the dark weight of his gaze, but not immediately responding. His feelings for this charmingly spirited young woman had undergone a marked change in the short time he had known her, and he spent a great deal of time thinking about her. Too much time. Too many inappropriate thoughts. They had been thrown together for the past few days almost constantly, and that had felt natural and right in a way Dominic had never envisaged. Although deeply concerned about Mrs. Darcy, Georgiana still found time to talk to him about anything and everything. She possessed good sense, asked intelligent questions, was interested in his travels, his medical experiences, but did not fill silences with unnecessary chatter.

That fool Halstead, with his proprietary nature and quite shocking want of civility, had brought out his protective instincts in spades. The man obviously had designs upon Georgiana, or more precisely upon her dowry. Dominic knew nothing to Halstead's detriment, but his every instinct told him he was a fortune hunter who would quell Georgiana's spirit, pursue his own pleasures, and leave her feeling miserable and neglected.

Dominic was fairly sure he had walked in on a proposal, Georgiana did not appear to be turning him down, and he was astonished by the degree of jealousy that caused him. She had suggested Halstead leave when he clearly didn't want to, but perhaps that was because he had not yet spoken to her brother. Damnation, this would not do! He had already decided he had no interest in matrimony, and if he became intimately involved with Miss Darcy, that was the only honourable outcome. Miss Georgiana Darcy, wealthy and protected heiress, used to the very best of everything Pemberley had to offer, becoming the wife of a country doctor? He couldn't imagine it, any more than he could see her married to the penniless major.

'The major wishes to marry you.' It was not a question, and she did not treat it as such. She merely shrugged, leaving Dominic to fill the ensuing silence. 'I am sorry if I intruded upon a private moment.'

'I have already told you that the interruption was welcome. I did not invite the major to speak to me, although he seems to think I expected his declaration.'

'I am so glad you did not,' he said softly, taking a step towards her, even though he knew it wasn't wise.

She blinked up at him. 'You are?'

'Very much so. You could do much better.'

She moistened her lower lip with the tip of her tongue, her expression reflexive. 'I liked the major when I first met him, but something in his attitude has changed since then. I cannot put my finger on what it is precisely, but there is definitely something about him that I find disagreeable.'

'My advice, for what it's worth, is to follow your heart.' He shrugged. 'Not that I have any experience in such matters. Never having thought to embrace matrimony, if I ever did, I would be guided by my instinctive feelings.'

'Yes.' Her gaze was fastened to his face as he took another step towards her, shortening the already slight distance between them. The rational part of his brain demanded to know what the devil he thought he was doing. The instinctive side ignored the voice of reason and continued to cause havoc with his determination. 'That is what Lizzy is always telling me.'

'You would be wise to listen to her.'

The atmosphere was tense with the anticipation that tugged between them like an invisible thread. It was up to Dominic to break its hold since he was the one who understood what it implied, and yet he was not in sufficient command of himself to do the sensible thing. Instead, he permitted himself to touch her face for the briefest of moments before withdrawing his hand. One man confusing her today was more than sufficient.

'I shall stay this evening,' he said, moving towards the fire and leaning down to scratch Hamish's ears, just for something to do with his hands. 'In the morning, if I am satisfied with Mrs. Darcy's condition, then I shall indeed return home.'

'Yes, I expect you shall.' She resumed her seat, looking pale, distracted. 'Mr. Sanford, may I request a favour?'

'By all means.' He sat across from her and sent her a vibrant smile. 'How may I be of service to you?'

'Well, this might seem a little unorthodox, forward even, but I must admit to a great curiosity about the Jordans. Having read about them in my father's journals, I must know how the story plays out.' She shrugged. 'That is the price one must pay for having an enquiring mind, I suppose. And so I wondered if you would take me with you when you make more enquiries.'

'Those enquiries will be done by correspondence in the first instance. In the event they turn up anything interesting, I might need to travel to Newcastle.' He sent her a speaking look. 'I am sure you will appreciate we can't go there together, unaccompanied.'

She bit her lower lip and blushed. 'No, I suppose not. Forgive me, I did not think it through.'

'What you can do for me, if you wish, is to continue reading your father's journals. There might be more to be learned from them.'

'Yes, I shall certainly do that.' She yawned. 'Oh, please excuse me.'

Dominic smiled, thinking how appealing

252

her pale, delicate profile appeared in the firelight. 'I have just sent your brother to his bed. Mrs. Bingley and Miss Bennet have both gone to theirs, and you should follow their example. You have barely slept these past few days.'

'I can't leave you alone.'

You had better, or I might give way to temptation and kiss you witless. 'Nonsense. I shall occupy myself and see you for dinner if you feel inclined to come down.'

'Now it is you endeavouring to be rid of me,' she said with a playful smile.

'Not at all.' He reached for her hand and pulled her to her feet. 'Now off you go,' he said, opening the door and ushering her through it. 'Doctor's orders must always be obeyed.'

'Very well then, but I shall see you for dinner, Mr. Sanford. I look upon it as a fixed engagement.'

★ ★ ★

James had not intended to leave Pemberley without matters between him and Georgiana being resolved. He slowed his horse, consulted his pocket watch and cursed. In spite of being all but ejected from the estate, he had still stayed longer than intended. It was

253

now twilight, and it would be a perfect time to pay a visit to Sanford's cottage. But if he did that, there would be no time left to visit Rose before he was required to report back to the garrison.

His mood lifted as he turned his horse in the direction of Kympton. Damn the button! Even if it was found, it could not be traced back to him. When he had realised it was missing, the sleeve of his tunic torn where it had been ripped from it, he had had the repair done not by his batman but by an anonymous tailor in Newcastle. No one would ever find him, even if they thought to look.

Rose was alone when he reached her cottage, which was a rarity. Her brother was always hanging around, and others were constantly coming and going. There was one rogue in particular whom she appeared to have formed an attachment to. If he tried to bed his Rose, James would tear his head from his body with his bare hands. He was damned if he would stand by while she shared her favours with other men. That was asking too much.

She appeared to be in a mellow mood and welcomed him with a saucy smile and open arms. A very short time later, they were in bed together, naked bodies entwined as they lost themselves in a mutual passion that transported him to a state of ecstasy he had never managed to achieve with any other woman.

'Is something amiss?' Rose asked when it was over. 'You seem preoccupied.'

'No, nothing.' He wasn't about to tell her he had failed to win Miss Darcy's affections. He had *not* failed, he reminded himself. It would merely require a little more effort on his part to bring her around. 'I have just come from Pemberley.'

'I heard tell that Mrs. Darcy has had her confinement.'

James told Rose all about that lady's brush with death and the sickly infant she had produced. Rose listened as she always did without interrupting.

'When is Sanford likely to return home?' she asked when he ran out of words. 'I have already arranged for the parish constable to make a call upon him. I should hate for Sanford to miss his visit.'

'Soon, I would imagine,' James replied, scowling. 'There is no occasion for him to remain at Pemberley now his patient is on the mend.'

'Now the roads are clear, I expect the constable will call tomorrow or the day after at the very latest.' She grinned. 'He would not want to give the miscreant time to get rid of his ill-gotten gains, would he now?'

James chuckled. 'You are never more lovely than when you're being devious.'

'Thank you.'

'Not many women would consider deviousness an endearing attribute, which is one of the many reasons why I love you so much.'

He waited for her to return the compliment, but of course she did not. 'I should like to send someone to watch the show, or go myself for that matter,' she said instead, 'but it's too risky.'

'Absolutely, it is.'

'Never mind. Just the thought of him being caught with stolen jewels he cannot account for will be enjoyment enough.'

'Are you absolutely sure about that?'

Rose leaned up on one elbow and sent him a probing look. 'Whatever do you mean?'

'Sanford won't be arrested. We both know that. You have spent so long plotting revenge against his family that I wonder if the fright he receives will satisfy your thirst for justice.'

'What else do you suggest?'

James ran a finger lazily down the side of her breast. 'We ought to rid ourselves of him altogether. He is the last of the Sanfords, and with him gone you will finally know peace.'

Rose seemed shocked. 'You would do that,

take such a risk, for my sake?'

James hadn't planned to do the deed himself, but Rose did not need to know that. He knew enough dubious types who would do it for a few guineas without a second thought. 'Certainly I would,' he drawled. 'Anything to secure your peace of mind.'

'Thank you, but I am no murderer. Let's see how the constable's raid goes, then we shall decide.'

Perdition, now was not the time for her to find her conscience, even though what she said was most likely true. She did not back away from violence, but did not embrace it either. As far as he was aware, she had never been involved in a murder, nor had she commissioned one.

'Whatever you say, my love,' he replied, pulling her back into his embrace.

17

Dominic had been back at the cottage for two days. As far as he could ascertain, no one had been near the place in his absence except Gibson, who had kept the range alight but not set foot anywhere other than the scullery. The rug that covered the under-floor hiding place remained undisturbed.

Satisfied on that score, if frustrated on others, Dominic lost himself in overseeing the work on the main house and writing letters to parishes in Newcastle and the surrounding areas, requesting information about the orphaned Watkins children. He sighed as he sealed the final missive, wondering if he was chasing shadows in an attempt to unravel a conspiracy that did not exist. Then he remembered the haul he had removed from beneath his floorboards and decided he was not.

He called daily upon Mrs. Darcy to check on her progress. During the first visit he told Darcy he would not be offended if he called in the physician from Newcastle whose services he had previously engaged. Darcy would not hear of it.

'You saved my wife's life, Sanford, and I shall always be in your debt as a consequence. I have absolutely no doubt I would have lost her, if not for you, and I have absolute faith in your abilities. Besides,' he added, grinning. 'You are cheaper.'

'Well, there is that.'

'Talking of which, you must send me your account.'

Dominic sent him an affronted look. 'Are you trying to insult me, Darcy?'

'You have to earn a living.'

'Not at the expense of one of my oldest friends.'

'Then I thank you. And my offer of some of my men to protect your cottage still stands.'

'Thank you, but Hamish and I can take care of ourselves.'

'All right, but if you change your mind . . .'

'You will be the first to know.'

Dominic felt the full force of Darcy's faith in him, and since the baby was still clinging to life and showing small signs of improvement, it might even be justified. He was increasingly optimistic about the infant's chances for survival.

On both visits to Pemberley, Georgiana had invited him to take tea with her. He had pleaded prior engagements, pretending not to see the disappointment in her expression. The plain fact of the matter was that he had spent far more time than was healthy thinking about her recently, and he did not consider it wise to feed his growing obsession by spending more time alone with his pretty young neighbour.

And so here he was now, in shirtsleeves on a frigid early December afternoon, chopping logs in the hope the physical activity would dampen his ardour. So far his efforts had proven to be a miserable failure. He paused in his endeavours when Hamish set forth with a volley of barks, and Dominic heard voices coming from the direction of the track. He straightened up, his senses on high alert, and leaned on the handle of his axe, waiting to see who his uninvited visitors were. Certainly, they were strangers, or Hamish wouldn't be making such an almighty racket.

A posse of four men emerged into the clearing. An older, portly man, with a profusion of whiskers and a wheezing cough that Dominic could probably cure for him if he felt so inclined, stood before him.

'How may I help you, gentlemen?' Dominic enquired affably.

'Forgive the intrusion, sir,' the large man said, looking warily at Hamish. At a command from Dominic the dog lay flat on the ground, his eyes never leaving the newcomers. 'I take it you are Sanford.'

'Indeed, and you are?'

'The name's Burton.' The man thrust out a huge hand, which Dominic shook. 'Parish constable.'

Ah, Dominic thought, so that's how they want to play it. 'It's a pleasure to make your acquaintance, Burton.'

'The pleasure is all mine, sir. Your parents were well-respected about these parts. Locals are glad to see the house being opened up again.'

'Well, as you can see,' Dominic replied, indicating the cottage behind him. 'At present, my accommodation is a little less salubrious. But you did not say what brings you to this out of the way spot.'

Burton clearly his throat. 'It's a delicate matter, you might say.'

'Indeed I might, if I knew what the deuce you were talking about.' Dominic raised a brow and allowed his impatience to become apparent. 'It's too cold for all this shilly-shallying about.'

'Well, sir, we've received a report.' He shuffled his feet awkwardly. 'I'm sure there's no valid-ity to it, but it's my duty to investigate.'

'Even though it has no validity?' Dominic was almost enjoying himself. 'I admire your dedication, Burton, but what has this report to do with me?'

'We've received a report of stole goods,' said one of the younger men at Burton's shoulder. 'We have to search.'

'Stolen goods in my house?' Dominic widened his eyes. 'Good heavens. Presumably they are concealed in the big house, if indeed they exist.'

'No, sir,' Burton replied, still looking acutely embarrassed. 'We've been told they are here in this cottage.'

'You astonish me, Burton.' Dominic was keen for more particulars regarding the origin of the report, but that question could wait until they failed to find what they were looking for. 'I can assure you I have nothing here that doesn't legitimately belong to me. Still, if your information is really that reliable, you had best do your duty and search.'

'You don't mind?' Burton seemed surprised by Dominic's ready acquiescence.

'I would not have you neglect your duty for any consideration.' The men looked a little alarmed when Dominic picked up the axe which he had been using to lean on and, swinging it over his shoulders, buried it in the block with considerable force. 'This way, gentlemen.'

Hamish stuck close to Dominic's legs, but

a growl continued to rumble in his throat as all the men trooped into the cottage, filling the restricted space in the main room with their bulk.

'Would you like to start in here?' Dominic asked helpfully. 'The only other room is my bedchamber, and there is a scullery.'

He wasn't the least bit surprised when they directed their attention to the area of flooring beneath Dominic's desk. Two of the men pushed it aside, another picked up the rug beneath it. Then they stared at the exposed floorboards and scratched their heads. If the situation hadn't been so serious, Dominic would have found it amusing. He watched them carefully, keen to observe which of them *happened* upon the loose floorboard in question. The only man other than Burton who had opened his mouth outside was the one to do so.

'Oh aye, what's this then?' he asked, sending Dominic a suspicious yet triumphant glare as the floorboard sprung up and revealed the space beneath it.

'I have absolutely no idea,' Dominic replied. 'What's in there?'

The constable and all of his men peered into the empty void. 'Nothing,' Burton said, breaking the silence. 'What do you say to that, Taylor?'

Taylor, the man who had found the hiding place, scratched his head. 'But I was told . . . I had it on the best authority — '

'Not such very good authority then,' Dominic remarked amiably. 'Would you like to search the rest of the cottage, Burton? I am entirely at your disposal.'

'That won't be necessary. We are very sorry to have inconvenienced you, sir.'

'Well then, in that case, Burton, perhaps you would like to have your men return my furniture to where they found it and send them on their way. Then you and I can enjoy a private conversation.'

'You heard the gentleman,' Burton said, saving a scowl for Taylor.

They replaced the floorboard, then the rug and returned the desk to its position beneath the window.

'Right, be off with you.'

The other two left happily enough, but Taylor seemed reluctant to go. Dominic gave a hand signal to Hamish, who obligingly recommended growling, causing Taylor to scurry after his companions.

'Now then, Burton,' Dominic said, indicating a chair beside the fire, which Burton lowered his bulk into. 'A little single malt to ward off the cold.'

'That's remarkably generous of you, sir,

seeing as how we came here under false pretences, all but accusing you of nefarious wrongdoing.'

Dominic sat in the chair opposite Burton's and savoured his drink. 'You are telling me then, that if you had found stolen goods in this cottage, you would have thought I knew something about them?'

'No one could convince me you are a thief, sir, but it would have looked deuced awkward. I didn't like hearing that rumour when Taylor came to me with it, but couldn't ignore it either. Still, I am very glad there was nothing in it.'

'Your friend Taylor, on the other hand, seemed disappointed.'

'He's not a friend exactly.'

'Then what?'

'I'm the only official constable for this district, sir, but the local justice of the peace — '

'Sir Walter Mead.'

'Aye, do you know him?'

'No, I have not yet had the pleasure, but I hear he is an honourable chap. He took over after my father died?'

'That he did. He has the devil's own job keeping order.' Burton paused to take a healthy sip of his whiskey. 'Damned fine malt this.'

'I brought it with me from Scotland.'

'Very sensible. Anyway, where was I? Oh yes, I expect you heard about the highway robberies in the district. You were just a boy at the time, but even so . . . '

'I think I recall something. But were the perpetrators not transported?'

'Indeed they were. Sir Walter had to reassure the populace they were safe after that. Mr. Ventnor, the constable at the time, retired, and I was appointed in his place. All has been quiet, until recently, when a few isolated thefts have been reported.'

'More highway robbers?' Dominic asked, his posture relaxed, his senses on high alert.

'No, thefts from properties.'

'I had not heard. I don't believe Mr. Darcy has, either. I have been to Pemberley a fair bit since my return and no mention has been made.'

'We're trying to keep it quiet until we're sure, to prevent people from panicking. It has taken that long for the farrago caused by the Jordans to die down, so the last thing Sir Walter wants is for the local populace to take the law into its own hands.'

'So you were hoping to find the loot hidden away here.' Dominic rubbed his chin. 'But even if I had criminal tendencies, I haven't been in the area for long enough to act upon them.'

'That's why I am glad we found nothing.' Burton shook his head. 'But that hiding place looked like it had been made specifically, and Taylor's information was so precise. It makes you wonder.'

'Tell me about Taylor and the others. If you are the only constable, how do you come to enjoy their services?'

'Sir Walter gives me leave to recruit assistance as and when I need it. Those men are the ones I call on when I do. Everyone around these parts knows that. They know the men too, and would be more likely to talk to them about their suspicions than to me. Some of them get their information from their own activities on the wrong side of the law, if you follow my meaning. But if they were to speak to me, I wouldn't necessarily be able to turn a blind eye.'

'I see, all too clearly. And you needed all three of them with you today to search this small cottage?' Dominic fixed the constable with a sardonic look. 'You must have thought me a pretty desperate fellow, likely to resist arrest, I suppose.'

Burton's face flushed a deep red. 'No offence, but it pays to be cautious.'

'No offence taken.' He waved the bottle at Burton. 'Top up?'

Burton thrust his glass forward. 'That's

very gracious of you, sir.'

'So,' Dominic said, leaning back in his chair and crossing one foot over his opposite thigh. 'From whom did Taylor get his information?'

'I gather it was from one of the servants who helped you get this cottage habitable. The information was quite specific. There was a hiding place beneath the floor, under the rug beneath your desk.'

Dominic wanted to laugh. That was complete rubbish. Apart from Gibson, who didn't have the wits, only the two girls were involved in the cottage's restoration. However, he did not tell Burton that. Someone had deliberately tipped Taylor off about the hiding place, wanting Dominic to be caught with the loot. The question was, whom? Presumably someone who bore him, or his family, a grudge. Someone connected with the Jordans. Perhaps his investigation into the identity of those children would not be such a massive waste of time after all.

★ ★ ★

Jane sat beside Lizzy's bed, baby Emma in her arms. Lizzy was propped against the headboard cradling her son.

'There are definite signs of improvement,'

Lizzy said, peering at Marcus's face. 'He opens his eyes with increasing regularity and feeds well.'

'I am perfectly sure he will grow up to be as big and strong as his papa,' Jane replied. 'And you will be up and about in no time.'

'I would get up now, except Will would skin me alive if I tried it. After the fright I gave you all, I could not do that to him.'

'He would not have left your side now if I had not agreed to sit with you.' Jane smiled. 'I don't think your husband trusts you to behave yourself, Lizzy.'

'Which is most unfair. It's not as though I caught a fever on purpose. And I don't suppose Marcus got twisted around the wrong way just to cause trouble.'

'I am sure he did not.' Jane shook her head. 'But I still thank goodness Mr. Sanford happened to be here and knew what to do.'

Lizzy grinned. 'He told Georgie after the event that although he knew the theory, the only time he had attend an expectant mother before now, the mother in question was a horse.'

Jane smothered a smile with the back of a hand. 'Thank goodness we did not know that.'

'Quite.' Lizzy concentrated her attention on her sleeping son. 'Georgie is totally besotted, you know. And this time, I think it might be the real thing.'

'Major Halstead called while you were still unwell, I mean really unwell, and she barely spared him the time of day. I think he was quite put out about it.'

'He would be. Major Halstead thinks very well of himself.'

'I thought you liked him, Lizzy.'

'I did to begin with, but recently . . . oh, I don't know, I can't cite anything specific, but I sometimes get the feeling he's putting on an act.'

'Pemberley *is* rather daunting.'

'Well anyway, my husband will be pleased about Georgie's change of heart. He has always been suspicious about the major's motives and doesn't think he's right for Georgie.'

'Would anyone be?'

Lizzy sighed. 'Actually, since Mr. Sanford saved my life, he can do no wrong in Will's eyes, so Georgie might get to have her way. If she can persuade Mr. Sanford to admit he admires her, of course.'

'You think he does not?'

'I think he has more pressing matters on his mind. He will never be satisfied until he finds out what happened to his parents.'

'And Georgie is determined to help him.'

'Yes, but he's keeping her at arm's length, probably because he thinks it might be dangerous.'

Jane sighed. 'Poor Kitty. She longs to see Captain Turner, but he does not come. Georgie, on the other hand, doesn't want to see the major and he calls continuously.'

'I am glad we no longer have to worry about such things, at least not for ourselves.' Lizzy paused, smiling as her sleeping son gripped her little finger. 'You were right, Jane. The love I feel for this tiny child is beyond imaginable.'

'Look at the two of us,' Jane replied. 'We have both made advantageous marriages to men we love and respect, and have borne them healthy children. Would you have imagined us so happily settled even in your wildest dreams?'

'Well, I knew we *deserved* to be, but — '

'Oh, Lizzy!'

'Talking of the men we love, have you heard from your Mr. Bingley?'

'Yes.' Jane's smile faded. 'He should be back tomorrow. He says Caroline is subdued and has lost her vitality. She refuses to speak about what happened here. He says it is as though she has blocked it from her mind, and Charles thinks it better not to press her.'

'Are they returning to Derbyshire with your husband?'

'They are coming, but in Mr. Hurst's carriage. Charles will come here to collect me first. We shall return home and they will arrive a few days later. They will stay, at least until the beginning of January.'

Lizzy reached out a hand and touched Jane's. 'And you are worried about that? Not that I blame you, of course. It cannot be easy for you, but rest assured that Will and I bear Miss Bingley no ill will, and if you think she is well enough, you are all welcome here.'

'Lizzy, that is too generous!' Jane's eyes widened in evident relief. 'After what Caroline tried to do to you, she does not deserve such consideration.'

'No, my dear, but you do. I have never liked Caroline, nor do I trust her, but there is nothing she can do to hurt me now.' Lizzy glanced at her sleeping baby to confirm her point. 'And so we shall not let her come between us.'

★ ★ ★

James slipped away from the garrison unobserved. If the new colonel noticed his absence, he would think of a way to account for it upon his return. Right now, the only place he wanted to be was in the taproom at Lambton inn since that is where the news of the raid on Sanford's cottage was bound to be made public. The locals would say they had always known there was something odd about Sanford's sudden return to the district and congratulate themselves on their extraordinary foresight.

James would have given a very great deal to be there and seen the arrogant upstart's reaction for himself, but had no legitimate excuse to go near the place. Rose had arranged for Taylor to point the search party in the right direction, and if his button was found . . . well, Newcastle was a garrison town, and military men in Lambton were a common sight. Any one of them might have lost that button.

Satisfied that he had covered his tracks, James settled into conversation with a few of the regulars, wondering how much longer it would be before Taylor put in an appearance. Presumably it would take a while to overcome Sanford's objections and Burton's disinclination to arrest such an outwardly respectable gentleman who enjoyed Darcy's influential support. Rose had little time for Burton, and considered him ill-equipped to fill the role of parish constable. That worked in her favour because she was absolutely sure he was too dense to catch on to her capers unless, as on this occasion, she gave him a helping hand.

James had barely completed that thought before Taylor pushed through the door. Too soon, surely? One look at his mulish expression and James knew things had not gone according to plan.

'What's up with you then?' someone asked. 'You look like you just lost yer last farthing.'

Taylor told a growing crowd of locals with a sixth sense for sensational gossip about the failed raid on Sanford's cottage.

'You really are dicked in the nob if you think Mr. Sanford's a thief,' someone said. 'He was in the village just the other day and gave me wife a linctus that cleared up our little one's cough overnight. Wouldn't accept payment for it, neither. The man's a real gent, and no mistake.'

'He saved Mrs. Darcy's life, and that of her son,' someone else said. 'How could you imagine he's a wrong 'un?'

The crowd was growing hostile towards Taylor, who was struggling to defend his position.

'We *did* find a secret hiding place under the floor,' he said defensively.

'But no loot?'

'He could have moved it on.'

'You're demented.'

There was nothing James could do to help Taylor without showing his hand. Damnation, would nothing go right for him? Sanford was coming out of this, not with his reputation in tatters, but with it enhanced. James caught Taylor's eye and nodded once, indicating he would break the bad news to Rose. She needed to know that not only had Sanford escaped arrest, but he had also, presumably, discovered the loot and removed it.

As James rode away, his thoughts dwelt upon that damned button. Even though it could not be linked to him, the prospect of it being in Sanford's possession was exceedingly unsettling.

18

'You have placed a wrong stitch,' Kitty pointed out.

'Botheration!' Georgiana threw her embroidery aside. 'It's no good. I can't concentrate.'

Kitty smiled. 'So I apprehend. You haven't listened to one word in ten that I've spoken to you, and I can easily guess why. Your thoughts are for Mr. Sanford.'

'I'm sorry, Kitty. I didn't mean to be rude.'

'You weren't rude. Merely preoccupied.'

Georgiana pouted. 'I don't understand why he is ignoring me. I thought we were friends.'

Kitty chuckled. 'Friends?'

'I like him so very much, Kitty.' Georgiana spread her hands. 'He is easily the most fascinating gentleman of my acquaintance.'

'I can understand why you feel that way. He is handsome, intelligent, elegant, interesting in so many unusual ways, *and* he saved my sister's life. If it were not for Captain Turner I would like him very much, too.'

'I thought he liked me.' Georgiana leaned forward, placed her elbows on her knees and rested her chin in her cupped hands. 'He was very obliged to me for finding all those references to the Jordans in my father's journals, but now he treats me as though I don't exist.'

'I know how that feels,' Kitty replied with a heavy sigh. 'Captain Turner treats me the same way.'

'I think the captain will prove to be constant in his affection for you and it is only his duties that keep him away, but Mr. Sanford has no such excuse.' Georgiana abruptly came to a decision and jumped from her chair in a swirl of muslin and righteous indignation. 'Well, I don't intend to put up with it.'

'Where are you going?'

'To visit him, of course,' Georgiana replied with determination.

'You can't!' Kitty stood also and grasped Georgiana's arm. 'Think what you are doing. Your brother will be furious if he finds out, and might forbid you to see Mr. Sanford again.'

'He will not do that. He is far too indebted to him. Besides, I shall not tell him, and he is too taken up with Lizzy and the baby to notice I am gone. I shall not be long. If anyone asks where I am, say you do not know.'

'Are you absolutely sure about this?' Kitty looked full of uncertainty. 'Won't it look as though you are throwing yourself at him?'

'Not in the least.' Georgiana elevated her chin. 'Miss Darcy of Pemberley does not throw herself at gentlemen.'

Kitty giggled. 'It seems she does now.'

Georgiana laughed too, but sobered again almost immediately. 'He agreed I could help him with his investigations, and I intend to make sure he keeps his word.'

'Would you like me to come with you?'

'No thank you, Kitty.' Georgiana squared her shoulders, her determination fuelled by her growing annoyance. Georgiana had had quite enough of being cosseted and protected. She had come of age, figuratively at least, and was ready to fight for what she was determined to have, which was Mr. Sanford. If he did not feel the same way about her, she would prefer to know it immediately. 'What I have to say to Mr. Sanford is for his ears only. I am tired of being invisible, and he has chosen an inadvisable time to treat me as if I am.'

Kitty looked rather startled. 'I have never seen you in such an intransigent mood before. Poor Mr. Sanford does not stand a chance.'

'Poor Mr. Sanford nothing.' Georgiana waved the suggestion aside. 'He has nothing to fear from me, provided he doesn't try to pat me on the head and send me away.'

'Take very great care,' Kitty said, her face creased with concern. 'It's freezing cold out there and looks as though it might snow again. I warn you now, if you are not back before dark, I shall give your secret away and tell your brother where you have gone.'

'I shall be back long before then.' Georgiana gave Kitty a swift hug. 'Thank you for being such a good friend.'

'Good luck.'

Dressed in a thick cloak, with the hood completely covering her hair, Georgiana set off across the park a short time later. Kitty was right. It was freezing cold, and the dark clouds directly overhead threatened snow. Georgiana, busy rehearsing in her head what she planned to say to Mr. Sanford, barely noticed the deteriorating conditions. She was wearing her warmest half-boots, but the cold still seeped through the leather. By the time she reached the edge of the estate, where it bordered Mr. Sanford's property, she was chilled to the bone.

She avoided the track that would take her past the big house and, as she had done once before, followed the path through the trees to the back of Mr. Sanford's cottage. This afternoon it felt as though the trees were closing in on her as a chill wind whipped through bare branches that cut out the dull afternoon light. She felt apprehensive for some reason and shivered as she quickened her pace, keen to be clear of the confining tunnel of shadowy trees. She hoped she would find Mr. Sanford at home. Only now did it occur to her that he may not be, and she was unsure if she would find the determination to make this journey for a second time.

As she stepped into the clearing that housed the cottage, she heard voices. She borrowed a curse from her brother's vocabulary, muttering it beneath her breath and allowing the forbidden syllables to roll quietly off her tongue. She could not possibly show herself if he was not alone. Hiding behind a stout tree trunk, she watched Mr. Sanford shake hands with a large man. He had his back to her, and she was unable to decide if she knew who he was. Thankfully, he took off down the track towards the big house shortly after the handshake, and Mr. Sanford was left alone, watching him slowly disappear from view.

Hamish must have picked up her scent. He lifted his head, sniffed the air, and then bounded towards her hiding place. Rather than have it seem as though she was spying on him, she stepped out and greeted the dog, who appeared deliriously happy to see her. He jumped up, almost knocking her from her feet and enthusiastically licked her hand.

'Hamish, what the devil . . . ' He blinked when he saw her. 'Miss Darcy, what are you doing here? Is something wrong with Mrs. Darcy?'

★   ★   ★

James strode into Rose's cottage without bothering to knock. She was seated beside the fire, her breast bared as she fed their baby. The sight stopped him dead in his tracks, and for the first time since leaving Lambton, he managed a genuine smile. The woman he loved had never looked more appealing. There was just something about the way his son greedily suckled her full breast that appeared so domestically serene as to make all his problems fade into insignificance. Why could they not live this way all the time?

Because, unlike Rose, James had ambitions that would not be served by living in what was little better than a workman's cottage. He was a gentleman and would not compromise his right to be acknowledged as such, not even for Rose. Besides, she would not marry him, so no compromise was necessary. Her unwillingness to give her entire self to him, to anyone, was all part of her addictive allure, ensuring the spark of desire burned bright between them.

Rose looked up and smiled at him, obviously in a mellow mood. Unfortunately, that situation was not destined to last. 'I did not expect to see you today,' she said.

The baby had fallen asleep. She gently detached him from her breast and laid him in his crib.

'I come with bad news,' he said, pulling her into his arms and kissing her because he couldn't help himself. 'Taylor didn't find anything at the cottage. The void beneath the floor was empty.'

'What!' She wrenched herself from his arms, anger frosting her eyes, and the tranquil mood was broken. 'How can that possibly be?'

James shrugged. 'I'm not in a position to know, but I assume Sanford found the loot and removed it.'

'That makes him as much of a thief as we are.' She folded her arms beneath breasts that were still naked since she hadn't bothered to replace her bodice. 'And a hypocrite to boot. He might pretend to be a fine gentleman, but when it comes down to it, he is just as tempted by the prospect of easy wealth as the rest of us. If that were not the case, he would have handed the jewellery over to the authorities, and we would have heard about it by now.' She threw back her head and roared loud enough to wake the baby and make him cry. 'I cannot stand it.'

'Hush, my love.' James reached out a hand and tentatively touched her shoulder. He knew how unpredictable she could be when roused and didn't know how she would react to his gesture since he had never seen her quite as angry as she was at that moment. He wasn't surprised when she shook off his hand. 'Come and sit down. You will make yourself ill if you carry on like this.'

She ignored him and paced the length of the room instead. 'How did he know about the hiding place? If it was discovered when the cottage was cleaned up, he could not have kept it quiet. Perdition, I thought it was secure there. I watched Patrick fashion that floorboard myself. There is no one better when it comes to working with wood than he is. Sanford could not possibly have found it by accident.' Her eyes blazed, dark and intense. 'If one of our people betrayed our secret, I will find out who it was and he will regret the day he was born.'

'I gather Sanford moved his desk to a position beneath the window. If he did so alone, he would have had to push it across the floor. I suppose it's possible that caused the board to spring up, if he happened to hit it in exactly the right place.'

'Yes, perhaps.' Rose threw herself into a chair, her anger replaced by the expression of stark determination James knew so very well.

'What shall we do about him?'

'He cannot be allowed to get away with stealing from me.'

James nodded, having expected such a reaction. The fact that the goods in question had been stolen in the first place did not seem to register with Rose, and James wasn't about to point it out.

'You want the goods returned, I assume.'

'Most certainly.' She fixed James with a look of malevolent intent. 'And I want rid of the Sanfords once and for all. I was not ready to entertain the idea when you first suggested it, but now I am. They have interfered in my affairs for the last time. I tried to be lenient and allow this particular one to get off with nothing worse than a damaged reputation. Even I must accept he was not involved in my father's transportation. But by stealing from me, he has signed his own death warrant.'

'You plan to kill him?'

'Not me, my dear.' Palpable excitement formed the bedrock of her expression. 'That privilege will fall to you, but only after he has told us where he has hidden the loot, obviously. I shall come with you and help you to persuade him it would be in his best interest to talk.'

James detested Sanford, partly because he was intelligent, a man of property and, presumably, independent means — but mostly because he had secured Georgiana Darcy's affections. The rogue had dazzled her with exaggerated stories about his travels and made her forget the passion she had once entertained for him. James disliked being bested by any man when it came to affairs of the heart. He did not love Miss Darcy, but he did need her money in order to persuade Rose away from a life of crime. Rose had a sharp mind and was as cunning as a fox, but her luck could not hold indefinitely, and James would die himself before he saw her incarcerated.

Rose was free of spirit, pure of soul, generous of heart, and it would break that spirit if she was caged. Had it been otherwise, he might well marry her and risk being ostracised by his family. The only person James Halstead would ever love more than himself, the only person's interests that featured higher than his own, were those of Rose Watkins. That was why he would never fail her, and would do whatever she asked of him in order to retain her admiration.

He would even commit murder, if that was what it would take for her to find the peace of mind that so eluded her. When previously offering his services in that respect, he had not seriously considered doing the deed himself. If Rose planned to be there, then he would have to. But before he agreed, he had to be sure she understood what the consequences were likely to be.

'If someone of Sanford's class is murdered, it will bring the full force of the law crashing down on this district,' he said, caressing her face with the tips of his fingers. 'It is always thus when a man of consequence meets an untimely end.'

'Bah, the law.' Rose snorted as she flipped a dismissive wrist. 'They are a bunch of old men, past their prime, who would not know where to start looking. They would not look at all if the murdered man was a farmer.'

'Don't make the mistake of under-estimating them. People around here were uncomfortable when Sanford's parents died suddenly. They approve of the son, and no rocks will be left unturned if he's found dead under dubious circumstances. All the people who work for you will be questioned, their activities scrutinised and interrupted. Can you be sure they won't point the finger of suspicion at you in order to save their own skins? Your hatred for the Sanfords is no secret amongst your followers.'

'You have a point.' She nibbled her index finger as she took a moment to think the matter through, sending him a captivating smile as she reached a decision. 'We shall just have to ensure his death does not seem suspicious.'

'You are contemplating staging a suicide?'

This time a decidedly calculating smile lit Rose's lovely features. 'Why not? He has been asking all sorts of questions about his parents since he returned to Derbyshire. When he could find no satisfactory explanation for their deaths, he was overcome with grief, couldn't face living in a house that held so many memories for him, and decided to end it all.'

'Very well,' James said, suspecting no one would be convinced, but prepared to go through with the scheme anyway, such was the hold Rose had over him. 'If you are absolutely sure you want to go down that path and are prepared to risk the conse-quences, then my services are, as always, at your disposal.'

Her eyes shimmered with hot intentions. 'I know they are, my love.'

He grabbed her hand and pulled her

towards the bedchamber. 'This requires careful planning,' he said. 'We ought to make a start.'

'We must act tonight,' she said as James set about removing her clothing. 'We cannot give him any breathing space or allow him the opportunity to ask probing questions about Burton's visit. If Taylor is implicated, he doesn't have the wits to make up a convincing story for knowing where the hiding place was.'

Tonight? Part of James had still been hoping to talk her out of her wild plan. He knew now that would be impossible. Perhaps that was all to the good. As long as he was careful to cover his tracks, he would never be suspected of killing the man. And with Sanford out of the way, Miss Darcy was as good as his, thus ensuring his future with Rose.

19

Dominic stood at the door to his cottage, watching Georgiana make a fuss of Hamish. Too much fuss. She was embarrassed by his less than fulsome greeting, he suspected, and was focusing her attention upon Hamish until she recovered her composure. He waited her out in silence, wishing her a thousand miles away, yet astonished by just how pleased he was to see her.

He had been denying his increasing attraction towards her since before his enforced stay at Pemberley. His feelings were as inappropriate as they were inconvenient, but there didn't seem to be a damn thing he could do to suppress them. She looked up at him from beneath the hood of her cloak, her eyes burning with an unfathomable emotion that made him want to pull her into his arms and offer reassurance in the manner that sprang spontaneously to mind.

The devil take it, this simply would not do!

'Who was that gentleman?' she asked.

'Come inside.' Dominic stepped forward and took her arm. 'You're trembling with cold, and the hem of your gown is soaked through. Presumably your feet are wet too. Are you deliberately trying to catch a chill? You should not have walked here in such conditions.' He paused. 'You should not have walked here at all.'

She paused on the threshold and pushed her hood aside. Her hair was a mass of hopelessly disordered curls that formed a dark halo around her head. 'It would not have been necessary for me to come, if you had not decided to cut me out of your investigation, leaving me to wonder what was going on.'

'I don't have the pleasure of understanding you,' he replied, understanding her very well as he stood behind her and removed her sodden cloak from her shoulders.

'At least do me the courtesy of not treating me like a simpleton.' She fixed him with an accusatory glare. 'I thought we had agreed to work together, but ever since I uncovered information that was useful to you, you have acted as though I don't exist. It is most insulting.'

She wagged a finger at him, her face now flushed a becoming shade of pink — whether from anger or as a result of the warmth in the cottage after her walk in the frigid conditions, he could not have said.

'I meant no insult. Come and sit by the fire and get warm.'

She graciously took the chair he indicated, and Hamish sat at her feet, gazing adoringly up at her.

'Then what did you mean?' she asked.

'The man who just left was Burton, the parish constable.'

Georgiana gasped. 'What did he want?'

'There were four of them initially. That is how many men it takes to search a small cottage for stolen jewellery, apparently.' Dominic didn't trust himself to sit. It would place him too close to her, and so he remained standing and paced the length of the small room. 'And they knew precisely where to look. They went straight to the floorboard that conceals the hiding place.'

'But did not find anything?'

'No, but that's not the point. I anticipated that someone would come looking, although I thought it would be the villains rather than the authorities.'

'What does that mean?'

'That is what I have been trying to conjecture.' He shrugged. 'I can only assume that whoever put the jewellery there was willing to sacrifice it in order to discredit me.'

'It was worth a great deal of money,' she said, her face losing the colour it had briefly gained. 'Someone must dislike you very much.'

'Evidently so.'

'But no one could suspect you of stealing it,' she said hotly. 'That is simply ridiculous.'

'The innuendo would be enough to destroy my reputation. However, I digress. I did not keep you informed because I did not wish to place you in harm's way. Your brother would have my hide if anything happened to you, and rightly so.'

'Who told Mr. Burton to look here?'

Dominic told her what little he had learned in that respect. She was correct about one thing, she had earned the right to know.

'It makes no sense,' she said, shaking her head.

'And it also means the situation is even more volatile than it was before Burton's visit.'

'Because whoever sent him, wishing to implicate you, will want to know what happened to the jewellery that was hidden here?'

'Precisely, and they will act quickly, before I have a chance to do any further snooping on my own behalf. That is why you absolutely must not be here.'

'Do you suppose it has anything to do with those children? The ones we think might have been Jordan's by-blows.'

'I dare say so, but I expect I shall find out soon enough.'

'Then you can't stay here either.' She leapt from her seat and grasped his arm. 'It isn't safe.'

'Thank you for your concern,' he replied softly, moved by her empathy, 'but I can take care of myself. It is your welfare that is my primary concern. If you oblige me by remaining safely at Pemberley, I can see this matter through without having to worry about you.'

'By getting yourself killed?' she asked bitterly.

The corners of his lips lifted. 'I have no intention of allowing that to happen.'

'Oh, sometimes I fail to understand you men!' She released his arm and whirled away from him with an exasperated sigh. 'You are in very real danger, have no idea who wishes you harm and when they might try to attack you, and yet you seem to be enjoying yourself.'

I am certainly enjoying your enticing company. 'Not enjoying precisely, but I need to know what — '

'I don't suppose you told Mr. Burton where the jewels are now, or asked him for help to protect yourself,' she said scathingly, turning to face him again and fixing him with a look of unbridled reproach.

'I might have done so, if I could be sure

Burton was trustworthy. I am sure he most likely is, but the men who work with him are not. After all, it was Taylor who knew exactly where to look for the jewels.'

'Yes, I suppose there is that.' Her face was invaded by a frown and she looked momentarily defeated. 'So, what shall you do now?'

'Make sure I am ready for my next uninvited visitors, I suppose.' He shrugged. 'One of the advantages of living in an isolated location, with so few means of approach, is that I will know they are coming before they get here. They can only use the track that runs beside the big house since, unlike you, they don't have ready access to the Pemberley estate. There are people in the house all day, so they will have to wait until dusk.'

He sensed he had lost her attention. She had turned away from him again, he heard snuffling noises and her shoulders were shaking. Dear God, she was crying!

'What is it, Miss Darcy — Georgiana?' He placed a hand gently of her shoulders and turned her towards him. Tears streamed down her face and she made no attempt to check them. 'What have I said to overset you?'

'What have you said? How could you be so insensitive?' Her eyes were filled with the coppery glitter of rage. 'You will be killed, and yet you can make so light of it.'

She was afraid for him. So afraid it had reduced her to tears. Dominic's efforts to keep his desire in check evaporated the moment he realised it. When did someone last truly worry about his welfare? Overcome, he pulled her into his arms. 'Thank you for your concern, but there is really no need to overset yourself. You forget, I am not alone.' She followed the direction of his gaze towards Hamish, lying full length in front of the fire. 'He is not always so docile, as well you know.'

'And a bullet or a knife would not stop him?'

'A bullet, if they were foolish enough to risk discharging one, but no one would get close enough with a knife before Hamish . . . well, I won't describe what he's capable of when roused, but rest assured, he would stop at nothing to protect me.'

She trembled in the circle of his arms and rested her head against his shoulder. 'Thank goodness someone is looking out for your interests.'

This was madness. Her tears had dried up so he ought to extract a promise from her that she would remain at Pemberley and then escort her home without delay. But doing the sensible thing whenever he was anywhere near Georgiana Darcy was an increasingly difficult ambition to achieve, especially when she looked up at him, an unfathomable something reflected in the depth of her eyes.

'Mr. Sanford, you should — '

'Dominic,' he replied softly. 'My name is Dominic.'

'Dominic.' She spoke his name quietly, rolling the syllables experimentally across her tongue as though testing them to see how well they fit. 'Don't put yourself in danger unnecessarily, I beg of you. There are others better qualified than you are to handle this matter. You have nothing to prove to yourself or anyone else.'

He ran the pad of his thumb gently down the curve of her face. 'Don't you understand yet that I must see this through?'

She lowered her head and shook it against his shoulder. 'No, I don't see it that way. I understand it is a matter of honour, of personal pride, and I respect you for that. But I still cannot persuade myself that it's worth dying for.'

Perdition, if he didn't take her home, or at the very least release her from his arms this very instant, he would not be responsible for his actions. She fit so perfectly against him, the top of her head reaching his chin, her soft curves a thrilling contrast to the hard planes of his own body as they collided against it. Rational thought disintegrated into pure sensation. Damn it, there was only so much temptation a man could resist. What he felt for Georgiana Darcy was more than just a passing admiration, but he was not in a position to do anything about it, and there was an end to the matter.

She deserved better than he could ever offer her. Wickham had already tried to compromise her for her fortune, and that blaggard Halstead was similarly minded. Dominic didn't need her money, but he was fiercely determined to develop his medical skills and help those most in need. That would take a lot of his own funds, and would not leave him with enough time to live within the top echelons of society, which was the life Georgiana had been brought up to expect. The life she deserved. They inhabited different worlds, impossible to breach without one or the other of them feeling isolated and unfulfilled.

He made a monumental effort to pull himself together and was about to suggest taking her home when she shifted in his arms, causing an explosion of desire to cascade through him, momentarily paralysing in its intensity.

'Please,' she said softly, looking up at him

through languorous, heavy-lidded eyes. 'There must be something we can do.'

Dominic didn't know if she was asking him not to put himself in danger's path, or for something more fundamental. He released his hold on her, pleased with his self-control, such as it was. But at the same moment she lifted a hand to his nape and tangled her fingers in the hair spilling over his collar. Her knuckles brushed against his skin, causing a riot of sensation to cascade though his body, sending scorching heat straight to his loins.

'Please what, Georgiana? What are you asking me for?'

'I don't want to be treated like a child.'

He chuckled. 'That is certainly not how I think of you.'

'I have been cosseted and protected for my entire life. You probably think I am young and silly, but I can assure you I am not.' She expelled a protracted sigh. 'I want adventure, Dominic, and if by admitting it I appear forward, I simply don't care. You are not indifferent to me. I can tell that much from your expression.'

Was she proposing to him? 'Georgiana, I admire and respect you very much.'

'I don't want your admiration and respect, I want — '

'I know what you want, but I am not in a

position to give it to you.' She looked on the brink of tears again, and he felt wretched for rejecting her. 'I am a slave to my duty, whereas you have a glittering future ahead of you.'

She stood on her toes and brushed her lips against his. Dear God, did she have any idea what she was doing to him? 'I have no interest in glittering, as you put it, but I shall not throw myself at you, either.' She removed her hand from his nape and her body from his arms. 'You have made your position crystal clear and there is nothing more to be said.'

'Georgiana, I — '

'No, don't make it any worse. I have already made enough of a fool of myself.' She stood with her back to him, arms folded defensively. 'I misunderstood the situation, clearly. I ought to go home. It's getting late, and I will be missed.'

'I will walk with you.'

'There is no need.'

'There's every need.' He cocked his head to one side when he heard a sound outside. Hamish leapt up and started barking. 'Stay here!' he said urgently to Georgiana. 'I shall see who it is.'

He and Hamish went to the door but Dominic peered through the small side window before opening it. He breathed a sigh of relief when he saw it was only Gibson and stepped outside, pulling the door closed behind him so he did not see Georgiana.

'Gibson, what brings you down here?'

'Grandma says as you're needed at the big house. A decision needs to be made about a bad patch of roof they've just found.'

'Damnation, can't it wait?' Gibson merely shrugged, leaving Dominic to think it through for himself. This was not the first problem to arise that required his intervention, and he knew Mrs. Gibson only sent for him when absolutely necessary. Presumably, if he did not go, the work would be held up. He didn't especially care at that moment, but knew he would have to go anyway. 'Very well, Gibson. Go back. I shall be there directly.'

'I have to go up to the house for a moment,' he said when he returned to Georgiana. 'Oblige me by remaining here until I return. I shall not be long. It is still only mid-afternoon, but I don't want you walking back alone.'

She appeared distracted but agreed to do as he asked.

★ ★ ★

When Dominic and Hamish left her, Georgiana returned to her chair beside the fire and stared sightlessly into the flames. Humiliation washed over her in unstoppable waves, causing fresh tears to flood her eyes. How could she have acted so shamelessly — little better than a light-skirt? She had thrown herself at Dominic, and he had rejected her. So much for her feminine wiles, she thought with a wry, humourless smile.

He thought more of his medicine than he did of her. She knew how important his occupation was to him, and she had thought she could be of help to him in that respect. She would persuade the local populace to place their faith in him and give his new methods a chance. They would listen to her, simply because of who she was. But he had made it abundantly clear he did not desire her help.

It confirmed what Georgiana already suspected. Men who needed her fortune were attracted to her for that reason and those who did not, found nothing about her to admire. It was as simple as that. And yet . . . and yet, when Dominic had taken her in his arms, she was absolutely sure he did so because he wanted to, even if his respect for her warred against his natural impulses. She closed her eyes, threw her head back, and relived the sublime feeling of his capable hands spanning her back, of the elusive light in his eye as he looked down at her, apparently at a loss for words. There was passion in his expression. She was perfectly sure of that, and felt encouraged by that knowledge. It went some small way to overcoming her mortification at being so summarily rejected.

Georgiana had spoken the truth. She *had* grown up since discussing Wickham with her brother, and now she had the courage of her convictions. She loved Dominic Sanford with a single-minded passion that made her previous entanglements seem pedestrian by comparison. She was also not convinced that Dominic was completely indifferent to her. It was just that she had approached the matters this afternoon all wrong. He was preoccupied, not yet ready to listen to his heart. In future, she would be more circumspect, make her partiality less apparent. When he had settled the matter of his parents' death, he would be at leisure to decide what he wanted from his future, which was her. He just did not know it, yet. Thus resolved, Georgiana was prepared to wait for him to see reason — provided he didn't get himself killed in the meantime.

Feeling restless, she stood up and walked around the small room. She glanced out of the window and noticed the clouds were even lower, the first fat snowflakes falling. If

Dominic didn't return soon, she had best make her way home before it got any worse. It would not do to be stuck here and have to rely upon Fitzwilliam coming to fetch her when Kitty told him where she was.

Recalling her resolve not to be too accommodating, she decided to leave right away. She reached for her cloak and heard the door open. Too late, he was back. That was fast.

Except it wasn't Dominic. She heard more than one pair of feet on the flagstones in the entrance hall, voices talking in whispers. A chill ran down her spine. Whom could it be if not Dominic? Surely, she would have seen anyone else approaching? Except she had been looking out the other window, not the one that overlooked the front of the cottage.

She made a mad dash for Dominic's bedroom, thinking to conceal herself in there. Before she could do so, a strong hand grasped her upper arm and swung her around. She looked up into a familiar face — one she had not expected to see here.

'Major Halstead!' she gasped.

20

Dominic inspected a large hole in his roof though which heavy snowflakes were making steady inroads. Even from his relatively protected position inside the attic rooms, an arctic wind still cut through him like a sabre, chilling him to the bone. No wonder the house was so cold all the time.

'Didn't know it was this bad,' his workman told him, scratching his head. 'We pulled off them slates and found all these rotted timbers. They will all 'ave to be replaced. You can't patch it up, Mr. Sanford. Would be a waste of money.'

'Can you replace the entire section in this weather?'

'Aye, we can, but it will be expensive.'

'How expensive?'

Dominic winced when the man named a figure. He took another look at the gaping hole, then looked down at the snow gathering around his feet *inside* his house, and nodded. He really didn't have any choice. If the roof wasn't properly fixed, then more damage would be done to the interior before the winter was through, and it would finish up being an even greater expense.

'Get started on it as soon as you can,' he said, escaping to the relative warmth of the kitchen, where Mrs. Gibson handed him a steaming mug of tea.

He didn't have time for tea, but he couldn't afford to offend Mrs. Gibson, either. He had a nagging feeling he ought not to have left Georgiana alone, even though common sense told him no harm could come to her in his tucked-away cottage when it was still full light outside. He drank the tea as quickly as he could, burning his tongue in his anxiety to escape.

'Right then, Mrs. G.,' he said, placing his empty mug on the kitchen table. 'I'd best be getting back before the weather gets any worse. You ought to think about returning to the village for the same reason.'

'Don't you worry none about me, sir. A little snow never hurt nobody.'

'Just so long as you are sure.'

With a final wave for Mrs. Gibson, Dominic, with Hamish at his heels, strode briskly through the now heavily-falling snow thinking about the interlude with Georgiana that he had handled so ineptly. How could he repair their neighbourly relationship without encouraging her interest in him? Friendship with the lively, much admired Miss Darcy was all he could allow himself. Whether it would be enough for him was another matter entirely, but he was older than Georgiana and knew their mutual attraction would not withstand the test of time. She would come to resent his obsession with his profession and the amount of time he dedicated to it and they would finish up drifting apart.

Georgiana deserved more than he would ever be in a position to offer her. He must stand firm and not permit his heart to rule his head. Georgiana was a compelling mix of spirited opinions and touching vulnerability. She was also highly desirable, which didn't help matters, and if circumstances had been different . . . but they were not.

Hamish disappeared into the bushes, barking and snarling at some invisible foe. At first, Dominic worried someone might be lurking there. Then he realised his dog was simply following the scent of some animal foolish or desperate enough to be abroad in such weather. Hamish was part hunting dog and chased anything that moved. He could be gone for two minutes, or two hours — Dominic had no intention of standing around until he discovered which would be the case on this occasion. The dog knew his way home, so Dominic left him to it and trudged on, relieved when he saw the smoke from his cottage chimney rising up to challenge the falling snow. If he was quick he would be able to deliver Georgiana safely to Pemberley before it came down any harder.

★   ★   ★

'Who is this?' Rose demanded to know.

'This is the oh-so-proper Miss Darcy,' James replied, his voice dripping with liquid venom, 'skulking about on the threshold of a single man's bedroom, no less.' He elevated one brow. 'Not so very proper after all, it would appear. If I had known you were quite so desperate to sample such pleasures, I would have — '

'What are you doing here?' Miss Darcy inverted her chin and adopted a haughty expression, but James could tell that was her automatic defence against the fear eating away at her. Her eyes gave her away. 'What is it that you want?'

'Damnation!' Rose thumped her thigh with her clenched fist. 'I thought as much, but didn't believe my eyes. We thought the place was empty. What are you doing here?' she demanded of Georgiana. 'This complicates everything.'

'Lost your little nest egg now, so you have,' Patrick said, smirking at James from behind

Rose. 'She'll never take you now.'

'If you, whoever you are, are implying that I would have married the major, then you have been grossly misled.'

'Spirited little thing, ain't she?' Patrick said, smacking his lips together. 'I wouldn't mind — '

'Be quiet!' Rose barked. 'I'm trying to think.'

Patrick was right, damn him, James thought. Miss Darcy would not take him now. Still, this was her second visit alone to Sanford's cottage that he knew of. There could have been more. It implied she wouldn't have taken him anyway. Humiliating though that realisation was, it made him feel a little better about the situation.

He shared a glance with Rose, both of them aware that Miss Darcy couldn't be permitted to walk away from this fiasco and expose James's involvement with the gang. Murdering Darcy's sister would make Sanford's demise appear trifling by comparison, but James was thinking only of his own survival now and would do whatever had to be done to save his skin.

'A lovers' pact,' Rose said softly, echoing James's own thoughts.

'Yes, possibly,' he replied.

James felt distinctly uneasy. Matters were

running out of his control. By even entertaining the thoughts now spilling through his head he had crossed some sort of invisible divide and there was no going back. Far from the comfortable future he had envisaged for himself, he would now be a fugitive. But only if he was caught. If they got away, he would find another heiress to charm — one was as good as another — and continue with Rose just the way he had always planned to.

They would have to act swiftly in despatching Sanford and Miss Darcy, before she was missed and a search party was sent to look for her. That meant Sanford would have to tell them where he had hidden the jewels, and tell them immediately. Fortunately, with Miss Darcy as a bargaining tool, he would not remain silent for long.

'I hope he was worth it,' James said as he ushered Georgiana to a chair, annoyed when jealousy twisted his insides. It shouldn't matter to him how she chose to entertain herself. 'I cannot commend your taste, but I do admire your rebellious nature. I clearly underestimated you since I didn't think you had it in you to act in any way that would risk your brother's disapproval.'

'Which just goes to show how little you actually know me.'

Patrick's vulgar laughter echoed around the small room. 'Seems you missed your opportunity,' he said to James.

'Where are your manners, Major? You haven't introduced your friends.' Miss Darcy impressed James with her convincing display of indifference. She clearly knew more about Sanford's circumstances than she had yet revealed, and also must realise her life hung in the balance. He would have expected tears, swooning, or pleas for mercy, not backbone and decorum. Perhaps she would not be so easy to replace after all. 'This, I assume, is Miss Watkins.' She nodded almost civilly to Rose and then turned her attention to Patrick. 'And you are her brother, I collect.'

'Well, well,' Rose said, placing a finger beneath Miss Darcy's chin and tilting her head backwards so she could take a closer look at her features. 'I thought you said she was a mousy creature, James, and yet she has a defiant spark about her.'

'Evidently, I underestimated her.'

'If you are hoping to see Mr. Sanford then you will be disappointed. He has gone into Newcastle,' Miss Darcy said with infinite politeness. 'I am awaiting his return because he is needed at Pemberley to attend to my brother's wife. We are expected back there directly. You are welcome to leave a message

310

for Mr. Sanford with me.'

James briefly panicked. If that was true then their time was indeed limited. Then it occurred to him that Darcy would not have sent his sister, but a footman, to summon Sanford. Rose clearly realised it too, because she laughed.

'Even *proper* ladies are given to telling clankers when the chips are down, it seems.' Rose walked restlessly around the room, picking items up at random and putting them down again. 'Perhaps we are not so very different after all.'

'You have the advantage of me, Miss Watkins.'

'*You have the advantage of me, Miss Watkins.*' Rose parodied Georgiana's cut-glass accent, chuckling to herself. 'We were hiding at the top of the lane, ready to come down here when everyone left the big house. But then we saw your precious Mr. Sanford heading for the house himself, *and* taking his brute of a dog with him. It seemed like too good an opportunity to miss, seeing as how this cottage would be empty. So we decided to take a chance and slip down the track when everyone else's attention was on his roof. We intended to form a welcoming committee for your lover, not knowing you would be here, which is a delightful surprise, of course.'

Georgiana gave a convincing display of boredom and hid a yawn behind her hand. 'I have no idea why you would want to see Mr. Sanford.'

'Oh, I think you do.' Rose prowled around her chair like a lithe cat, her eyes gleaming with spiteful anticipation. 'And because you are here we won't have the slightest difficulty extracting the information we need from him.'

★   ★   ★

Georgiana felt giddy with fear, but knew better than to let it show. She accepted no one was likely to come to her immediate rescue. If these interlopers had been seen from the big house, Dominic and the men working for him would have rushed to her aid by now. She was unsure whether to be relieved or disappointed when they failed to materialise. Of course, she wished to be rescued, but they would not harm her all the time Dominic wasn't here. When he arrived, that situation would quickly change and she was not optimistic about their chances for survival.

Patrick Watkins was a large man, but she didn't fear him nearly as much as she did his sister. There was something about her, a malevolent look in her eye that truly terrified Georgiana. Whoever said the female of the species was more ruthless than the male was clearly acquainted with this vindictive woman. Georgiana's best policy would be to keep them talking, and hopefully Dominic's return would be detained. She absolutely didn't want him or Hamish to walk into this trap. The snow was now falling quite heavily. It would blanket any footprints they had left on the track, so he would not have advance notice of the intruders' arrival.

Yes, she must definitely keep them talking, and perhaps Fitzwilliam would come in search of her. It was a vain hope since she would not yet have been missed, but she clung to it with tenacious determination. It was either that or fall apart, and she refused to give the major or his friends the satisfaction of hearing her beg for mercy.

'I am disappointed to discover you are a criminal, Major,' she said conversationally. 'But not altogether surprised.'

'One man's criminal is another man's hero, Miss Darcy.'

Georgiana toss her head. 'Is that how you justify your behaviour?'

'I have hidden depths you once found

attractive.' He curled his upper lip disdainfully. 'Until Sanford came along and turned your head.'

'You flatter yourself. I was once briefly attracted to you, it is true, but that attraction did not stand the test of time. I thought you handsome and charming, but not as handsome and charming as you yourself appear to think you are.' She shook a finger at him. 'Vanity in a man is not an endearing characteristic.'

'If you say so.' He bowed his head politely, but Georgiana suspected she had dented his pride, just as she intended to. Angry men did not think rationally.

'I very soon realised it was my money, and not me, that you wanted, and so your suit was doomed to failure. Besides, I studied you at unguarded moments and could tell your heart was not really in it.' She sent him a scathing look. 'If you were that desperate for my fortune, you might at least have tried a little harder to make a good impression.'

Patrick Watkins snickered. Major Halstead and Miss Watkins shared the sort of speaking look that committed lovers used as a means of communication — the sort of look that her brother and Lizzy often exchanged. That explained a lot. The major was infatuated by Miss Watkins, but if she was involved with the thefts it would be difficult for him to marry her and retain the respectability he set so much stock by. There again, perhaps he was just thirsty for adventure and wanted to line his own pockets with the proceeds from their crimes.

Georgiana knew Major Halstead's position in society was important to him and even if Miss Watkins' background did not become common knowledge, an alliance with her would see society's doors closed to him. Georgiana bit her lip, feeling almost sorry for him. She was perfectly sure that the strength of her passion for Mr. Sanford would overcome any such obstacles. Presumably the major felt the same way about Miss Watkins and had wanted to marry Georgiana only to maintain his respectability. No wonder his heart had not really been in it.

'Will you not share your reasons for being involved with Miss Watkins's criminal ways?' she asked politely, perfectly sure it was the sister who ruled over her much larger brother.

As she waited for the major to respond, Georgiana wondered if there was anything she could do to help herself out of this dilemma. She eyed the poker, sitting within arm's reach in the grate. So near yet so far. She could cause considerable damage to one of them with it, she supposed, but she would never get past all three. No, it would be better not to try it, and let them think she was a helpless female, a wilting violet, until they relaxed their guard around her. But she would not forget about the poker. Perhaps an opportunity to wield it for something other than its intended use would present itself, if she was patient.

'It is really none of your concern,' the major replied.

'Perhaps not, but we must either sit here and look at one another, or make conversation while we wait for Mr. Sanford. The choice is yours.'

The major and Miss Watkins shared another of their looks, and Georgiana knew then that they would humour her. She had read somewhere that people who thought they were clever liked to boast about their feats. Miss Watkins was clearly no exception to that rule, but before they could answer her, the door burst open. Georgiana's heart lurched and a gasp of dismay slipped past her guard. She heard Dominic stamp the snow from his boots as he called out to her. But where was Hamish? Why wasn't he making the devil of a racket?

'I'm sorry to have . . . ' He stopped dead in his tracks when he walked into the sitting room and found Major Halstead standing directly behind her, a knife to her throat. 'Halstead,' he said slowly, murder in his eyes as he took in the scene. 'I should have realised.'

21

'Are you all right?' Dominic looked towards Georgiana with concern. 'Have they harmed you? Touched you inappropriately?'

Dear God, if they had, he would find a way to make them pay. Never had he known such feelings of impotency to war with quite such a murderous, blood-curdling rage.

'No, we were having the most interesting conversation. I am so glad you could join us.'

Dominic looked at her askance. Why wasn't she swooning? She must be petrified, but to look at her, no one would know it. Dominic had never admired her more. He swore beneath his breath, called himself every sort of fool for leaving Miss Darcy here alone when he knew assailants were out for his blood. He had arrogantly assumed they would not come calling until after dark, and by underestimating them, he had probably forfeited Georgiana's life, to say nothing of his own. They could not be allowed to walk away from this situation. That much was absolutely certain. Damn it, what a time for Hamish to be off chasing rabbits! Even if the dog came back now, it would be too late for him to help them since he wouldn't be able to get into the cottage. The front door was closed, and if Dominic tried to open it again, the intruders would feel the wind whipping through the cottage and know it at once.

Halstead? Dominic had taken a dislike to the man on first acquaintance but had not for one moment considered he might be involved in this business. Presumably the button he had found had been detached from his tunic. Not that he would be able to prove it, but at least he knew the answer to that tantalising question, even if he did not know what had possessed such a man to become involved.

'These people are Rose and Patrick Watkins,' Georgiana said with commendable poise.

'Ah, I see.' Dominic had already assumed that was who they must be, but pretended surprise. 'To what do we owe the pleasure?'

'Don't play coy with me,' Rose replied, glaring at Dominic with unmitigated dislike. 'I have long waited for this moment and intend to enjoy it.'

Dominic offered her an exaggerated bow. 'Then I am delighted to be of service to you.'

'Make sure he's not armed.'

Patrick searched his pockets but came up with nothing more dangerous than a pocket handkerchief.

'Where is my jewellery?' Rose asked.

'Why did you choose to hide it in my cottage?'

'It was symbolic,' Rose replied with a vindictive smile. 'And very safe. Even if anyone had known to look for it, they would never think to search this hovel.'

'You learned to steal at your father's knee, I suppose,' Dominic said conversationally, stepping further into the room, discouraged to see that the dagger being held at Georgiana's throat had not wavered in Halstead's hand. She looked deathly pale, but there was a defiant spark in her eye which reassured Dominic, even though he didn't yet have a clue how to get them both out of this situation. Or if he could. But he refused to dwell upon that gloomy prospect.

'Don't you dare mention my father's name!' Rose's eyes blazed with resentment, confirming Dominic's suspicions about her dedication to the man fuelling her thirst for revenge. 'You are not worthy to shine his boots.'

'Do they wear boots in the antipodes?' Dominic asked mildly.

Rose roared and threw herself at Dominic, her fingers reaching for his eyes. Dominic was easily able to hold her off, but that situation would change if in the blink of an eye if

Patrick joined the fray. Before he could do so, and before the major's attention towards Georgiana could be diverted, giving her the opportunity to escape him, Rose recovered herself. She shook her shoulders, held Patrick off with a wave of one hand and swallowed several times.

'Be careful, my love,' Halstead said reprovingly.

Ah, so that's the way the wind blows. 'Did I say something to anger you?' Dominic asked, feigning concern.

'I will not ask you again,' Rose replied, placing her admittedly beautiful, albeit enraged, face inches from his. 'Where is my property?'

'Since it was stolen, I don't see how you can claim ownership,' Dominic replied indifferently.

'We don't have time for these games. Tell me, or the young lady dies.'

Dominic's soul pitched at the prospect, but he disciplined himself not to look at Georgiana for fear his expression would give away the depth of his feelings to the miscreants. He realised at that moment leaving the jewellery with Chandler had not been such a wise move after all. In order to get it back, he would have to visit that gentleman's office in person. Rose couldn't let Georgiana go along because she must realise a huge search would be started for her long before they could reach the solicitor's office. A chill travelled down his spine when he accepted there was only one other thing they could do with her.

Perdition, what the devil was he supposed to do to save her?

'As a matter of interest,' he said calmly, 'why have you taken me in such dislike? I realise you blame my father for what happened to your own parent, but he was only doing his duty. And I was just a child myself at the time. It was nothing to do with me.'

'But you are still here, living the life of a gentleman,' Rose spat back. 'Whereas mine is on the other side of the world. My mother couldn't live without him and killed herself. Patrick and I were sent to the workhouse.' She glowered at Dominic. 'Have you any idea what those places are like?'

'I'm sure it cannot have been pleasant,' he replied, refraining from saying that perhaps Rose should blame her mother's selfishness for the predicament she and her brother found themselves in. Either that or her father's felonious ways.

'Pleasant, huh!' She threw her hands in the air. 'I was twelve the first time the overseer raped me. Twelve! What do you say to that?'

Dominic winced. 'I am truly sorry,' he said, meaning it.

'He didn't do it again.' Her eyes sparkled with a malicious expression Dominic was already starting to recognise. 'I fashioned a spike from a piece of wood and the next time he came near me, I used it in a place that ensured he could never operate as a proper man ever again.'

Dominic actually felt sorry for her. To suffer such indignities at such a tender age, to lose her childhood in such a brutal manner, was unimaginable. But he could not afford to feel pity. She was very clever, yet unbalanced, and would take his and Georgiana's lives without a thought for the consequences unless he did something to prevent her.

'You carried on with the business your father had started, but were wise enough not to terrorise your victims.'

'My father and half-brother were not brutal, either.'

'But the victims, they all said — '

'Oh yes, they all *said*. But they exaggerated beyond imagining and, of course, because they were gentry, they were believed.'

Ah, now Dominic understood. She resented every one of his class because their word was accepted over that of a thief.

'Perhaps your relatives didn't terrorise their victims but they *did* steal their possessions and knew what the consequences would be if they were caught. All things considered, they were fortunate to escape with their lives.'

Rose fixed him with a scathing expression. 'You think they turned highwaymen out of choice?'

Dominic merely shrugged. 'I have no way of knowing.'

'My father was a skilled carpenter, and made a good living. He supported his wife and my mother and us, and we were all happy with that arrangement.'

'Your mother did not wish to marry him?'

Rose tossed her head. 'Females in my family don't set much stock by marriage. We are free spirits.'

'I see.' Dominic inclined his head. 'Excuse me, I interrupted you. That was rude of me.'

'You upper classes,' she scoffed. 'Your life hangs in the balance but you still apologise for forgetting your manners.'

'I am sorry if you find that distasteful.'

'Since you are so interested, I will tell you how Papa was forced to turn to robbery. Some gent he was working for accused him of taking liberties with the daughter of the house. It wasn't true. The girl chased after him and then told tales when Papa rejected her.' Rose's eyes flashed. 'Needless to say, the girl was believed, Papa was thrown off the job, his reputation never recovered, and he could no longer find honest work.'

'I am very sorry to hear it. If he made that hiding place beneath this floor, then he was very skilled indeed.'

'That was Patrick. He inherited our father's skill.'

'Forgive me, but you do not operate a band of highwaymen in this district. Word would have reached the authorities as to their activities by now if you did.'

Rose flashed a superior smile. 'I did better than that. After dealing with the overseer at the workhouse, I taught some of the brighter children how to pick pockets.' Dominic nodded, anticipating what she would say next. 'A lot of them already knew how; I simply helped them to perfect their art. Everything they stole came back to me, I had a circle of fences on hand to receive the loot, and the orphans got their share. By the time I left that workhouse, I had half a dozen bands working all across Newcastle,' she added proudly. 'Everyone expects pickpockets in big cities and the powers that be have yet to realise they are so well organised.'

'Congratulations.'

She inclined her head in an ironic bow. 'Thank you.'

'And yet in spite of your admirable organisational skills, you are not living in the lap of luxury.'

'She gives most of it away,' Patrick said, speaking for the first time.

'I won't see other families suffer in the way that we did,' she replied acerbically. 'I take enough for my needs, and that of my son — '

'You have a baby?'

She glanced at Halstead, and Dominic knew then whose baby it was. 'Very altruistic. I can understand what motivates you, and might almost sympathise, but for the fact that you killed my parents.' Dominic's tone was silk on steel as he fixed Rose Watkins with an accusatory gaze. 'My father merely did his duty, and my mother was guilty of nothing at all. How could you live with yourself after committing cold-blooded murder?'

'I didn't kill them,' Rose replied. 'I was too young at the time to think of it, or be in a position to do anything about it even if I had.'

'Then who . . . ah, of course.' Dominic nodded slowly as realisation came crashing in on him. 'Your mother.'

Rose shook her head. 'No, her brother. He sent the threats, and promised Ma he would finish the job. She couldn't wait to see it. She was heartbroken and killed herself. Stupid woman. No matter, I have spent the intervening years waiting for the opportunity to finish what she started and wipe out the last of the Sanfords.'

'Which is what you hoped to do by setting Burton on me. I would not be dead, of course, but my reputation would be beyond redemption since there is no smoke without fire.'

'Precisely, but you foiled my plan by finding the contraband.'

'That happened by the merest chance. Your brother's handiwork is indeed exceptional.'

'I would have sacrificed the haul, just for the satisfaction of seeing you humiliated. Since that did not happen, I would like it back, if you please.'

'I don't have it here,' Dominic replied. 'I am not that mutton-headed. I knew someone would come looking for it, but did not expect you quite so soon.'

'Then where is it?' At a nod from Rose, Halstead held the dagger closer to Georgiana's throat. He watched her swallow down her nerves and implore him with her eyes to do something. Anything. Never had he felt more impotent. Now, at this most inappropriate juncture, Dominic allowed himself to admit that he truly loved Georgiana. Loved, respected, and adored her, but he might never get an opportunity to tell her so. 'This is your last chance, Sanford. Tell me at once or your lady friend dies.'

'Even you would not be foolish enough to murder Miss Darcy,' Dominic replied, thinking that since she was so deranged she very likely would be.

'My advice is not to put that theory to the test.'

Whatever happened, Halstead would not use that dagger on Georgiana; upon that point Dominic was fiercely determined. He would throw himself at Halstead before he permitted it to happen and accept the consequences, which would be the loss of his own life. That appeared to be a foregone certainty anyhow, and his actions might conceivably afford Georgiana the opportunity to escape in the ensuing melee. If she could just get out of the cottage, she could run for her life, back to Pemberley. She knew the way. They did not.

'Well,' he said, strolling across the room and winking at Georgiana. 'Since you ask me so persuasively . . . '

★　★　★

Georgiana wanted to scream at him not to tell. She somehow managed not to tremble when Major Halstead, the man who had actually wanted to marry her, tightened his hold on her and made ready to cut her throat. She looked helplessly at Dominic, and he stared right back at her, his expression filled with love and regret. Or so she chose to believe. If one was about to die, presumably it was all right to make assumptions that had no foundation in fact. If she believed Dominic actually loved her, it would make it easier to forfeit her life, although she would infinitely prefer not to have to when she still had so much of it ahead of her.

There was definitely admiration in his expression, she decided as their gazes clashed and held. She wasn't imagining it, nor had she dreamed up the dark flame of desire leaping in his eyes. She couldn't possibly die, not now that she had found a man she loved with such an enduring passion her heart was too small to contain her feelings.

Do something, she silently implored, casting covetous sideways glances at the poker. They were neither of them intended as figures in a Shakespearian tragedy. But what could he do? He was outnumbered and had no weapon. It was hopeless. She ought to accept the fact and spend her last few moments drinking in the sight of his dear face.

Dominic took a step towards Georgiana and winked at her. God in heaven, did he actually have a plan? Afraid to move her head because the dagger would pierce her skin if she did, she cast her eyes sideways and stifled a gasp when she saw what had obviously just become evident to Dominic. Salvation was on the other side of the window, salivating, fangs exposed. She had never been happier to see Hamish in her entire life. But the window was closed, it was old and probably warped. Dominic would not be able to open it before he was set upon and she was killed.

Dominic clearly thought otherwise. He took one step backwards, lifted the latch and the window swung smoothly open. Dear Lord, he must have had them overhauled when the cottage was cleaned up. She thanked every deity she could think of for his thoroughness. Before the intruders could realise what was happening, Hamish leapt threw the gap, teeth barred. Patrick was foolish enough to step in the dog's path. Hamish attached himself to his shin, and didn't let go.

Patrick howled and tried to kick him off. Major Halstead was distracted by the disturbance and loosened his hold on Georgiana just fractionally. It was enough for her slide out of his grasp and curl into a protective ball on the floor. Dominic crossed the room in one stride and confronted Halstead with a murderous glare.

'Be careful, Dominic! He has a dagger.'

Dominic actually grinned as he evaded Halstead's right hand, in which the dagger was clutched, and struck his face with his clenched fist with considerable force. Georgiana wanted to applaud when, after a brief tussle, he managed to land a blow squarely in the centre of Halstead's face. He was magnificent in his anger and protection of her. Blood spurted from Halstead's nose, and Georgiana had the satisfaction of hearing bone splinter.

Her attention was diverted when she heard a howl and glanced around to see Rose trying to attack Hamish with a dagger of her own. Infuriated, Georgiana simply would not permit that to happen.

'No!' she screamed.

Rose took no notice of her whatsoever, appearing to think she was too feeble, too timid, to do anything to prevent her from harming Dominic's beloved dog. That was a grave miscalculation. Georgiana reached for the poker and, face contorted with fury, brought it down over the back of Rose's skull with all the force of her released fury. Rose looked up at her, momentarily startled, and then slowly crumpled to the floor.

Blood poured from Hamish's flank, but he clung determinedly to Patrick's shin. The man was now deathly pale, howling with pain as he too fell to the floor. Georgiana felt a moment's pride at discovering what she could achieve when those she loved so very dearly — Dominic and Hamish — were threatened.

'Give it up, Halstead,' Dominic said when the major tried another attack, which Dominic easily parried, relieving him of his dagger in the process.

The front door burst open and Georgiana gasped when she saw Captain Turner standing there, two other men in red coats at his shoulder.

'Don't tell me you are involved in this business too, Captain,' she said.

22

'N-no, Miss Darcy,' Captain Turner replied tersely. 'I am not involved, but I am surprised to s-see you here. Is e-everyone all right? Are you all right?'

'Yes, just a little shaken,' Georgiana replied, reeling on her feet as the enormity of what she had just done struck home.

It was Dominic who reached her first. 'You were incredibly brave,' he said softly, touching her shoulder and helping her to resume her seat. 'You stopped Rose from hurting Hamish with your quick thinking.'

'But he is hurt,' she said anxiously. 'Don't worry about me. Attend to him instead.'

'How could I not worry about you,' he whispered intently, running his fingers down the side of her face, his eyes burning with an unfathomable emotion. 'When I think how this might have turned out, I . . . '

He shook his head, apparently overcome and didn't finish his sentence. Their gazes held for a protracted moment, until a whimper from Hamish drew Dominic's attention. He crouched beside his dog and examined his wound. Captain Turner and his men were busy binding the hands of the three criminals, who were cursing fit to turn the air blue — Rose especially.

'Good boy,' Dominic said, his brow creasing with a frown as he stroked his dog's head. Hamish managed a brief flap of his tail, but a worrying amount of blood continued to flow from the gash on his thigh.

'You cannot let him die!' Georgiana cried, tears spilling from the corners of her eyes. 'He saved us.'

'He won't die if I have any say in the matter. Fetch my black bag from the bedchamber, if you please, Turner, and then take Miss Darcy home. I need to attend to Hamish.'

'I want to stay.'

'You cannot,' Dominic said, flashing her a wry smile. 'Surely you must see that. Captain Turner must explain his part in all this to your brother. I will see you again as soon as I can and offer my own reassurances to Darcy regarding your part in all this. Your reputation will not be tarnished.'

'Oh, hang my reputation!'

Georgiana wanted to stamp her foot with frustration, but Captain Turner returned and she could see Dominic was too concerned about Hamish to have time to mollify her feelings. Georgiana watched in a daze as

Dominic opened his bag and concentrated all his attention on the ragged tear in his dog's thigh. Hamish appeared to have lost consciousness, but Georgiana refused to accept he was dead. It would be more than she could bear. She was vaguely aware of Dominic's soothing voice and Captain Turner's harsher one as he ordered the miscreants to be taken away. More curses spilled from Rose's lips, but Major Halstead actually tried to bluff his way out of things.

'I came here to help Miss Watkins recover some property. I was not aware it was stolen. Come, Turner, you know me better than that.'

'D-do I?'

'He was going to slit my throat,' Georgiana said, causing Captain Turner's expression to turn thunderous.

'I would not have done it.'

'Stop trying to save your sorry hide, Halstead,' Dominic said, not looking up from stitching Hamish's thigh. 'I have a button in my possession.' Georgiana glanced at Halstead and watched as his complexion paled. 'It was torn from a military tunic when someone hid jewellery beneath my floor. I suspect, if you look at Halstead's cuffs, Turner, you will find one of them has been repaired.'

Captain Turner grasped the major's bound hands, inspected his tunic and nodded grimly. 'That rather s-seals your fate, Halstead.' The captain shook his head, looking truly bewildered. 'I did not want t-to believe it when I was told you were mixed up in this b-business. How could you do such a thing?'

'Damn you to hell and back, the whole lot of you,' Halstead replied as Captain Turner's men pushed him from the room. 'I would not expect you to understand.'

'Will he be all right?' Georgiana asked, referring to Hamish, not Halstead.

'I hope so.' Dominic glanced at her, then Captain Turner. 'I assume you were set to watch Halstead, Turner.'

Captain Turner gave a brief nod. Kitty will be pleased, Georgiana thought. His preoccupation had nothing to do with his diminished feelings for her, but was a reflection of the strain he felt at having to prove one of his closest friend's involvement in criminal activity.

'I don't have time to hear the particulars now,' Dominic said tersely. 'I must concentrate on saving my dog, much as he just saved us. Take Miss Darcy home at once,' he added, his gaze once again briefly lingering on profile, her lips . . . and lower. 'She is in shock.'

'No, I'm fine. Really.'

But when she tried to stand, her knees gave out, and if Captain Turner had not caught her, she would have fallen to the floor.

'Definitely delayed shock,' he said, sweeping her into his arms and returning her to her chair. 'P-perfectly understandable given the circumstances.' He found her cloak, draped it around her and pulled the hood over her head. Then he picked her up again.

'I can walk.'

'No, she can't,' Dominic said. 'There's a shortcut, Turner. Miss Darcy will show you the way. Now go before the snow gets worse.'

'You will come later?' she asked.

'Of course.' Dominic sent her a searing look and seemed reluctant to snatch his eyes away again. 'Just as soon as I can.'

★ ★ ★

'Good heavens.' Lizzy gazed out of her chamber's window and thought she must be seeing things. 'Is that Georgie, being carried by Major Halstead? She must have fallen and hurt herself. But what is the major doing here?'

'What!'

Will leapt from his seat beside her bed and

337

peered through the window also. A red-coated figure appeared through the snow, definitely cradling Georgiana in his arms.

'It's not Halstead but Turner.' Will scowled. 'What the devil is going on?'

'Whatever it is, I want to know,' Lizzy said, sending Kitty, also in the room, a probing glance. 'And so does Kitty. Have them both come up here.'

'You are in bed,' Will pointed out unnecessarily.

'And entirely respectable,' Lizzy replied, pulling her shawl more closely about her shoulders. 'Something of import has occurred, and I shall only fret if I do not hear the particulars immediately.'

'Very well.' Will sighed. 'If you are absolutely sure, I shall have them come up.'

'Why on earth is Captain Turner bringing Georgie home?' Kitty asked when Will had left them. 'She went to call upon Mr. Sanford — '

'Ah, I rather thought she must have done so. I knew you were not being honest earlier when you said you did not know where she was.'

'I was sworn to secrecy. Georgie thought Mr. Darcy would not approve. You know how protective he can be.'

Lizzy rolled her eyes. 'I am sure he will

frown at her behaviour. But as long as there is a reasonable explanation for her being carried back home, he will get over it. Since Mr. Sanford saved me and our baby, he can do no wrong in Will's eyes.'

'That is very good news from Georgie's perspective. She likes Mr. Sanford very much.'

'Yes, so I collect.'

'But why on earth was Captain Turner at Mr. Sanford's cottage, and why is it him and not Mr. Sanford bring Georgie home?' Kitty fidgeted with impatience. 'I do not understand what's going on.'

'Patience, Kitty. I am sure we shall soon find out.'

Will returned at that moment with a dishevelled Georgiana and Captain Turner in tow, his hair damp from the snow. Georgiana embraced Lizzy and then Kitty, but seemed shaken and withdrawn.

'Whatever happened to you?' Lizzy asked. 'You look all done in.'

Georgiana sighed. 'I have had the most terrible fright, but I am fine now, thanks to Hamish and Captain Turner.'

'Intriguing,' Lizzy muttered to Will, who was occupied with frowning at Turner and looking concerned for his sister.

'Mrs. Darcy,' Captain Turner said. 'I

apologise for the intrusion, but your husband said you were anxious to know w-what has been going on.'

'We are all anxious to know that,' Will replied.

'I must apologise if I h-have neglected you over recent weeks,' the captain replied, his gaze fixed on Kitty as he spoke with little sign of the stutter that plagued him when he was feeling anxious. 'But I had rather unpleasant orders to f-follow, which I could not discuss with anyone. I did not go to visit my f-father shortly before Colonel Fitzwilliam's wedding, as I had led you to believe, but rather I w-was called to a meeting with our new colonel.'

'About the growing number of pickpockets operating in and around Newcastle?' Will suggested.

Captain Turner raised a brow. 'You know about them?'

'I made it my business to ask a few people, given that Sanford had found jewels hidden beneath his floor.'

'Quite so. There were r-rumours of an officer in our regiment being involved. I was not prepared to believe it at f-first, especially when Halstead's name was suggested, but agreed to keep a covert eye on him, i-if only to prove his innocence.'

'Major Halstead is part of the gang?' Lizzy

asked, widening her eyes in shock.

'Unfortunately, yes.'

It was Georgiana who took up the story. She explained how she had called on Mr. Sanford that afternoon, just as Mr. Burton was leaving, and the subsequent events. There had been some kind of struggle in the cottage, from what Lizzy could make out, and Hamish had saved the day. She suspected Georgiana was playing it down, but Will looked ready to burst with anger.

'You were in danger.'

It was not a question, and Georgiana merely nodded in response to her brother's terse comment.

'Halstead wanted to marry you so he could keep his mistress in style?' Once again Georgiana nodded. 'It's very fortunate for him he is now in gaol, otherwise . . . I knew there had to be a good reason why I didn't like the man.'

'Your instincts were right, my dear,' Lizzy said, touching his hand. 'Mine let me down on this occasion.'

'W-we managed to get to one of Rose Watkins's inner circle. He t-told us everything he knew in an effort to save his own skin,' Captain Turner explained. 'He k-knew Rose was about to show her hand today. Unfortunately, due to a series of misfortunes t-that I will not trouble to relate, we lost sight of her and Halstead this afternoon, and it t-took us a while to discover where they had gone. That is why we were n-not on hand earlier to rescue you, Miss Darcy, for which I apologise.'

'That's quite all right, Captain. Hamish saved the day.' Georgiana wiped away a tear. 'I pray he will not pay for his bravery with his life.'

Lizzy patted her hand. 'Your Mr. Sanford will save him. Never doubt it.'

Far from seeming placated, Georgiana burst into tears and fled from the room.

'Let her go,' Lizzy said when Kitty went to go after her. 'Perhaps you will take Captain Turner downstairs, Kitty,' she added. 'I am sure he could manage a cup of restorative tea or, given the circumstances, perhaps something a little stronger.'

'Please, Miss Bennet.' The captain proffered his arm. 'Tea would be very welcome, as would the opportunity to converse with you.'

Kitty left the room on her captain's arm, a radiant smile gracing her features.

'Well,' Lizzy said to Will as they watched them go. 'Unless I mistake the matter, my sister is about to get her heart's desire.'

'But what of my sister?' Will asked glumly.

Lizzy sighed. 'What indeed. It would be

best to leave her to her own devices for a while. She has had a terrible time of it, but I suspect if Mr. Sanford should happen to call, she will recover with remarkable speed.'

★ ★ ★

Georgiana had a long soak in the bath, replaying the events of the day in her mind as she attempted to rein in her oscillating emotions. Every time she thought of the cold steel pressed against her neck, of the stark determination in the major's expression, she became paralysed with renewed fear. He really would have killed her without a second's regret. Relief at Hamish's timely intervention made her head spin with gratitude.

It was snowing heavily when she finally got out of the bath, but she was sure that would not prevent Dominic from calling later. He knew just how worried she was about Hamish, and he would want to set her mind at rest. Or otherwise. *No, don't think the worst. Hamish cannot possibly die.*

Dinner time came and went with no sign of him. She tried to be her usual cheerful self, especially since Captain Turner had remained to dine, and Kitty positively glowed beneath the full force of his attentions. Well, at least one of them was happy. Georgiana toyed with her food, having no appetite to speak of. After everything they had been through, how could Dominic abandon her so summarily? Had she misinterpreted his expression, read too much into it? By staying away, was he trying to let her down gently? Oh dear, this was all so confusing, and she wished she had someone she could apply to for advice. Normally she would speak to Lizzy, but she was still recovering from her own ordeal. Georgiana could not burden her with her own problems, which would seem trifling by comparison.

She replied to some remark her brother addressed to her and then returned her mind to Dominic. She recalled their conversation *before* Rose and Halstead invaded the cottage — was that only a few hours ago? It seemed more like a lifetime. She had not believed he was indifferent towards her then, and subsequent events had reinforced that opinion.

So why didn't he come?

She slept badly and dressed the following morning in an old gown, not much caring about her appearance, determined to wallow in her justified anger at Dominic's neglect. She sat with Lizzy for a while, but avoided Kitty because she didn't want to spoil her happiness with her morose mood. At a loose end, she wandered into the small salon where she had nothing to do except enjoy an uninterrupted view of the steadily falling snow. And brood.

It was almost time for luncheon, but she still had no appetite. Perhaps she could think of a reason not to go to table. She was not in any mood to be exposed to company. It was exhausting feigning normality when one's heart was breaking.

She didn't hear anyone approaching, but sensed Dominic's presence before she turned and saw him standing in the open doorway, looking at her, filling the aperture with his glorious masculinity. She was determined to remain indifferent, but her heart lurched and a small gasp escaped her in spite of her best efforts to contain it.

'I did not know you were here,' she said coolly.

'I have been with your brother.'

'How is Hamish?'

'Weak, but he will recover.'

That news justified a smile, and she duly obliged. 'Thank goodness.'

He moved to stand in front of her. 'More to the point, how are you?' he asked gently.

'I will recover, too,' she replied.

She sounded sharp, ungracious, but didn't much care, just so long as she kept her dignity intact. He did not want her, and she refused to beg. Even so, remaining vexed with him when his stance conveyed such strength and integrity was a difficult ambition to achieve. Every fibre of her being urged her to go to him, to fling her arms around him, and fight for what she wanted. He was allowing his pride to stand in the way of their happiness, she was absolutely sure of that, yet had no idea how to fix the situation. He regarded her with an intense, searing expression, as though he could see into her heart and read what was written there. The deep lines etched on his forehead were erased when the corners of his mouth lifted into a devastatingly engaging grin that captured her delight and left her giddy with anticipation.

Anticipation of what?

'I couldn't come last night, much as I wanted to. I sat up all night with Hamish, and I have been occupied all the morning with the authorities. But don't worry. They will not be bothering you. I have made sure of that.'

'Thank you.'

He fell silent, seeming hesitant, unsure of himself. 'You know I plan to remain in the district and pursue my profession.'

Ah, so he *had* decided to stay and didn't want her to bother him. 'Yes.'

'The life of a country doctor is far from glamorous.'

'But rewarding.'

'Nothing like what you are accustomed to.'

'What does it have to do with me?'

'That rather depends upon you.'

'I — I don't understand.'

'Georgiana, when I saw Halstead holding that knife to your throat, I was ready to murder him.' He ploughed a hand through his hair, agitated, angry. 'I have never felt so powerless, so incapable, in my entire life. I thought I had lost you,' he said bleakly, his voice breaking.

Hope brought Georgiana's jaded spirit to life. 'I wasn't too optimistic about my prospects, either.'

'It took a life and death situation to make me realise how quickly you have captured my heart.'

Georgiana blinked at him, convinced he hadn't actually said the words she so wanted to hear. 'It did?'

'Hmm, I planned to throw myself upon Halstead, before he could use that knife.'

'But then he would have used it on you.'

'I expect he would, so we must be thankful Hamish returned when he did.'

'And that you had the foresight to have your windows overhauled.'

'That too.' He fixed her with a penetrating gaze. 'Life is too short for dissembling, Georgiana. Recent events have at least taught us that much. We have not known one another for long, but it doesn't take long for a man, for this man, to know he has met his heart's desire.'

Georgiana swallowed. 'It does not?' Goodness, she sounded like a simpleton, but the smile that refused to be contained made formulating more than a few words next to impossible.

'If you are willing to compromise your standards, live in a draughty old house that has not been used for fifteen years, and put up with being woken at all hours by patients in urgent need of my services, then I would be honoured if you would consider becoming my wife.'

'Yes!' she cried joyously, jumping from her seat and throwing herself into his arms. 'A thousand times yes.'

'You will be sacrificing so much. Are you sure you don't need to think about it?' His lips hovered above hers. 'It is a big step to take. Your brother has given me his consent to address you, but the decision is yours to make.'

She widened her eyes. 'Fitzwilliam agrees?'

'It seems his wife warned him to expect a call from me.'

Georgiana smiled just as the whole world ought to smile with her. 'Lizzy is the wisest woman I know.'

'If she is responsible for your brother's agreement, then we have much to thank her for.' Dominic held her by the waist and looked into her eyes. 'I love you, Georgiana, but are you absolutely sure you don't need more time to consider? This is a huge step to take.'

'I love you too, Dominic,' she replied, tears streaming down her face. 'So very passionately. And the only thing I need to think about, is how long it will take you to kiss me and seal the bargain.'

We do hope that you have enjoyed reading this large print book.

Did you know that all of our titles are available for purchase?

We publish a wide range of high quality large print books including:
Romances, Mysteries, Classics
General Fiction
Non Fiction and Westerns

Special interest titles available in large print are:
The Little Oxford Dictionary
Music Book
Song Book
Hymn Book
Service Book

Also available from us courtesy of Oxford University Press:
Young Readers' Dictionary
(large print edition)
Young Readers' Thesaurus
(large print edition)

For further information or a free brochure, please contact us at:
Ulverscroft Large Print Books Ltd.,
The Green, Bradgate Road, Anstey,
Leicester, LE7 7FU, England.
Tel: (00 44) 0116 236 4325
Fax: (00 44) 0116 234 0205

Other titles published by Ulverscroft:

COLONEL FITZWILLIAM'S DILEMMA

Wendy Soliman

Lady Catherine de Bourgh has invited herself to Pemberley, intent upon bringing about an engagement between her daughter Anne and Colonel Fitzwilliam. But her ladyship has failed to take into account the remarkable improvement in her daughter's health and spirits since the arrival of her new tutor, the charismatic Mr. Asquith. Meanwhile, enchanted by the widowed Celia Sheffield, Colonel Fitzwilliam is perturbed to learn that her fortune is being contested by an individual in Jamaica — from whence Mr. Asquith also hails. And when the obsequious Mr. Collins shares grave rumours concerning the tutor's character, further suspicions are raised . . .

MISS BINGLEY'S REVENGE

Wendy Soliman

Elizabeth Darcy is determined not to be found wanting when she and her new husband throw their first house party at Pemberley. Of course, Miss Bingley will be there, but Lizzy has nothing to fear from her old nemesis — or so she thinks. Miss Bingley has convinced herself that Mr. Darcy made a mistake in his hasty marriage to Lizzy, and is determined to save him from his own folly. When Lydia Wickham puts in an unexpected appearance, and Miss Bingley learns that Wickham himself is also in the neighbourhood, an unlikely alliance is formed between two people with very different reasons for wanting the Darcy marriage to fail.

TO DEFY A DUKE

Wendy Soliman

Elias Shelton, the Duke of Winsdale, has a duty to produce an heir. Completely indifferent, he leaves his mother to invite the most suitable candidates to a house party at Winsdale Park, promising to choose one of them as his duchess. Returning home after several days of pre-nuptial carousing, he falls from his horse and badly injures his head. His life is saved by a mysterious woman who fascinates and enthrals him: Athena Defoe, who, along with her young twin sisters, is hiding from her past in a tumbledown cottage on Eli's estate. Can Eli help his new love escape her pursuers before it is too late?

A BITTERSWEET PROPOSAL

Wendy Soliman

When Marcus Rothwell, Earl of Broadstairs, is forced to spend the night alone with Harriet Aston he willingly does the honourable thing. In this marriage of convenience, Harriet determines to engage Marc's affections. However, she is brutally attacked, and whilst suspicion falls upon the dowager countess, who disapproves of Harriet, there's the village beadle's unaccountable behaviour to be considered, as well as Marc's Machiavellian steward. Wanting to protect Harriet, Marc delves into the mystery surrounding her attack. Now he must examine his feelings for the woman he married on a whim. But he too is in mortal danger . . .